WAITING FOR YOU

Praise for Elle Spencer

30 Dates in 30 Days

"Spencer is adept at dropping an emotional bombshell at just the right time for maximum impact. She adds her own brand of flair, making the romance formula feel new and fresh."—*Lesbian Review*

"I'm an Elle Spencer fan. I want to say that this was surprisingly good, but I guess I shouldn't really be that surprised. She generally delivers on everything I love about reading romance. Feelings, chemistry, conflict, angst, tears, and happiness. The characters were likable. Fun situations. Great chemistry. A slow burn romance that satisfies in the end."—*Bookvark*

"As usual with Spencer, the characters are wonderfully layered and flawed, [and] the chemistry is out of this world."—*Jude in the Stars*

"Spencer imbues the story with some great humour and witty banter that brings the characters to life, and the romance works wonderfully. I really enjoyed this one–it hit all the right notes for me and left me with a bit of an aw, shucks smile on my face when I finished."
—*C-Spot Reviews*

"Ms. Spencer knows how to build the tension so thick that you could cut it with a proverbial knife. The intimate scenes are really hot… Overall, a clever, funny and light romance with great chemistry and a superb cast."—*LezReviewBooks*

Private Equity (in *Hot Ice*)

"This story had a lot of heart and quite a bit of depth for so little time. This was the strongest among the three novellas."—*Bookvark*

The Road to Madison

"The story had me hooked from its powerful opening scene, and it only got better and better. I feel like Spencer tailored this book just for me. For anyone who has read my reviews, it's no secret that I love romances that include lots of angst, and *The Road to Madison* hit the bull's-eye."—*The Lesbian Review*

"Elle Spencer weaves a tale full of sadness, remorse but one filled with those little moments that make you have the flutters. Her characters are well developed, the dialogue is seamless and natural, you really get thrown right into Madison and Anna's world. You feel what they feel. This book grabbed my attention and had me turning the pages through the night. A delightful story that I thoroughly enjoyed. I cannot wait for the next adventure Elle Spencer takes me on."—*Romantic Reader Blog*

"Elle Spencer is fast becoming one of my favourite authors. She transports me into the story and I feel like I'm living vicariously through the characters."—*Les Rêveur*

Unforgettable

"Across both novellas, Elle Spencer delivers four distinct, compelling leads, as well as interesting supporting casts that round out their stories. If you like angsty romances, this is the book for you! Both stories pack a punch, with so much 'will they or won't they' that I kind of wondered how they'd turn out (yes, even though it's marketed as romance!)"—*The Lesbian Review*

"I was stunned at how Elle Spencer manages to make the reader feel so much and we end up really caring for the women in her novels…This book is perfect for those times you want to wallow in romance, intense feelings, and love. Elle Spencer does it so well."
—*Kitty Kat's Book Review Blog*

Casting Lacey

"The characters have a chance to really get to know each other, becoming friends and caring for each other before their feelings turn romantic. It also allows for a whole lot of angst that keeps things interesting. *Casting Lacey* is a compelling, sexy, angsty romance that I highly recommend to anyone who's into fake relationship books or celebrity romances. It kept me sucked in, and I'm looking forward to seeing more from Elle Spencer in the future."
—*The Lesbian Review*

"This is a very good debut novel that combines the fake girlfriend trope with celebrity lifestyle…The characters are well portrayed and have off-the-charts chemistry. The story is full of humour, wit, and saucy dialogues but also has angst and drama. I think that the book is at its best in the humorous parts which are really well written…an entertaining and enjoyable read."—*Lez Review Books*

"This is the romance I've been recommending to everyone and her mother since I read it, because it's basically everything I've been dying to find in an f/f romance—funny voices I click with, off-the-charts chemistry, a later-in-life coming out, and a host of fun tropes from fake dating to costars."—*Frolic*

By the Author

Casting Lacey

Unforgettable

The Road to Madison

30 Dates in 30 Days

Waiting for You

Hot Ice
(with Aurora Rey and Erin Zak)

Visit us at www.boldstrokesbooks.com

WAITING FOR YOU

by

Elle Spencer

2020

WAITING FOR YOU

ISBN 13: 978-1-63555-635-3

This Trade Paperback Original Is Published By
Bold Strokes Books, Inc.
P.O. Box 249
Valley Falls, NY 12185

First Edition: May 2020

CREDITS

EDITORS: Barbara Ann Wright and Stacia Seaman
PRODUCTION DESIGN: Stacia Seaman
COVER DESIGN BY Tammy Seidick

Acknowledgments

As always, thanks to Rad, Sandy, and the entire Bold Strokes team for all of your hard work and support. I couldn't ask for a better publishing experience.

Thanks to my awesome editor, Barbara Ann Wright, for making each book better, and for getting me and my writing.

I'm grateful for the support I've found in this writing community and the authors who have become friends along the way. Thanks to Carsen, Georgia, Kris, Melissa, Sandy, and so many more for looking out for me, cheering me on, and making me a better writer by what I learn from you every time we're together.

Sandra, thank you for letting me use Brooke's name in this book. Hugs forever.

Paula, you're everything I want to be when I grow up. Please be my BFF in this life and all of the others too. #allthecookies

And to Nikki, who's been killing it since 2015 and before, and loves me with all her might, I can't even with how much I love you right back. You and me, baby.

In memory of Brooke Fagundes,
who left this world too soon.

PROLOGUE

L indsay woke with a start and nudged Patty. "Wake up."
"I'm just resting my eyes," Patty mumbled.

"Patty, wake up." Lindsay was more forceful this time. Her confusion over what had just happened left her feeling disoriented and vulnerable. And Patty's insistence that the blinds in her room be closed—"for effect," as Patty had put it—meant she couldn't see a damn thing. Lindsay was over it. "I'm not kidding. This whole thing was stupid. Get. Up."

Patty snorted and smacked her lips together. "But I'm so relaxed."

Stuck between the wall and Patty's dead weight, Lindsay scooted to the end of the twin bed and stood. "You won't be when your dad catches us ditching class."

Patty bolted up. "What? Is he home? Shit!" She grabbed the bottle of peach schnapps off the nightstand.

"Calm down. No one's home." Lindsay took the bottle and gave Patty a gentle push back onto the bed. "All I meant was, it was stupid to do this, this, past life bullshit." Lindsay yanked on the cord and opened the blinds. The midday sun caused both of them to slap a hand over their eyes.

"God, Linds. You couldn't just twist the rod like a normal person and gently ease us back into reality?"

Lindsay stomped over to the bed and sat so she could put her shoes on. Maybe they could get back in time for gym class, and she could burn off some of this unexplained anger and frustration. "I'm over it, okay? Let's get back to school before we get caught."

"Okay, calm down, crazy person. At least we got a nap in before the party tonight. And since when are you dying to get back to that shithole they call a *learning* institution? We're so above that place."

Lindsay never should've gone along with Patty on this one. She'd humored her before with the Ouija board and the tarot cards, but when they found a set of past life regression CDs at a tag sale, Lindsay should've never agreed to buy them. "No nap for me. Just…"

Patty sat up again. "Just what?"

Lindsay leaned over and rested her face in her hands. It all felt so real, but that didn't make any more sense than watching the Ouija spell out "Satan." Because of course that was what it would spell for two girls who were looking for a cheap thrill in the form of a good, hair on the back of your neck standing on end, scare. It took Lindsay a whole month before she could sleep without her lamp on. She eased back up and turned so they were face-to-face. "I don't know for sure. Maybe it was just a dream."

"While you weren't napping?" Patty raised her eyebrows. "Tell me."

Lindsay felt embarrassed. She'd never thought of herself as bisexual, but this was Patty, her best friend in the whole world, who definitely had a thing for girls. If she couldn't tell Patty what had happened, who could she tell? "Okay, listen," Lindsay said. "I'll tell you, but only because of our status."

Patty raised an eyebrow. "Tell me more about this status. Because if we're a thing and I didn't even know it, I'm going to kill myself."

"Our BFF status, dummy. I trust you to keep this between us."

Patty zipped her lips and threw away the key. "I got you, boo."

"Okay, here goes nothing." She took a deep breath and said, "I was in love. Madly in love. With the most beautiful girl."

"You were in love with a girl!" Patty squealed with excitement.

"Not a girl. A woman. We were both grown-ups."

"Like grown-up, grown-up? Like, old?"

"I don't know. Like, in our late twenties, maybe. Thirties?" Lindsay covered her face with her hands. "It felt so real. I can still smell the smoke."

"Smoke? Was there a fire?"

"On her breath," Lindsay said. "When she kissed me."

Patty's eyes widened. "Oh. Was it gross?"

"Not like that time Eric Brown kissed me after he'd smoked half a pack at Fly's house. That was like licking an ashtray."

"Not the smoking, dork. Kissing a girl. Was it weird?"

Lindsay shook her head. "Not at all." She took in a deep breath and covered her chest with her hands. Just thinking about it made her heart beat faster. "We were so in love, but people wouldn't leave us alone."

"Who?"

"I don't know. I just felt like people were, you know, after us." She shrugged. "It's hard to explain, but all the feelings were there except everything was blurry. Everything except her. Roo."

"Roo? As in, kangaroo? I'm kinda getting confused here, Linds."

"I don't know. I guess. I mean, that's how she wrote it. R-O-O." Lindsay understood Patty's confusion. How could she make sense of it when Lindsay couldn't find the right words to express how real it all was? The passion. The fear. The longing. The heartbreak. Words failed her in that moment.

"Okay," Patty said. "So you're dreaming about making out with a chick, and people are after you, and she's, what? Signing autographs? So she's famous. Cool. And—"

"It was a letter," Lindsay interrupted.

"What?"

"I was holding a letter in my hand. She signed it, 'I will love you forever. Always, Roo.'"

Patty tilted her head. "What kind of a name is that for a girl?"

"Or anyone." Was she making this up? How had her mind conjured up such a silly name for such a beautiful woman? "Maybe it's a nickname. How should I know?"

Patty put a hand on her arm. "But you loved her?"

She had to hold back tears. "With all my heart," she whispered. "Yeah. I loved her."

"Wow, Linds. Your past life was way more interesting than mine."

"I'm pretty sure you slept through yours." Lindsay gave her a slug on the arm. "Besides, in this life there's no Roo, just Ben."

"Who you haven't done more than kiss yet."

Lindsay shrugged. "Who knows? Maybe I'll go all the way tonight."

"Ha! You're too much of a prude."

Lindsay scowled. "I am not."

"Linds, I adore you, but you just used the phrase 'go all the way' to refer to sex with your boyfriend. You, my innocent child, are a prude."

"Oh, I'm sorry. Would it be cooler if I talked about *banging* him?"

"Not until he asks you to go steady and gives you his class ring to wear around your neck. You don't wanna be known as the school hussy."

"I hate you."

Patty got off the bed. "Hussy." She bolted out of the room, laughing. "Hussy, hussy, hussy!"

Lindsay heard the bathroom door slam. She would've chased her, but her thoughts went back to that smoky kiss. And a girl named Roo.

CHAPTER ONE

The eyes seemed right.

Or were they? Lindsay took a step back from the painting she'd worked on through the night. A woman this time.

It had been months since she'd painted the young boy who'd come to her in her dreams so many years ago. His face had never been as clear as the woman who now stared back at her. He was more of an impression on the canvas. Cloudy. Muddled. Unrecognizable. But still someone she felt compelled to bring to life. She loved him. She loved him the way she loved Brooke. Not as much, not really, but still. She felt his absence in the way she felt Brooke's when soccer practice ran late, or she was out on a date. He was somehow missing from her life.

Lindsay glanced at the paintings stacked against the wall of her backyard studio. All were of the boy. None would bring any money unless she took them to the local gallery. She'd reached the point where she was no longer a starving artist, but she had to sell paintings to keep doing what she loved. That meant selling ones she didn't want to. She'd sold enough over the years to know the boy could define her as an artist. According to some critics, he already had:

"A strangely relatable, yet transcendent look into a young man's mind."

"Hall seems to reject the notions of time and space, instead delivering something so indescribable one can only call it love."

"In an age of pointless portraits, aka selfies, what could be more meaningful than the portrait of the boy who doesn't exist? Who is this Timmy? And why do we want to know him so desperately?"

Every time she took a painting of him in, it broke her heart a little. She only did it when she had to.

"Mom?"

Lindsay jumped at the sound of Brooke's voice behind her. "Yes, honey?"

"Did you get up early? Who's she? We're out of yogurt. Dad's picking me up in ten, and I haven't eaten anything."

Curious. Inquisitive. Accusatory. Dependent. Obviously, Brooke was a teenager. And lately, she had been killing it with the hard-done-by teenager act. If they didn't have the particular thing she wanted for breakfast, she considered the fridge and cupboards empty. "Have a bowl of cereal," Lindsay said.

"I can't eat a bowl of cereal in the car. You know how Dad drives."

"Explain to me again how you're old enough to go to Europe alone, but you can't work out breakfast."

"Mom," she said with that charmingly exasperated tone Lindsay had to work hard not to laugh at. "It's a senior trip. No one's going anywhere alone."

"Oh good. Then the whole show choir can wander around Europe *together* wondering what's for breakfast."

Brooke gave her a playful shove, then put an arm around her. Lindsay knew enough to enjoy the lighthearted moment while it lasted.

They stood side by side and stared at the painting. Lindsay was a good five foot eight, but Brooke's recent growth spurt meant she would forever look up to her daughter. If Brooke felt the balance of power shift, Lindsay did not. At five foot nine and a half, Brooke towered over most of her friends, including the boy she had a crush on. She hated her long legs, but one day she'd appreciate them. Lindsay was sure of that much.

They had the same dirty blond hair and dark blue eyes, and most days, they shared the same hairstyle, a messy bun or ponytail. A thousand years from now, when aliens excavated their house, they'd find hundreds of hair ties and wonder why these people hoarded them under sofas, behind clothes dryers, and on doorknobs.

Up until this year, they'd shared clothes and makeup, enjoyed the same food, liked the same TV shows and movies. They'd been mother and daughter, but they could hang out together like friends. Lindsay missed that. She wondered if Brooke did too, but she was afraid to ask.

Lindsay wanted to believe it was only teenage hormones that had driven a wedge between them, but she knew the truth. It was also the divorce. Brooke hadn't seen it coming. They'd done a good job of keeping their problems from her. No reason for her to worry about their marriage. But it hadn't been good for a long time, and although they'd never want Brooke to know it, she was the reason they'd stayed together for so long.

It wasn't like that was a conscious choice. They didn't sit at the kitchen table one day and say, "Let's continue this charade for Brooke's sake." It was more that it just happened. Brooke kept them busy and distracted, particularly since they both doted on their only child.

When Brooke started asserting her teenage independence, Lindsay found herself with more time to think about what her life would have been like in a different time with a different person. It was easy to see that the late nights spent in her studio had become an excuse to avoid going to bed until Ben fell asleep.

Now they'd been separated for two years and divorced for one. Brooke seemed hell-bent on doing anything and everything to piss off both of them. Take the recent shaving of the sides of her head. It was called a side cut, but Lindsay preferred to call it a gutless attempt at rebellion. Why not a neon pink mohawk with spikes? Or just shave it all?

Ben had made a fuss. Yes, some of the soccer team had done it, but that didn't matter to him. Lindsay didn't see the point in giving Brooke what she was looking for: another reason to yell and slam doors.

Truth be told, she found Brooke's rebellion slightly charming. She wanted to yell, "Come on, kid. Commit!" If Lindsay had to do it all over again, she would have rebelled the same way. Stupid side cut and all. Okay, fine. She might have thrown in some black or bleach-out white to make things interesting. But when Lindsay was in school, punk still existed. She consoled herself. At least Brooke didn't color it gray.

They'd tried to keep things as normal as possible after the divorce. Brooke was still sleeping in the same room she'd had since she was eight years old. Ben still took her to school every morning before his shift. They both made every effort to attend all of her volleyball games. Together. Lindsay wanted her daughter to stay young and carefree for as long as possible.

At seventeen, Brooke might have been far from the best self Oprah intended, but Lindsay had never had the luxury of pointless, unearned teen angst. She'd be damned if she'd deny her daughter the opportunity to be a complete pain in the ass.

Lindsay put her arm around her waist while they continued to stare at the painting. "There might be a yogurt in the minifridge, and there's some trail mix in my purse."

"Mother of the year." Brooke took a step closer to the painting. "She's intense. Who is she?"

Fuck.

Lindsay desperately wanted to tell Brooke that the woman in the painting was a paying client, but she hated lying to her daughter. Brooke wasn't a surface info kind of girl. She'd want names and places of residence and social media accounts. Maybe a background check and a quick image search. Nosy kid. She'd always shown interest in the people Lindsay painted. When she was younger, she'd sit by Lindsay's side and make up stories about them as they came to life on the canvas.

That was how the boy became Timmy. The name was perfect. But that was all Lindsay said. Brooke would talk about his family. How his name was Timothy, but *they* called him Timmy. He was a precocious only child who longed for siblings. His parents weren't around. Not together, anyway. Brooke seemed to feel he was missing something. "He's so lonely," she'd say, not knowing it broke Lindsay's heart to hear it.

When Brooke was very little, she'd leave her teddy in front of Timmy. Once, she'd left her little blanket, the one with the soft silky edge she called her na-na. Clearly a big deal. But Brooke didn't last more than an hour before she and Teddy shuffled across the backyard and into the studio and lay down next to the blanket in front of the painting. Lindsay smiled as she remembered watching the scene from a cracked door.

As Brooke grew older, she wanted to know the actual story behind the real faces. Paying clients. So they would spend hours in front of the computer researching. Brooke's interest had never waned.

"Mom?"

Lindsay stepped up to the painting, then turned and folded her arms. "I don't know who she is, honey." Not entirely true, but she wasn't ready to talk about it with Brooke.

Her eyes narrowed. "What do you mean, you don't know?" She thought she knew everything about everything, another teenage trait she had in spades.

"Honey, it's not a big deal."

"Not a big deal?" She jabbed her finger at the stack of paintings. "You refuse to sell Timmy, and now you're painting another stranger? How are we supposed to live? How am I supposed to go to college?" She tilted her head. "You were up all night, weren't you?"

Lindsay stayed quiet while Brooke stomped to the minifridge and grabbed the yogurt. It was pointless to say they had plenty of money for college, and Brooke had never gone without in her entire life. Okay, fine. They might have scraped by on ramen a few times during the early years, but Brooke never lacked the necessities.

All details that would be lost on Brooke at the moment. Sometimes silence was the best option. Brooke was almost out the door when she turned and grabbed Lindsay's purse. She dug through it, then held up the trail mix along with a twenty-dollar bill. "Thanks for the hearty breakfast, Mother. At least now I can have some lunch."

The door slammed shut as Lindsay shouted, "Love you, honey!" She made a mental note to subtract twenty dollars from

Brooke's lunch fund. She might have her guilty moments, but she'd be damned if her purse would be up for the taking.

She turned back to the painting and promised herself it wouldn't be like before. Lindsay wouldn't lose her ability to paint anything but this woman for weeks on end like she had with Timmy. No. That would definitely not happen again. In fact, she'd march right over to the gallery and sell it. Not the woman she'd just painted, of course. It would need time to dry. And Lindsay needed time with her. She'd sell a painting of the boy. Right after she took a nap.

CHAPTER TWO

R en pulled over to the side of the two-lane highway and lowered the top on her convertible Mercedes E450. She leaned back, closed her eyes, and took in the fresh, familiar air. Salt Creek held a special place in her heart. The first time she'd visited the small town in the Berkshires, she was nineteen. Deb, her college roommate, had brought her home for a long weekend, and from the moment she stepped out of the car, she felt a strong sense of belonging. She wasn't sure if it was the mountains and rivers, the slow pace of life, or the fact that she could escape her parents' never-ending arguments. Whatever it was, something drew her back year after year. It helped that Deb always seemed thrilled to have her visit, even with little or no notice.

She glanced at her watch. It wasn't a surprise she'd made better time than planned. Driving the speed limit wasn't a strong character trait, as evidenced by the state trooper—a statie, as Deb would call him—getting out of his car behind her. She got her driver's license out of her purse and the insurance card from the glove box.

The officer took off his sunglasses. "Ma'am."

"Officer." Ren tried for a sincere smile. "Is there a problem?"

"Oh, nothing too serious. Just the fact that you were driving twenty-two miles over the speed limit. May I have your license and proof of insurance?"

Ren took a deep breath. After a long week of exhausting negotiations, the last thing she needed was another one. But it looked as if she was going to have no choice in the matter since

ELLE SPENCER

another speeding ticket would make her insurance rates skyrocket. She handed him her information and said, "Medical emergency? No? How about, I'm carrying a live organ in the trunk, and if I don't get there in time—"

"A small child will die?" He chuckled. "No, really, what's the big rush?" He looked at her license. "Miss...oh, I see. You're from New York. Let me guess. All the gridlock keeps you from experiencing the true joys of driving this nice car? Or how about, you recently ended a relationship and needed to experience the freedom of the wide-open road." He wiggled his fingers by his ears. "Feel the wind rush through your hair."

Okay, that last one wasn't far off, but she wasn't about to let Officer I Do Standup on the Weekends know he'd hit his mark. "You're using up all of my excuses, Officer."

"I know. I could go on all day." He grinned.

Dare we dream? Ren gave him a slight smile and said, "I'm sure you could."

"Yup, I've heard 'em all, Miss Christopher." He leaned down and looked her in the eye. "Or is it Mrs.?"

Oh God. He was flirting. And not particularly well, either. If Ren had to guess, she'd say he was short on practice. She found herself at the edge of a fine line. Be polite enough to keep from pissing off Officer McFlirtFace while letting him know in no uncertain terms that his efforts were misplaced. Wildly.

"It's sweet of you to ask," she peered at his name tag, "Officer Hall, but I'm afraid I haven't met the right girl yet. Unfortunately, the last one was a bit too..." She paused, trying to think of the best way to describe her brief association with Kerry, the Drama Queen. "A bit too out of touch with reality to be marriage material."

"I'm not here to judge." He laughed. "I'm divorced myself. Here's to getting out." He held up his ticket pad as if he was going to toast with it.

"Glad to know someone can commiserate. And Officer, next time you want to know if a woman is single, well, first, try to pick a straight one. But then look for a ring. It's a bit more subtle."

"You thought I was flirting with you?" He stepped back in mock horror, then put his hands up in a show of innocence. "I was just trying to be inclusive. Ask you your pronouns and stuff."

Ren wasn't sure if he was serious. Did he really think Miss and Mrs. were pronouns? God, she hoped not. "Well, excellent. And she and her will do just fine." Just in case it was indeed a teaching moment.

"Good to know, but I hope you know I was kidding about the pronoun thing." He smiled. "And I still need to know where you're headed in such a hurry."

She took it as a good sign that he hadn't opened his ticket pad or pulled out a pen. "I'm going to see a friend in Salt Creek."

"I see. Well, we are a friendly place." He winked and gave her a quick once-over. "You forget Bruiser at home?"

"Who?"

"The car. The suit. You look like a character in that movie." He paused and cleared his throat. "You know, *Legally Blonde*."

Ren glanced at her pink silk blouse and matching skirt. Good thing he couldn't see her three-inch nude Blahniks. Her hair was more of a golden brown than blond, but she'd take a comparison to Reese Witherspoon all day long. "Touché. I'd have guessed you were more a John McClane guy than Elle Woods."

"What can I say? I'm comfortable with my masculinity." He grinned. "Actually, my ex loves that movie. So does my daughter. Seen it more times than I'd like to admit."

"Aw, you're a good dad."

"I do my best." He leaned on her car with both hands. "I'm from Salt Creek, by the way."

"Is that so? Do you know Deb Stewart?"

"Of course." He patted his stomach. "I've probably put on five pounds since she opened that new coffee place. Her baked goods are out of this world."

Ren pointed at him. "That's the one. She made the best sugar cookies back in our college days."

"Still does." He looked at her driver's license again. "Okay,

Ms. Christopher." He handed it back to her. "I don't want Deb spiking my coffee with something horrible, so I'm going to forget I ever met you, okay?"

"You're a nice guy, Officer."

"Nah, I just love my coffee and pastry. Have a good day, Ms. Christopher, and slow down."

She saluted. "Will do." She put her license back in her wallet and grabbed a hair tie. She'd drive the last few miles with the top down. And just under the speed limit as a thank you to Officer Hall.

❖

Change had always been slow to come to Salt Creek. For years, whenever Ren visited, she saw the same people doing the same things. Shirley and her husband ran the hardware store. Becky waited tables at the pizza place. She could rely on this place. She always loved that.

But change was inevitable, and Salt Creek wasn't a sleepy town anymore. Ren was appalled to see a Taco Bell where the walk-up soft serve place used to stand. She was still ranting about it in her head when she passed a shiny new garage and a modern convenience store with a neon sign announcing the jackpots for Powerball and Mass Millions. She groaned when she saw the sign announcing the availability of Keno.

It wasn't that she couldn't deal with change. She simply had a low tolerance for it. And besides, the Sooper Dooper Quik Mart and Package Store lacked the charm of its predecessor, Gene's Auto. Gene's place had two gas pumps outfitted with the latest in 1970s technology. They had analog meters and didn't take credit cards. But that didn't matter. If he wasn't working on a car, Gene pumped the gas for people anyway. Ren wondered if he had retired. She hoped he hadn't been pushed out...or worse.

She breathed a sigh of relief when she saw the Merrill's Hardware sign. At least that was still there. She'd stop in at some point and buy a jar of Shirley's famous honey. Was it a small-town cliché? Yes. And that was exactly what Ren had always loved about

Salt Creek. It was as clichéd as small towns came. Or at least it used to be.

She looked out her window at what used to be Stewart's Pharmacy before a big box store popped up in the next town over and put Deb's parents out of business. She pulled into an empty spot and stared in disbelief at the carved wooden sign hanging above the door.

You Mocha Me Crazy.

Now she knew why Deb had refused to tell her the name of the new shop. She was too embarrassed. Ren mumbled, "Deb Stewart, you have got to be kidding me."

Ren and Deb couldn't have been more different. In fact, the first time they were introduced, their mutual friend had said, "Uptown, meet Small Town." But somehow, their friendship had stood the test of time. This sign could be a deal breaker. Was she serious? *You. Mocha. Me. Crazy*? She got out of the car and put her hands on her hips. "WTF, Deb?"

Deb burst out the door. "I know what you're going to say."

Ren pulled her sunglasses down her nose. "I doubt it."

"You're going to say it's the best damned name anybody ever came up with for a coffee shop. That's why I didn't tell you. I wanted it to be a surprise."

Ren tilted her head again. "It's…"

"Where's your luggage? Never mind. Get over here, Ren Christopher. Let me hug that smug look off your face."

Ren stepped onto the sidewalk and opened her arms. "We've been over this, Deb. The smug look actually is my face. It's here to stay." She fell into Deb's arms and stayed there for a moment. Deb gave the best hugs, and Ren always found them comforting. She was warmth and love and laughter. And most important of all, a safe place for Ren to be herself. "It's good to be here," she said.

Deb hugged her tighter. "Took you long enough."

Ren pulled back and got a good look at Deb. There were a few lines around her pretty blue eyes, but not any gray in her brown hair, and in Ren's estimation, they both carried their thirty-eight years pretty well. "Still running?"

Deb grinned. "I try to get in twenty miles a week."

"It shows," Ren said with a shrug.

"Still have the hots for me, Soda Pop?" Deb's nickname for her came the first day of college. As soon as she realized her initials were RC, Deb decided the matter was settled. It stuck even though RC Cola wasn't widely available anymore. The more she thought about it, the more she realized the ridiculous name of the coffee shop shouldn't have surprised her.

"The hots for you? Absolutely," Ren joked. "And guess what?"

"You're about to say, 'If only you were gay, Deb Stewart,' and then I'll pretend to get all embarrassed except that we both know I love it because Ren Christopher is a goddamned catch if ever there was one."

Ren shook her head. "No. Actually, I was going to tell you that they don't need me in Paris until the fifteenth, which means I can stay an extra week if you'll have me." She actually couldn't believe her luck. She loved Paris and was thrilled to take on a new challenge running the estates business for Christie's in Europe. Even so, an extra week in Salt Creek, decompressing and hanging out with her favorite person, felt like the perfect break between her old life in New York and her new one.

"Oh." Deb looked away. "So you don't wish I was gay anymore?"

Ren rolled her eyes. "Really? That's all you have to say?"

"Well, I just need to make sure because I know your taste in women. You like the hot ones."

Ren put an arm around Deb's shoulder and urged her to the door of her cute little shop with the awful, awful name. "And you always liked the hot, sweaty, jockstrap wearing—"

"Gross!" Deb pulled away and put her hand on the door. "I refuse to let you say the word *jockstrap* right before you enter my masterpiece."

Ren laughed under her breath. "That's what she said."

Deb slapped her forehead. "Oh God."

Ren cleared her throat and made a show of trying not to laugh.

"I promise to never say the word *jockstrap* before entering your..." She covered her mouth and laughed. "I can't even say it."

"The shop, Ren. Not my—"

"Masterpiece?" She burst out laughing and stomped her feet a few times. "I can't with this. You realize what you've done, right? It cannot be undone. This is like Newton's fifth law of vagina naming."

Deb rolled her eyes. "Yes, I realize my vagina has a new nickname. Now, do you want to see my—"

Ren put up a hand. "No!" She doubled over from laughter. "Let me use my imagination."

"Well, I have a feeling your imagination has you picturing checked tablecloths and fake flowers."

Ren stood up straight and cleared her throat again. "Is that what straight chicks are into these days? You make tiny little tablecloths for your..."

"Oh my God! My shop. Not my master...fuck!" Deb shook her head and giggled.

"Yes. That's exactly what I pictured." She barely got the words out before she doubled over again.

Deb opened the door for a customer. "Hey, Monty. You're just in time to nab the last cinnamon roll."

"Thought I'd mix things up and try one of your sticky buns." He looked at Ren, who was once again shaking with semi-silent laughter. "Did I say something funny?"

Ren shook her head. "No. In fact, I can't wait to get my hands on Deb's buns even though I particularly enjoy a good muffin."

Monty turned to Deb. "Does she know about your famous muffin?" He turned his attention back to Ren. "My wife considers it her special Saturday morning treat. You should try it. It's called the cherry bomb."

Deb urged Monty through the door. "Go get your sticky bun before we run out, Monty. And say hi to Renee for me." She turned back to find Ren with her hand over her mouth, shaking uncontrollably. "Get a hold of yourself."

"Oh, come on. He just said his wife likes your famous muffin. How am I supposed to pretend that didn't happen?"

Deb put her hand on her hip. "How do you manage to function in the real world when *everything* people say has a sexual undertone to you?"

"Cherry bomb, Deb?"

"Yes. Like that. You have such a dirty mind, Soda Pop."

Ren shrugged. "I keep my laughter on the inside most of the time. But I don't have to do that with you, do I?"

"Of course not. Now promise me you'll keep yourself together for the next five minutes. This is a place of business, for cryin' out loud."

"Okay, okay. I promise." Ren gathered herself and took a deep breath. She held up two fingers and said, "Scout's honor."

Deb shook her head. "That's a peace sign, Soda. Now, come on." She put her hand on the door again. "Prepare to be amazed."

Ren walked in, took off her sunglasses, and gasped. Deb had turned her parents' drugstore into a modern, inviting space with not a single fluorescent light to be found. Instead, a zebrawood bar flanked by wooden stools wrapped around a large serving area. Soft globe lights hung from metal rods in the twelve-foot ceiling. A large industrial espresso machine stood out in the otherwise natural space. The pristine kitchen was visible through a large glass window opposite the bar. Three huge mixing bowls sat on a stainless steel countertop. All manner of utensils clung to a long magnetic bar running across the wall. Racks of baked goods waited to dismantle the willpower of any unsuspecting dieter.

"It's stunning, Deb. Absolutely stunning."

Deb let out a deep breath. "You have no idea how good that is to hear."

"I knew it would be amazing, but this…" She waved at the space, then squealed. "Oh my God. What do your parents think?"

"They haven't seen it yet. They're still on the never-ending RV trip. All they said was to do something I love with the building and make sure I pay the property taxes."

Ren laughed. "Good Lord. I thought I was overly practical."

"At least you're finally self-aware."

"Oh, you're hilarious, aren't you? So what does Colby think? Does he love it?"

"Oh, you mean the sweaty jockstrap I married?"

"I told you, you have a type."

"Yeah, maybe I do. Anyway, his hands are full with his real estate business, but he thinks it's great." She clapped her hands in excitement. "You really like it? Yours is the only opinion I care about."

"Ha!" Ren scoffed. "You always said my opinions were too high-minded, whatever that means."

"What I said was highfalutin, and I may also have said something about you being a pretentious fuck." Deb shrugged. "But I just wanted to keep you grounded. I guess that's a lost cause now that you have a fancy new job in Paris."

"Don't romanticize it too much. It's going to be grueling. Besides, I had a fancy job in New York too."

"Paris? Grueling? Cry me a River Seine, why don't you?"

"It's true." Ren flashed a smile and put her arm around Deb. "Which is why I'm here. To see my favorite friend in the world and find two weeks of peace and quiet. No drama. No demanding clients. No conference calls. Did I already say no drama?"

"Did you forget I have three kids? They live for drama. And forget peace and quiet. Also, they're demanding as hell. Especially number two."

"Colby Junior?"

"No, the third one," Deb said. "His name escapes me, but he shits his pants a lot. Hence the nickname."

"You're talking about your two-year-old who still wears a diaper?"

"Caleb. That's his name." Deb chewed on her thumbnail for a second. "Or is it Corey?"

Ren rolled her eyes. "I think Corey wouldn't speak to you for a week if she knew you were implying she still wears a diaper. How is she? Has she decided on a college yet?"

"She's great, actually. She has her moments, but I think I'll keep her. School's another story. She and Brooke have this plan to go to the same school and room together. They've narrowed it down to about three hundred fine schools. But hey, they have a whole two months to ger their applications in." Deb leaned against the coffee bar. "Can you believe I'm that old? Seems like just yesterday we brought her home from the hospital."

"Seems like yesterday you and I were roasting marshmallows over that crappy little hot plate in our dorm room." Ren sighed. "Ah, the good old days."

Deb grabbed her by the shoulders. "Hey! Colby built a firepit in our backyard last summer. It's perfect for roasting marshmallows and getting drunk on questionable wine."

"Cutoffs and hoodies?"

"iPod and singing at the top of our lungs?"

"You still own an iPod? I'm so there," Ren said. "How about a cup of this famous coffee I've heard so much about."

Deb went behind the counter. "You have? From who?"

"The statie who pulled me over this morning. He couldn't stop talking about your famous muffin."

"That's Ben Hall, and he did not."

"Fine. He said your baked goods are out of this world, and your coffee is almost as good as Dunkin' Donuts."

"I hate you. And please tell me he let you off easy."

"He was afraid you'd spike his coffee with something horrible if he didn't."

"Nah," Deb said with a shrug. "I just wouldn't sell him any of my pastries. That'd be payback enough." She pointed to an empty table. "Have a seat. I'll be right there."

Ren sat at a table by the window. She hadn't had much chance to laugh until her eyes watered. Especially lately. But that was what Salt Creek and Deb did to her. This place always made her feel at ease, a far cry from her normal state of being.

After her last visit, she'd considered buying a home here so she could visit more often without intruding on Deb and her family. There were some smaller postwar homes just west of Main Street that would suit her perfectly. She could pay someone to take care of the yard when she wasn't here. That dream flew out the window with the Paris job on the table. When Samantha King called to tell her about the position, she'd jumped at the opportunity.

The job was perfect. Most of her career had been in estates. She'd moved up over the years and developed an impressive list of contacts. The work itself was what drove her, though. Something about the family stories and the complex dynamics made it all so interesting. She loved digging into the provenance of a piece of art. Finding out how a family came to possess certain treasures often uncovered far more than most families were willing to let on in their early meetings. More than once, she'd been involved in returning a piece to its rightful owner. She knew she'd be exposed to a whole new world of possibilities in Paris.

Still, being back in Salt Creek made her pause. Just for a moment. Was she doing the right thing with this huge change? Ren wasn't sure. But her reasons for going outweighed any reason to stay.

Sure, there was Deb and a town she loved but didn't grow up in. There was her Manhattan co-op, but that pretty much rented itself. Lord knew Kerry the Drama Queen wasn't a selling point.

Ren sighed. Had she been so caught up in work that she actually didn't see just how self-centered and fake Kerry had been? Actually, yes. The irony wasn't lost on her either. The idea that she'd be so caught up she didn't notice the glaring character flaws was pretty self-centered on its own. She didn't love that about herself. All the better that she'd resolved to avoid all relationships *and* all drama in Paris.

Deb set a cup and saucer on the table and sat across from her. She pointed at the heart she'd made in the foam. "I made a heart for two reasons. One, my heart is happy you're here. And two, so you'll never forget that I was hands down a better barista than you back in the day."

"Which is why I got fired and they made you shit supervisor."

"That's *shift* supervisor to you, ex-barista."

"Right. Well, I haven't, nor will I ever, forget that you were the queen of the campus Peet's." Ren lifted the cup to her nose. "Mmm.

Smells delicious." She took a sip. Then another. "And I bow to your greatness, queen of You Mocha Shop with a Messed-Up Name."

Deb rolled her eyes. "See? You give me a huge compliment, and then you mock the name of my shop. You realize I can go home for this kind of abuse, right?"

Ren lifted the cup to hide her grin. "Happens a lot, huh?"

Deb folded her arms and huffed. "The name fits. You all Mocha Me Crazy. Every last one of you."

"Ah. Well, you could always run away to Paris like I'm doing."

Deb leaned forward. "Not that you don't look as fabulous as ever, but is everything all right?"

"Crap. That ridiculous breakup is written all over my face, isn't it? I thought I'd managed to hide it with a cover stick."

"Then you laughed about my hoo-ha until you cried, and now I can see those dark circles under your eyes. Serves you right, vagina mocker. I trust this is about Krazy Kerry?"

"Krazy with a K. Yes." A giggle bubbled up inside Ren, but it didn't take long for her demeanor to turn serious again. "It's been kinda rough lately. I know I joke about Kerry, but she's had a tough time letting go of the whopping six months we dated." Deb took her hand. Ren returned the reassuring squeeze. "It's fine. I'm just glad to be away. It's definitely time for a break."

Deb stood, still holding her hand. "Let's get out of here."

"No way." She picked up her mug with her free hand. "Not without a to-go cup."

CHAPTER THREE

Lindsay covered her mouth and yawned. "Sorry. Late night." She waited while Patty filled out the consignment form. Patty's art gallery was contemporary and minimalist, designed to showcase the art, not the gallery, while accommodating a wide range of rotating exhibitions. Straight lines and wide-open spaces allowed the work to be easily accessed and showcased by strategically placed spotlights.

Patty slid the contract across her desk. "Is the portrait business slow, Linds?"

Lindsay picked up a pen and signed it. "What are you talking about?"

"I'm talking about how even when I beg you to class up this place with some of your work, you refuse. I can only sell so many of old Mrs. Stokely's pastoral scenes and still keep the lights on, you know."

Lindsay walked to a bronze sculpture of a woman flanked by two old men reaching inside her abdomen to take hold of her uterus. "This doesn't seem like a Stokely. In fact, if I'm not mistaken, this is Kleber." Lindsay turned the price tag over. "Twelve five? Yeah, I'm pretty sure the lights will stay on."

"I got lucky with the Kleber. Her regular gallery thought the piece was too political."

"Idiots. Last I checked, it's art," Lindsay said. "If it doesn't sell, I might make an offer."

Patty pointed to a rural landscape on the far-right wall. "Could you make an offer on a Stokely instead? I love the old woman, but damn, she can be cranky when a piece sits unsold for too long."

"I'll have you know that Mrs. Stokely is the only reason I'm an artist at all." Lindsay walked to one of the smaller paintings and examined it closely. It was clear by the signature that Mrs. Stokely's hands weren't as steady as they'd once been. "She convinced me I had a God-given talent that I shouldn't let go to waste."

"And I wholeheartedly agree with her. Lucky for me, the tourists who come through here don't know she's been painting from the same vantage point on her back porch for years. As long as I only keep one on the wall at a time, they think they're getting something unique."

Lindsay turned back. "It's sweet of you, Pattycakes. I know us artist types aren't the easiest people in the world to deal with."

"Flighty, temperamental, self-absorbed, grandiose—"

Lindsay put up a hand. "Okay. You don't have to go all stereotypical. Unless you're looking for me to throw a fit and grab my painting and haul it back out of here as I inform you—at the top of my lungs—just how far beneath me this gallery is."

"Well, you wouldn't be the first." Patty plopped into her chair and piled her curly hair on top of her head and secured it with a hair claw. *Secured* might have been too strong a word since several strands broke free. Lindsay would've pointed it out, but the strands were actually framing her face quite nicely.

Lindsay put up her index finger and made a circling motion. "This whole art gallery thing…you're killing it, Cakes. Don't let anyone tell you otherwise."

Patty grinned. "You think my dad would be proud?"

"So proud, hon. So proud."

When Patty's father had died, he'd left the southwest side of Main Street to her on the condition that she keep all of the lessees at their current rate for another five years. After that, it was hers to do with as she pleased. His reason behind that decision was simple. He wanted to give his longtime leaseholders time to find other options. That and he wanted to make sure any changes were slow to be adopted, the way small-town life was meant to be.

Since she had to wait out the five years, Patty had decided it would be fun to turn what had been her grandfather's old camera store into an art gallery. It was meant to be more of a hobby, but she put her art history degree to work and turned out to be a fantastic curator, discovering new talent and bringing in work other gallerists only dreamed of acquiring.

Her complaints about being able to keep the lights on were just a ploy to get Lindsay to bring in more work. She was doing just fine even without the aforementioned southwest side of Main Street. Lindsay couldn't imagine how Patty would walk away from what she'd built. She couldn't imagine losing her best friend, either. But she understood that Salt Creek wasn't the best place in the world for a single lesbian. The gay population was small. It pretty much consisted of Patty; Mrs. Stokely and her late, longtime companion Mildred; the two guys who opened a bowling alley, of all places; and of course, that one gal's husband. With the exception of Patty and the bowling alley guys, all of this was pure speculation on Lindsay's part.

Salt Creek had little to offer in that respect. Boston or Northampton maybe, but not Salt Creek. Lindsay would miss her terribly if she decided to move on, but Patty had spent most of her adult life alone. Lindsay wanted more for her.

Patty leaned forward and rested her elbows on her desk. "Why bring a painting in now, Linds? Should I be worried about you?"

"What? No. Business is good. Better than ever, actually. I have a waiting list."

"Should I pretend to be surprised? Because I'm not." Patty got up and pulled her into a hug. "Seriously. That's amazing."

"It would be if I could focus on my clients' faces instead of—" She looked at the portrait of the boy again. She needed to leave before she changed her mind. "Just get what you can for him, okay? And don't worry about framing it. They'll either like it enough to pay for framing themselves, or they won't."

"Oh yeah," Patty said. "I'll just hang it on a flimsy nail and hope for the best, just like I do with every artist. Hope and pray it doesn't fall when someone slams the front door."

Lindsay sighed. "Okay, fine. I trust you to do whatever you think is best. Just get rid of it, okay?"

Patty went back to her desk and picked up the painting. She set it on an empty easel and stepped back. "Honestly, I can't believe you're selling one."

"Are you trying to talk me out of it? You know it wouldn't be that hard."

Patty wagged her finger. "Oh no, you don't, Lindsay Hall. You're not taking it back now." She grabbed Lindsay's shoulders and pushed her toward the door but stopped and wrapped her arms around her from behind before she could leave. "Whoever that boy is, you know I love him too, right?"

"I know."

"Then trust me to do my job. I'll make sure he goes to someone who sees him."

"No asshole investors who made their money in hedge funds?"

"Linds. Seriously? You know me better than that. I'll make sure he goes to someone who loves him."

Tears threatened to fill Lindsay's eyes. She and Patty had been friends since grade school. They kept each other's secrets, and in a small town like Salt Creek, where gossip spread like wildfire, it was important to have a friend like that.

Patty was also the only person she allowed in her studio besides Brooke. She released herself from Patty's embrace and turned to face her. "I know, Pattycakes. And I love you for it."

"And you'd tell me if something was up, wouldn't you?"

Would painting the face of a woman she'd only seen in her dreams for sixteen hours be considered troubling? She wasn't ready to talk about the painting with anyone. Not even Patty. "I'm not like Mrs. Stokely. I don't sit in the same place, painting the same picture." But she did exactly that, didn't she? "I mean, he's not a photograph I have clipped to my easel."

Patty took hold of her shoulders. "I know that. He's up here." She tapped Lindsay's forehead. Then she pressed her palm to Lindsay's heart. "And here. Hold on. My phone is buzzing." She went to walk away but stopped. "Seriously, Linds? I know what you look like when you're worried. What's wrong?"

"It's nothing—" Lindsay stopped herself. "Actually, there is something. I was in the studio all night. Brooke caught me. She wasn't happy."

Patty waved the comment off. "Oh, she just wants you to be like all of the other boring moms in this town, but you're a badass painter of CEOs and politicians. And a beloved pet every now and then." Patty went back to her desk. "And by the way, I think you're talented as hell, but anyone who'd pay your rate for a painting of their cat has too much money."

Lindsay took a few hesitant steps back into the gallery. "It's a woman." Her words were barely audible. A part of her hoped Patty hadn't heard. Why couldn't she just keep these things to herself?

"What did you say?"

"Nothing. Forget it."

"No, I heard you." Patty stood there with a look of shock. "You promised, Linds. Back in high school, you said I'd be the first to know if you were ever with a woman."

Lindsay remembered it clearly. *I don't just like boys, you know.* It was a truth she would have shared eventually, but at that moment, she'd been lamenting the fact that her life had quite suddenly and very unexpectedly been mapped out for her. What that had to do with the woman in the painting escaped her. "Why bring that up?"

"You just said Brooke caught you in the studio with a woman."

Lindsay slapped a hand over her eyes. "Oh God. OMG, no!" She spread her fingers apart just enough so she could see Patty, who was scowling. She took her hand away. "How could you think I'd bring someone out to my workspace to, I don't know, screw around?"

"How could I possibly have had a crush on you almost our entire senior year? When you smelled like baby vomit? And your boobs got ginormous, and you'd stopped showering? How desperate could I be?"

Lindsay gasped. "I never stopped showering. I was just young and depressed because I was forced to marry a boy I didn't love. And also, what crush?"

"Oh, shut up, Linds. You know I was crushing on you in high school. I hated that you had to marry him. For me and for you. So, yeah, you bring up some woman in the studio, and I...I...kind of want to kick her ass back to wherever she came from. Is that wrong of me?"

"Yes," Lindsay said. "High school crush or not, it's not your place to kick anyone's ass, and you couldn't anyway because she doesn't really exist."

The silence was deafening.

"I spent all night painting her, just like I did the first time I ever painted Timmy, you know?"

Patty softened her tone. "I don't know. Not completely. You have this other world that I can't see. You have memories I don't have. And I can't see the pictures in your head, Linds."

Lindsay nodded.

"I know something has you obsessing over a boy you've never met. And now you're telling me there's a woman? Is it Roo?"

Lindsay winced. Patty respected that she felt she'd lived before, in another time, another place, with a woman she only knew as Roo. But Patty didn't fully understand, couldn't understand. "Yes, it's Roo."

"How do you know?"

Images of a woman with dark brown hair and red lips flashed through Lindsay's mind. She was walking on a beach in a floral summer dress. She turned around and smiling, said, *I love this beach, and I love you, Katie Jane.*

The feeling was most certainly mutual. To Lindsay, it was as if she could feel everything Katie felt for Roo. All of the love and passion. All of the pain. Everything. This woman, Roo, belonged to her.

"Linds?"

Lindsay opened her eyes. "I know what Roo looks like. I know her face. Every freckle. Every laugh line. The small scar above her eyebrow. It's Roo. I've never painted her before, but for some reason, I had to last night. She had to come out of my head and onto a canvas."

Patty seemed surprised. "Never? I mean, I kind of always figured you had paintings you didn't show anyone. Not even me."

Lindsay shook her head. "Not of Roo. I just, I don't know, I guess I always wanted to keep her just for me."

"I'd love to see this person you think you shared another life with. Is she pretty? Is she happy and smiling or sad and crying? What is she wearing? You said she has freckles. Lots of them or just a few? I'm dying to know, Linds. I've wanted to know ever since the first time you told me about her in high school."

To Lindsay, it felt as if she'd always known Roo, but the memories only came to her by accident. Or fate, depending on how she looked at it. She and Patty had been bored on a rainy Saturday afternoon, so they'd gone to a tag sale looking for a cheap video. They'd found a set of CDs that were supposed to guide people through a past life regression. What had happened next would change Lindsay's life forever, in more ways than she could count.

"I think I've never painted Roo because I've been afraid that if I did, I'd lose the memories of her. Of us. Together. It's like, Timmy comes to life on canvas. With Roo, she already comes to me alive. You know?"

"No, I don't know. But you've said you and Roo were like, together, together, right? Do you have memories of that part?"

Lindsay nodded. "Yeah. Together, together."

"Huh." Patty shrugged. "Maybe it won't be like Timmy. You've only painted Roo once."

"Yes. But it wasn't like painting a client's portrait." Lindsay tried to think of a better description. "It was like I was experiencing her, not painting her."

"I don't mean to be flip, but it sounds kind of erotic."

Lindsay turned away and walked over to the window. She could feel her cheeks heating up. "I don't know if that's the right word for it, but kinda, yeah."

Patty let out a long, low whistle. "Wow. I need to see this painting. Can I come over for dinner tonight?"

Lindsay turned back around. "How did my emotional turmoil turn into me making you dinner?"

"Well, you've got to eat, and it just so happens I find myself unexpectedly free."

"Did you break up with that hairstylist? What was her name?"

"Oh! You mean, Stacy—I love your curls, now let me cut them all off—Peters? Yeah, I don't care how good you are in bed, you don't mess with the hair. Plus, the forty-five-minute drive was kind of killing me."

"Right. They always say true love wins. Unless there's an inconvenient commute."

"Or a bad haircut." Patty had thick, curly brown hair that she hardly ever cut. She loved her damn hair, but Lindsay wouldn't have minded seeing what Stacy had in mind. She'd never met Stacy, but she empathized with her desire for a new look.

"Come by around seven," Lindsay said. "I'll make your favorite." She opened the door and noticed that the accompanying sound of a little bell had been replaced with a computer-generated gong. "Where's the bell? I love the bell."

"I updated the security system. Can't have anyone stealing Mrs. Stokely's 'originals.'" She put finger quotes around the last word.

"I'll miss it," Lindsay said. "It always made me feel at home."

Patty threw her hands in the air. "Fine, I'll put the ancient bell back on the door. God, I hate how wrapped around your little finger I am."

Lindsay shouted over her shoulder, "Don't be late, or I'll feed your share to Sir Barksalot!"

❖

Brooke stopped dead in her tracks and sniffed the air. "Is Aunt Patty coming over for dinner? I smell tater tot casserole." She dropped her backpack on the floor and sat at the kitchen island.

"She is." Lindsay dipped her pinkie finger in the vinaigrette and tasted it. "More mustard. Wasn't Corey supposed to stay for dinner tonight?"

Brooke grabbed a few grapes from a bowl of fruit sitting between them. "That car she drives isn't free, Mom. It comes with lots of strings attached." She sighed. "It sucks being a kid. I can't wait until I can choose my own breakfast cereal and movies and boys."

Lindsay quirked an eyebrow. "I don't choose the boys you hang out with." She shrugged. "Much as I'd like to sometimes."

"It's Dad and his unreasonable expectations," Brooke said. "Those boys are just kids too. They don't need to have their whole lives planned out right now. And besides, he's such a hypocrite."

"Your dad? How so?"

"He didn't even wear a condom. Only *tools* do that."

Lindsay sighed. "He was young, Brooke. I was young. It just happened. And P.S., it's the whole reason you're here."

"Oh my God," Brooke exclaimed. "Do you have any idea how much trouble I'd be in if I came home and said, 'it just happened. Hope you're ready to be grandparents at thirty-four'?"

She had a point. Evidently, Patty thought so too. She came into the kitchen and set a bottle of wine on the counter. "You'd be grounded until your poor child, God help him, her, or however that beautiful little cherub identified, turned thirty-four. Then and only then would you be allowed to have a life."

Brooke threw a fist in the air. "Preach, sister."

Patty grabbed Brooke by the chin. "If you even think about getting pregnant before you're twenty-five, I'll tie those tubes with my bare hands."

Brooke's eyes widened. "Wow, Auntie Pattycakes. Way to escalate that shi...oot, is something burning?"

Lindsay smirked. "Nice save. And listen to your auntie. She's a very wise old woman."

Patty gasped. "We're two months apart!"

"Your hair and clothes say different."

It was Brooke's turn to gasp. "Mom!"

"What? The tie-dyed muumuu look screams, I don't shave anything. Ever."

"Mom!" Brooke's mouth hung open. She turned to Patty and whispered, "Really? Nothing?"

Patty laughed. "First of all, muumuus are in now. They're the new yoga pants. And don't argue with me because if it's in *People*, it must be true. Second, don't listen to your mom. I would like to have sex again sometime this century. Not that my privates should be a topic of dinner conversation." Patty glared at Lindsay and made a slicing motion across her neck.

"You can say *vagina* in front of me, Aunt Patty. This kitchen island…" Brooke made a circling motion with her hand. "Is a safe zone. Anyone can say anything they're feeling or thinking as long as you start with the words *I'd like to be in the safe zone right now*. Oh, but don't cuss, or you'll owe a buck to the swear jar. Five if it's an f-bomb."

"Gee," Patty said. "I'm so old, I remember when an f-bomb was only fifty cents."

Lindsay shrugged. "Inflation."

"Yeah, but I've basically funded Brooke's college education, which I have to wonder, was that your goal all along? And if so, when does it stop?"

Brooke turned to Lindsay. "Yeah, Mom. It's kinda pointless since I'm, you know, almost an adult. It's not like I haven't heard every single swear word there is to hear. Plus, it's embarrassing. It's not like any of my friend's moms have a swear jar."

"None of them have Patty Potty Mouth for a best friend, either." Lindsay threw her hands in the air. "Fine. No more swear jar."

Patty and Brooke gave each other high fives and a couple of hip bumps. Lindsay opened the oven and checked on the casserole. She turned back around to find Patty staring at her. "What?"

"Is this safe zone a real thing? Like, you can really say anything, and it'll be okay?"

Lindsay rolled her eyes. "Oh God."

Brooke pulled Patty over to the kitchen island. "Just say the words I told you to say."

Patty cleared her throat. "I'd like to be in the safe zone right now."

Lindsay wanted to laugh when Brooke gave Patty a reassuring

pat on the back. But then she realized there was a real look of fear in Patty's eyes. "What is it, Cakes?"

Patty took a deep breath, looked Lindsay right in the eye and said, "Linds, I've never liked your tater tot casserole."

Brooke's eyes widened. "But it's your favorite, Aunt Patty."

Lindsay's mouth gaped open. "What?"

Patty put her hands on the island. "I'm in the safe zone." She squeezed her eyes shut, then opened just one.

"Since Brooke was born it's been your favorite," Lindsay said. "I've probably made it a hundred times for you."

"More," Patty said. "I swear, I've eaten those tots at least three hundred times."

"Four hundred-ish," Brooke said. "You know, if you really do the math, 'cause I'm seventeen, and if you figure twice a month for seventeen years—"

"That's enough, smarty-pants." Lindsay teased. "And three or four hundred-ish times, you chose to what, gag down the meal I'd worked so hard on?"

Patty put up her hands. "Okay, just hear me out. I had a good reason because for a long time, it was all you knew how to make when company came over, so of course, I complimented you on it. We were kids, Linds, and I wanted you to feel like you were being the grown-up you were forced to be. No offense, Brooke."

"None taken." Brooke looked at Lindsay. "I love your tater tot casserole, Mom. No lie. Corey too. Yeah, she drowns it in ketchup, but she drowns everything in ketchup."

Lindsay's anger turned into hurt and disappointment. "What kind of a friend would lie for years like that?" She shoved the oven mitts on her hands, pulled the piping hot casserole out, and tossed it on the stove.

"Well, first of all, in my defense, I would like to point out that I have not—after all these years— been apprised of the existence of the safe zone. So like, WTF is that?" Patty folded her arms across her chest. "And really, Linds, this is good news if you think about it. I'm mean, you don't ever have to go to so much effort on my account again. We can order pizza or tacos. Help me out here, Brooke. You're the one who got me into this mess."

Lindsay glared at her. "Brooke can't save you when you've been lying for our entire friendship. How can I ever trust you again?"

Patty made a circling motion with her hand. "What about the safe zone?"

"But that was harsh, Aunt Patty. Like, savage harsh. The safe zone is for stuff like, I tried smoking a cigarette, but I promise never to do it again. Or I'm thinking about having sex, but not really. You circled around to casserole, so you're kinda on your own there."

Patty threw her hands in the air. "I didn't know there were parameters! And how is casserole a bigger deal than sex?" She rounded the island. "Linds, please."

Lindsay backed away. "I'm going to my studio. You two can fend for yourself." She pretended to be furious, but she gave Brooke a quick wink on the way out the door.

❖

Ten minutes was longer than Lindsay thought it would take, but she had a beer waiting for Patty when she showed up at the studio door. She kept her eyes on the pencil sketch in front of her and held out the bottle. Patty took the beer and sat where she always did, on an old stool Lindsay had picked up in a secondhand store. Sometimes she needed distance from her work, and the stool by the door gave her just enough. "Don't touch anything."

"You say that every time."

"And I mean it every time." Lindsay took another sip of beer. "Don't tell Brooke I keep beer out here."

"Little Miss Nosy Pants doesn't already know? She's like a freaking investigative journalist. You can't even keep Christmas presents hidden from her."

Lindsay rapped her knuckles on a tall box she'd covered in drop cloths and set behind her easel. "As long as she has access to the other minifridge with the yogurt and coffee creamer, her nosy little ass never imagines Mom would hide another fridge, right?"

Patty's eyes widened. "Oh my God. What else do you keep in there? Chocolate?"

"Of course. And maybe some weed."

"You do not. I haven't seen you smoke since—"

"Last fall on the cape?" Lindsay opened the fridge and pulled out a beer for herself. "I know I grew up fast, but come on. I'm hardly in a retirement home."

"No, love, you're just a recluse." Patty took a swig of her beer. "Don't worry. I'm not going to give my standard-issue 'it's time you thought about dating because you deserve to be happy' lecture." She set the beer down and gave Lindsay a smile. "You know, Linds, it was good to see Brooke stick up for you back there. I think she's so lucky to have a mom as cool as you."

Patty's tone had softened. Lindsay knew she'd meant well, but sixteen years was a long time to lie to your best friend. "You don't have to suck up. Like you said, I don't ever have to make that fucking casserole again." Lindsay swiveled her stool so they were face-to-face. "But keep telling me what a cool mom I am."

"Cool in every way. I mean, look at you. You make paint-splattered overalls look sexy. Whose were they, your grandpa's?"

Lindsay put her leg up on her knee and pulled some of the loose strings from the frayed hem. She'd had to cut a few inches off the legs but had never bothered to hem them again. "I like to imagine they belonged to an old farmer who milked cows and plowed fields in them."

Patty put up her finger. "Or maybe they belonged to a lesbian who refused to conform to societal norms, and she worked on trucks and tractors in them. Maybe even rode a Harley in them."

"She sounds badass." Lindsay yanked on a thread and unraveled more than she'd planned. "Either way, I'm happy to have them now, but I think it's safe to say I'll be their very last owner."

"Linds?"

Patty had that contrite tone in her voice again. It was so out of character it made Lindsay uncomfortable. "Just say it, Cakes."

"Did I blow my chance to see the painting? You know, with the whole casserole thing? Are you still going to let me meet her?"

Lindsay lifted an eyebrow. "Meet her? You make it sound like she's a real person."

"She is to you."

"God, I love you. Thank you for taking me seriously." Lindsay glanced at the covered painting sitting on an easel in the corner. She sighed heavily. "Now that I've painted her, I'm worried she's going to haunt me even more."

Patty glanced at the paintings of the boy. "You're a complicated woman, Lindsay Hall." She stood as if ready to leave.

"Wait." Was she making too much of this? That was always Ben's complaint. *You hoard paintings of that kid like they're your most prized possessions.* "It's not a big deal, right?" Her statement didn't sound convincing, but she hoped Patty would believe it.

Patty shrugged. "If you say so."

With a careful hand, Lindsay lifted the cloth off the painting and let it fall to the floor. She didn't look for Patty's approval. She just stared at it and waited.

"If a ghost was going to haunt me, I'd want it to be her," Patty said. "Hot AF."

Lindsay took a step back. "She is beautiful, isn't she?"

"She's orgasmic. And she's looking right at me. Or through me. Jesus, Linds. It's just this side of scary. Like, I can't decide if she's going to fuck me into next week or kill me and bury me with her own hands."

"Hey, watch it. You're talking about my past life love, you know."

"Artists are so sensitive. I'm evaluating the work purely as a gallerist. That was my professional observation."

"Right. I've been trying to put the feeling she evokes into words, and you're here all of five minutes and—"

"And nailed it, didn't I? She's irresistible. And dangerous. And irresistible."

"Are you going to climax right on that stool? Stop repeating yourself and wipe the sweat from your brow." Patty put a hand on her forehead, and Lindsay laughed. "I was kidding, Cakes." She picked up the cloth and covered the painting back up. "Also, I'm starving because someone ruined my appetite earlier."

"Brookey ordered pizza," Patty said. "It should be here by now." She took another gulp of her beer and poured the rest into the small utility sink. "Gotta destroy the evidence. And, Linds, your secrets are safe with me. All of them."

"I know." Lindsay put her bottle in the sink and wrapped her arm around Patty. "But I still haven't forgiven you for what we'll now refer to as the TTL."

"The what?"

"The Tater Tot Lie."

"Can't we just call it the Teeny Tiny Tater Tot Tale?"

Lindsay huffed. "More like the Big Ass Tater Tot Travesty." She opened the door and locked it behind them.

"But I'm still your Pattycakes, right?"

Lindsay put her arm around Patty's shoulder and walked close to her down the dark path that led to the house. She knew it by heart, but Patty wouldn't know when to duck to avoid hitting her head on the willow tree branch. "No. You're my Tater Tot now."

"Oh, bite me."

Lindsay laughed. "Only if you're wrapped in cotton candy and dipped in chocolate. Watch your head."

"Is that combo even possible?" someone said.

Lindsay stopped short and yelped. Patty screamed and shouted, "Brooke, you can't just stand there silently in the dark like a creepy stalker!"

"Sorry, but the pizza's here." Brooke broke out in a big grin. "Can I call you Auntie Tater Tot now?"

"No," Patty shouted. "Do you people even understand what a safe space is? Like, at all? In fact, you're banned from using those words ever again, under any circumstances."

"I can't say *tater tot*? Like, ever?" Brooke turned to walk inside. "My life sucks so hard right now."

Patty stopped and folded her arms. "Yeah, she's got it so hard. Terrible parents, not a single brain cell in her head, short, stubby legs like mine. Did you know I have to get on my tiptoes to hug her now?"

"I hear you. It's so demoralizing, isn't it? I knew we should have fed her more processed food."

"Don't think that would have helped with the teen angst. My God, they act like they invented it."

"I try to cut her some slack even when I really don't want to," Lindsay said. "She's still working through things with the divorce, and Ben tried to tell her she couldn't go on that Europe trip with the school choir. Apparently, he has some concerns that the choir is going there just to party."

"Kids in Europe? Party? What?" Patty shook her head. "He's being an idiot. I'd overrule him, Linds. They've been fundraising for that trip for over a year."

"I know. My Cherokee has never been so clean with all the car washes they've done."

"I've bought everything they've sold because I thought Brooke would be going."

Lindsay grabbed Patty's arm and led her to the house. "Yes, I'm sure it was a great hardship eating all of that chocolate and popcorn."

"They were like drug dealers, pushing it on the corner in front of You Mock Me Like Crazy. I'm a victim, damnit."

"It's You Mocha Me Crazy," Lindsay said. "But I kinda like your version better."

CHAPTER FOUR

Deb's old wrought iron bed squeaked with every move Ren made, but that was part of its charm. She'd slept on a piece of family history going back to 1828. John Quincy Adams had signed the original deed to the family's land. As for the bed, she imagined many a child had been conceived on it. And maybe a few had even been born on it back in the day.

She'd cracked the window open for some fresh air the night before, so the room felt cool but not cold. The kids had already run up and down the stairs several times, probably having been sent back up because they'd forgotten to put on socks or brush their teeth.

Ren snuggled under the covers and closed her eyes in the hope she'd fall back asleep for another hour. The house fell quiet after a final slam of the front door. She took in a deep breath and slowly exhaled. Maybe she'd sleep for another two hours, then stop by the coffee shop.

The door slowly squeaked open. Ren opened her eyes and saw Caleb with his little hand gripping the knob he could barely reach. He was naked except for a diaper. Ren sat up. "Hey, little man. I thought everyone had left."

Caleb trotted over to the bed. He grabbed the sheet and tried to climb up, but the bed was too high. "Climb in?" he said with a grunt.

"Reach up." Ren pulled him up, and they both settled under the covers.

"Caleb?" Deb shouted from the bottom of the stairs. "Number Two, where are you?"

Caleb whispered, "Uh-oh."

"Yeah," Ren said in a louder than normal voice. "Big Mama is looking for you." She lifted the covers. "You better hide."

"You did not just call me Big Mama." Deb made it to the top of the stairs and put her hands on her hips. "You're both in so much trouble."

Ren threw the covers over her head and whispered, "It's worse than I thought. We better both hide." Caleb cuddled in close and covered his eyes. Ren shrugged and did the same thing. "It's worth a try," she whispered.

Deb played the game for a few minutes, looking everywhere but the guest room. As the tension grew, Caleb couldn't contain himself. He threw off the covers and shouted, "Wen is in here, Mommy!"

"Oh, you ratted me out." She ruffled his messy blond hair.

"Never trust a two-year-old. They have zero loyalty." Deb grabbed Caleb and put him on her hip. "How did you sleep?"

Ren sat up and rubbed her eyes. "Like a baby with a tummy full of milk." She patted the bed. "You didn't buy this new mattress just for me, did you?"

"Of course not. Everyone in this town decided to retire at the same time and travel. Which means when they come back, they'll be sick of the RVs they sold their homes for and will want to shack up with their kids. Colby's mom bought the mattress and said she'll disown us if we let this guy wet his pants on it." Deb poked Caleb in the stomach, making him giggle.

"Oh God. I could've been responsible for you losing your inheritance? You really can't trust a two-year-old."

Deb rolled her eyes. "Trust me, there won't be anything but an old RV to inherit, and I love Colby, but there's no way we'd survive driving from Walmart to Walmart in a tin can together. We'd kill each other at a KOA in Nebraska and end up on *Dateline*. They'd interview the kids one by one, and Corey would cry and say there's no way my dad could've killed my mom. Then Colby Jr. would say something really smart like, that last Facebook post my mom made should've tipped us off that something was wrong, but we're selfish children who don't pay much attention to anything she says. We regret that now."

Ren laughed. "And what would that final Facebook post have said?"

Deb tapped her chin. "Oh, something really vague like, kids, I'm going to kill your father tonight. In his sleep. With that little pistol he keeps in the glove box. If you have any last words for him, you better text him now."

Ren tilted her head. "Should I start checking Facebook more often?"

"Nah. I'm not raising this little traitor on my own." She checked Caleb's diaper. "Number Two strikes again." She kissed his cheek. "You're lucky I love you so much, little guy." She shouted from the hallway, "There's juice and yogurt in the fridge. See you at the shop later?"

"I'll be there!" Ren shouted back.

❖

Ren tugged on the heavily worn boots she saved for her trips to Salt Creek. "Still a perfect fit." She stood and stomped a few times. "Best thing I ever stole from you, Deb."

She couldn't remember exactly when she'd absconded with the old Blundstone boots, but it had to be going on ten years. The only pair of heels she brought was the pair she had on her feet when she arrived. The rest of her trip would be heel-free.

She grabbed her phone and a long wool sweater in case the sun decided to hide behind the clouds on her way into town. In October, it was best to be prepared for any kind of weather.

She tied the sweater around her hips. Yogurt would have been a fine breakfast, but the alternative was decidedly better. Breakfast could wait until she got to the coffee shop.

Deb lived three blocks from Main Street, so it wouldn't be a long walk. Just enough to get some fresh air and maybe do a little window shopping along the way. It was a far cry from Fifth Avenue, but that was what she loved about Salt Creek. She could let her hair down and not worry about impressing clients.

In Paris, she imagined it would be even more important to wear the latest styles. Not that it was a hardship to dress up. Ren loved her shoe collection, even though it took up way too much space in the criminally small closet of her apartment. She loved her Chanel suits and Versace dresses. She loved fancy parties and rubbing shoulders with wealthy art collectors. She fit in well in that world, thanks to her pretentious parents. Well, that and her love of history and the finer things.

Salt Creek offered something different. It grounded her. She felt safe in its simplicity. Unlike New York, she could wear whatever she wanted, and no one would bat an eye.

The air felt cool and crisp, and there wasn't a cloud in the sky. It was the perfect start to her two weeks off. No pressure. No drama. No clients. Just Deb, her family, good coffee, a craft beer or two, and if all went well, one of those cinnamon rolls would soon light up her life.

Ren stopped short when she turned the corner. "*Main Street*. On Main Street. That's new." Or new to her, at least. She couldn't help but wonder what kind of art could be found in Salt Creek. Sure, they got plenty of tourists on their way to see summer stock in Great Barrington or Pittsfield, but who in this town could afford a piece of fine art?

Ren opened the door to the gallery. A loud bell rang out, announcing her arrival, and someone yelled, "Be right there, Mrs. Stokely."

Ren could've shouted back that she wasn't Mrs. Stokely, but she found herself speechless as she stared at the painting in front of her. She hadn't expected to see something so exquisite. So beautifully executed. So full of emotion. She set her water bottle next to a ceramic vase and moved closer.

❖

"Mom, you really need to give up this charade," Brooke said. "You don't even like the dog."

Lindsay opened the front door, leash in hand. "I don't know what you're talking about. I love the dog. And hurry up. Your father's waiting."

With a dramatic huff, Brooke grabbed her backpack off the coat hook. "Yeah, right. That's why you bought a boy dog a pink leash with fake diamonds on it. Not passive-aggressive at all."

"I don't put limitations on Sir Barksalot. He can express himself however he wants."

Brooke stepped out the front door and put up her finger. "Okay, number one, that's not his real name, and number two, you make it sound like he picked out the leash himself."

"He did." Lindsay bit her lip to try to hide her grin and locked the front door behind them. "And heaven knows he needs a good walk."

"Pugs are supposed to look chubby," Brooke said.

"Not that chubby." Lindsay held the leash up and waved at Ben. He rolled his eyes and shook his head. *Good. Mission accomplished.*

Brooke opened the truck door. "Hey, Dad. Hey, boy." She scratched Sir Barksalot behind the ears, then set him on the ground and said, "Sorry for what you're about to endure."

Lindsay bent down and secured the leash on his collar. "Isn't joint custody fun, Sir Barksalot?" He licked her wrist. "Ew, don't do that."

"I'll pick him up tomorrow night," Ben said. "And don't lose him by 'accident.'" He put finger quotes around the last word.

Lindsay held up the pink leash. "We're going to strut down Main Street together. Sure hope some of your buddies see us."

"Oh God, Mom." Brooke slammed the door and covered her eyes.

"Love you, honey!" Lindsay gave them a big wave as they drove off. She looked at Chubby McChubberson and shook her head. "I couldn't lose you if I tried." She rubbed behind his ear the way he liked. God, she loved that damned dog. She tried to pretend it was just an arrangement for the sake of the divorce, but the truth was, she hated sharing him.

Lindsay checked the pocket of her fleece jacket to make sure she had two plastic bags since the pug was famous for needing more than one pit stop on a fifteen-minute walk. Finding herself to be appropriately stocked, she announced, "Okay. Let's go, Barksy."

❖

A woman came out from the back room and stopped dead in her tracks when she saw Ren. "Oh!"

"I'm not Mrs. Stokely, obviously. Sorry, I should have said something."

"No, it's quite all right." She laughed. "You're most certainly not a grumpy elderly woman here to scold me about why I haven't sold one of her paintings this week."

"Ah. Nope. Not elderly or grumpy. Well, not grumpy after my second cup of coffee in the morning. I'm Ren. Ren Christopher."

"Wait. Ren? Kevin Bacon's Ren?"

"Good catch. Most people assume I'm named after the bird. It's a lot easier than explaining my mom's obsession with *Footloose*." She pointed at the painting she'd been admiring. "Can you tell me anything about the painting and the artist? I don't think I've seen their work before."

"The artist is local. And she's been very secretive about this one. I actually had to convince her to sell it, and trust me, it wasn't easy. She only brought it in this morning." She backed away. "Do you mind if I make a quick phone call?"

Ren wasn't in a big hurry, but she did want to get to Deb's place as soon as possible. "I actually need to meet someone. I'm very interested in that painting, but I don't see a price on it."

"Yeah, I didn't expect to have a buyer so soon. Maybe you could come back another time?"

She needed some serious coaching on how to treat a prospective buyer. Ren wasn't about to let her get away with such bad service. She offered her hand. "I didn't catch your name."

"Patty. I own the gallery."

Okay, so this was progress. "Nice to meet you, Patty." Ren pulled her credit card out of her phone wallet. "I'd like to purchase that painting." She noticed the beads of sweat on Patty's forehead. "Are you okay?"

"I...I really need to call someone."

"Okay. Um, I can wait." Ren watched closely as Patty sat at her desk and put her phone to her ear. They stared at each other until Patty looked away and began whispering. Ren stepped closer so she could listen in.

"There's a woman here, an art dealer, I think. Anyway, she wants to buy the boy—Timmy—she wants to buy Timmy. I know I begged you to sell it, but now I'm feeling like I pressured you, and I'm not sure what to do."

"Sell it to me?" Ren flashed Patty a winning smile when she turned. "I promise it'll go to a good home."

"Call me," Patty said into the phone. She set it on her desk and stood. "It's just that I made a promise to the artist."

"I get it," Ren said. "Artists can be fickle. Sounds like we have a very hesitant seller here?"

"You could say that. And since I don't really know anything about you..."

"What would you like to know? In fact, why don't you just google me." She put up a hand. "Wait. Don't do that. My ex has been posting crazy stuff on Facebook."

"Oh God. I hate it when that happens," Patty said with a groan. "They think they're being all sly with vague posts about betrayal and heartache and letting go, as if all of their followers are complete idiots and have no idea who they've been dating for the last few months. I mean, just grow up, Stacy."

Ren threw her hands up. "Right? Grow up, Krazy Kerry with two Ks. No one cares that you've lost your voice from whispering my name over and over."

Patty scrunched her nose up. "Really? A dude posted that on Facebook? He's brave."

"Krazy Kerry is a woman who, I regret to say, seduced me with her amazing smile and quick wit and then proceeded to turn my world upside down, and not in a good way."

"Oh, I've been there. Women." Patty tried to smooth her wild, curly hair but quickly gave up and proceeded to twist it up into a spikey puff on her head.

Ren stared in fascination at the dexterity and quick tucks that held it all in place without any pin or barrette. She waited a few seconds, expecting it to explode, but it held. "Wow, that's impressive. I wish I could do that with my hair. You should put that on YouTube. It's like watching hands shuffle cards or knead dough or build tiny things."

"Oh, it's nothing." Patty waved a hand. "You're making me blush."

"Well, I feel we're moving in a more positive direction, Patty."

"Yeah, sorry about that. Can we start over?"

"Absolutely. Let's start over by you ringing me up for that painting over there."

"I was thinking more along the lines of a song. 'Hello' by Lionel Richie."

Ren managed to barely hold back her laughter. "A song. Okay. Are you singing the song, or am I?"

"For some reason, ever since you walked through that door, I felt like I needed to belt out that song. Like, just sing it from the top of my lungs. Just get it out there into the universe, you know? I do that with all the new girls in town."

Patty's phone vibrated on the desk. She grabbed it and said, "Linds? Yeah, never mind. I got this. Me and Lionel Richie have totally got this. I got your back, babe. You are under my umbrella, if you know what I mean. No, it's a song. No, not a Lionel Richie song. Rhianna!" Patty slammed the phone down as if that somehow ended the call the way it would with a landline.

Ren gestured at the phone. "I think I can hear her yelling for you."

Patty hit the end button and set the phone back down. "Okay, here's the deal. You can buy the painting."

Ren rubbed her hands together. "Now we're getting somewhere."

Patty put up a finger. "Ah. Not so fast."

"Oh, right. The Lionel Richie song." Ren grabbed a letter opener off the desk and offered it to Patty. "I usually need a microphone when I belt out a song."

Patty sat on the edge of the desk and held the letter opener to her mouth. "The urge to sing has passed, but it's important for you to know that my BFF is the artist, and if anything bad were to happen to that painting, I would be forced to hunt you down."

Patty continued to hold the letter opener like a microphone while she waited for a reply. Ren reached for it, and Patty handed it over. She put it to her mouth and said, "I promise that won't be necessary."

Patty took the letter opener back and pushed off the desk. "One more thing." She walked to a small landscape that hung on the wall. "You will also purchase this painting done by a local artist named J. Stokely. It's a package deal or no deal at all."

This was quite possibly the strangest negotiation Ren had ever experienced while purchasing artwork, but she felt utterly amused by Patty, and she really wanted that painting, so she offered her hand. "Ah yes, the famous Mrs. Stokely. Her reputation precedes her. Consider it done."

❖

Sir Barksalot gave Lindsay that pathetic look again. "Nope. Not falling for it, mister. Your dad might cave under that kind of pressure, but I won't."

Sir Barksalot sniffed the air, licked his chops, and whined.

Lindsay also got a whiff of what could only be Deb's famous, at least in the Hall household, caramel shortbread cookies. "If you weren't on a diet, Barksy, I'd share one with you." She tied his leash to the bike rack, knowing full well she'd buy one of those homemade doggie treats Deb kept in a jar by the cash register. "Stay, Barksy.

And don't let anyone steal that fancy leash of yours. The diamonds aren't real, but not everyone knows that, you know?"

He sat back on his haunches and whined again.

Lindsay backed away and shook her finger at him one last time. "Be a good boy. I'll be right back." She walked into You Mocha Me Crazy, stopped, and closed her eyes. "Oh my God, it smells good in here."

Deb gave her a wave from behind the counter. "Hey, Linds. Same as always?"

"If by same as always you mean two cinnamon rolls, a half dozen shortbread cookies, a doggie treat, and a tall Americano, extra hot, then yes, same as always."

Deb laughed. "I wish all of my regulars placed big orders like that." She grabbed a paper cup and held it up. "To go?"

"Yeah, I'd love to stay and chat, but I have a rotund canine waiting for me."

Deb looked past her. "He looks fine to me. And look, he misses you."

Lindsay turned around, and there Barksy was, blocking the door and trying to make everyone think he'd been abandoned. "Oh, he just wants one of your cinnamon rolls, and believe me, he's not too proud to beg. Get some pride, Barksy!" She turned back to Deb. "Actually, when it comes right down to it, I'm not too proud to beg either. Please tell me you haven't sold out of them already."

"You're in luck."

"Oh, thank God," Lindsay said. "Brooke would not be a happy camper if she knew I indulged in her favorite treat without her."

"Yeah, I can't hide anything from Corey either," Deb said. "Those two should be private detectives."

"Their interrogation techniques alone, am I right?"

Deb's eyes widened. "I've often wondered if they didn't take an online course at some point because Corey can sniff out a lie faster than that dog out there could find raw hamburger in his doggie dish."

"You lie to your children, Deb? I'm shocked. Just shocked."

Deb slid the cup across the counter. "I'm not even going to try with Caleb. I'll let Corey and Colby Junior decide how long they want to keep him in the dark about Santa and the Easter Bunny and the tooth fairy, etcetera."

"How do you keep all of those C names straight? I have a hard enough time with Brooke and Ben."

Deb shrugged. "They all have nicknames, even if some of them are just in my head."

"Oh, this should be rich." Lindsay leaned in close. "Spill it."

"Corey is Coreo, like her favorite cookie. That one I say out loud. When she's being a hormonal teenager, I call her Corgesterone. Core the Bore tells meandering stories about the teachers at school as if I'd never spent a day in high school or had exactly the same teachers back in the day because apparently, they never leave."

Lindsay giggled under her breath.

"Oh, your kid's not off the hook either," Deb said. "When Corey won't get off the damn phone, I know it's Babbling Brooke we have to thank."

"Totally fair," Lindsay said with a laugh. "I don't think she talks to me in an entire month as much as she talks to Corey in an afternoon. Tell you what, though, when she acts like we live in poverty because we won't let her do this or that, I'm going to call her Brokey."

"Oh, that's Junior's schtick too. He always needs money. Plus, his feet smell like rotten cheese, so I call him Colby Jack."

"And your little one?"

"He's Number Two because it seems like his diaper is always full."

Lindsay laughed out loud. "Oh my God, this is fantastic."

Deb grabbed a pastry box and started packing it with Lindsay's order. "Good thing I already set aside a cinnamon roll for my houseguest. You're clearing me out."

Lindsay took her coffee to the condiment station and added a little bit of milk and sugar. "Friends in town?"

"Yup, my old college roommate." Deb pointed at the door. "Oh, she's here."

Lindsay put the lid back on her cup and turned so she could introduce herself. Her mouth gaped. She waved in a futile effort to grab a chair or table before she lost the will to stand.

CHAPTER FIVE

Lindsay woke with a start. The ceiling wasn't white with an orange peel texture like the one in her bedroom. There were pipes and air ducts and concerned faces. "Ow." She grabbed the back of her head and found a goose-egg-sized bump. "What the hell happened?"

"You fainted, dear. Did you forget to have breakfast this morning? If you remember in fifth grade, you fainted in my classroom because your blood sugar was too low."

Lindsay appreciated Mrs. Stokely's concern, but she had the story all wrong. Fifth graders had dropped like flies due to a heat wave. The AC wasn't working in the portable classroom they'd put in the school parking lot while they renovated their regular classroom. It was all Ethan Thomas's fault. One day, he'd decided to set his desk on fire just to "see what would happen." How could Mrs. Stokely forget that part?

Deb knelt next to Lindsay and put a cold cloth on her head. "I can't have customers dropping dead in my shop, Linds. It's bad for business." Deb gave her a wink and moved the cloth to Lindsay's cheek.

"Just tell them I died from too much pleasure while eating your masterpiece of a—" Lindsay stopped when she heard someone laugh. She turned her head, and there she was again, sitting in a chair with her elbows on her knees, old boots on her feet, and a smile on her face that Lindsay would never in a million years forget.

And for some reason, she had a painting of the boy leaning on the chair next to her. It was too much for Lindsay's brain to comprehend. She was obviously in the upside-down because as sure as the sun would set tonight and rise again tomorrow, Lindsay knew she was looking at Roo. Or the present-day version of Roo.

As her emotions welled, Lindsay had to blink tears away so she could see Roo more clearly. "Hi," she whispered.

The woman put out a hand as if she wanted to help Lindsay to her feet. "Hi. I'm Ren."

Ren, not Roo. Lindsay wanted to repeat the name over and over. She felt more tears welling. The rest of the world faded away. There was only Roo. Or Ren. She swallowed the lump in her throat and said, "Sorry, I'm, um…" She trailed off, unable to think of her own name.

Ren withdrew her hand. "Lindsay."

"How did you—"

"Deb's said it about fifty times trying to wake you up."

"Oh. Right." God, she was so beautiful. Her eyes were perfect. Such a deep brown. So full of emotion. So expressive. Much like Roo's eyes.

"I think she might be a little confused from the fainting," Deb said. "Let's get her up off the floor."

"Lindsay!" Patty rushed into the shop. "Oh God! What happened?"

Lindsay sat up. "I'm fine. Really. Just a little light-headed."

"Fine? Why are you on the floor?"

"Can you give me a lift home, Cakes? I just need to rest. Then I'll be fine."

"Of course. Let's get you up." Patty leaned down and grabbed her arm.

Deb and Patty helped her stand. A headache was setting in, and the bump on her head throbbed. She took a deep breath and paused to get her bearings. "I'm so embarrassed. I don't know what that was."

"I'll pack up your order and bring it over later," Deb said. "I'll want to check on you anyway."

A burning sensation on Lindsay's chest caused her to look down. Coffee covered her white Henley and jeans. Her face burned from embarrassment, but her chest was just plain burned. She always ordered her coffee extra hot, but today that turned out to be a mistake. She grabbed Patty's hand to steady herself and turned to Deb. "Do you have some ice you could put in a bag for me?"

"You should see a doctor."

Lindsay turned to protest and found Ren standing less than an arm's length away. She resisted the urge to step closer out of fear she'd completely lose control of her emotions. She couldn't fall into a stranger's arms and cry on her chest. She couldn't breathe her in or feel her skin or get lost in her voice. She'd get so drunk on the feeling that she'd say or do something inappropriate. "I'll be fine," she said. But she couldn't look away. Every day for the rest of her life, she'd regret it if she didn't spend these precious seconds committing that face to memory.

"You fell hard." Ren stepped even closer. "And your chest is red. I think maybe the coffee burned you. Deb, hurry up with that ice!"

Lindsay felt faint again. Dizzy. The sound of Ren's alto voice felt like a healing salve on a long-open wound, but at the same time, it was all so confusing. And so painful.

Hard as she tried, she couldn't hold Ren's stare. She dropped her gaze and questioned if this person was real or if this was just another dream she'd wake up from. The pain in her head, the burning on her skin, and the tightness in her chest told her it was real. But how could this be real? And why now? It was going on eighteen years since she'd had the past life breakthrough, so what did it all mean?

There were no clear answers. She had no idea where her past life took place or who Roo was then. And now, here was Ren. One look at her, and Lindsay had known she was looking at Roo. And the next thing she knew, she was flat on her back. It was all too much. She needed to get out of there before she humiliated herself again.

"I'll be fine." Lindsay backed away. "I just need to get home and rest a bit."

Mrs. Stokely piped in. "You'll do no such thing. I'll drive

you to the clinic myself." She dug into her purse for her keys. "I remember that stubborn streak of yours, missy, and I'll have none of that today."

Oh, fabulous. Could this get any more embarrassing? Lindsay didn't want to make more of a scene than she already had. She'd just have to climb into Mrs. Stokely's 1979 Buick LeSabre that she got on her fortieth birthday and had been driving ever since. Everyone knew the exact year and model because Mrs. Stokely didn't refer to it as *her car*. It was always, "my 1979 Buick LeSabre." It became a joke with the kids. They'd admire her car and ask what year it was just so they could hear Mrs. Stokely call it a LeSabe-ruh, as she chose to pronounce it, painted in what the Buick designers called Saffron Firemist. So basically, a rusty colored car.

Back in the day, it was considered a badge of honor if you managed to get a ride in what the kids called the Mistmobile. Bets were even waged. Dares made. Lindsay hadn't ever participated in those dares, so this would be her first ride. She always thought Saffron Firemist would be a good name for a superhero. In fact, she'd be loath to admit it, but Saffron Firemist was her online username.

She would have to convince Mrs. Stokely to take her straight home, bypassing any doctor visits. If she went home and climbed under the covers for a hundred years, maybe that would be long enough for everyone to forget this moment of humiliation. A hundred years would be perfect, actually. She could meet up with Ren or Roo or whoever in the next life. Forget this one ever happened.

Ugh. Why couldn't she have been chill about the whole thing? Just act like it was no big deal. Be cool and say sophisticated things in a low, slightly gravelly voice like, "I see you bought my painting. I'd be happy to put a personal note on the back of the canvas. Have a Sharpie, by chance? No? Me neither because who carries a Sharpie with them?" *Not cool, Lindsay. Not even close.*

"Get your things, dear." Mrs. Stokely took Lindsay by the arm and whispered, "Do you think Deb's friend knows whose paintings she just bought?"

Lindsay hadn't noticed Mrs. Stokely's smaller landscape sitting on the table. She leaned in and whispered, "Can we not tell her? If she knew it was me, she might want to return it."

"Nonsense." Mrs. Stokely puffed up her chest as much as an elderly woman with a slight hunch could and turned to Ren. "Whatever you paid for that boy, it was a steal." She winked at Lindsay and turned to leave. She didn't let go of Lindsay's arm, apparently intending to drag her out of the shop.

"I know," Ren said.

Lindsay paused for a few seconds, then turned to look at her.

Ren stood there with her arms folded. "It's extraordinary, actually. Exquisite." Ren looked at the painting again and back up at Mrs. Stokely. "Do you know the artist?"

Lindsay shook free of Mrs. Stokely and was out the door before anyone could answer. She spotted the Mistmobile across the street and rushed over to it. It wasn't surprising that the car was unlocked. One of the many benefits of living in Salt Creek.

The door felt heavy and closed with a force. She scanned the dashboard. It looked like one of those private jets she'd seen in the movies with the shiny wood grain and silver knobs. The steering wheel looked too skinny. Nothing like today's cars. And right in front of her, above the glove box, was an actual clock. Not a digital clock, but one with a second hand that was ticking away.

The tan velour felt soft under her fingers. It showed very little wear and tear. She wondered what the horn would sound like and reached over to push it right when Mrs. Stokely opened the driver's side door. "Don't you dare blow that horn at me, young lady."

Lindsay pulled her hand back. She knew better than to help Mrs. Stokely with her purse, or "pocketbook," as Mrs. Stokely called it. The woman valued her independence and let everyone know it. "I just wondered how loud it is."

Mrs. Stokely got situated behind the wheel and pushed hard on the horn. "Loud enough to get your heart beating a might faster, and I'm not afraid to use it."

Lindsay jumped at the sound. Talking with Mrs. Stokely always made her feel like she was a kid and could be grounded at any moment if she said the wrong thing. She was pretty sure that's exactly how Mrs. Stokely saw her. "Yes, ma'am."

They both jumped at the sound of a knock on the passenger window. Surely, with the right person behind the wheel, the Saffron Firemist would be a great getaway car. Big engine roaring, tires shrieking. But an elderly woman driving as if she'd just robbed a bank only happened in the movies, and even then, it was a stunt man wearing a gray wig. Unfortunately, Mrs. Stokely was no stuntman, so she chose to keep the car in park, ensuring Lindsay's further humiliation.

Since there was no escaping this nightmare, Lindsay turned toward the window and forced a smile. Ren gave her a wave and held up a pink leash. "I think this is your dog," she shouted.

Oh, God! Lindsay was such an idiot. First, the fainting, then she forgot a *whole* dog. She'd run right past him, hell-bent on extracting herself from that horrendous scene with Ren. Because Ren. *Ren.* Lindsay's gaze fell to the gap in Ren's blouse. She could see the curve of her breasts. The light freckles on her smooth skin. She looked nothing like Roo, but she was just as intriguing.

The whole thing was crazy. It was just the painting of Timmy and the beautiful woman and the low blood sugar like Mrs. Stokely said. All of that, with the déjà vu? Who wouldn't have fainted? Lindsay knew the answer to that. No one else would have fainted.

By the time Mrs. Stokely interrupted Lindsay's train wreck of a thought process, she was horrified to discover she was still ogling Ren's breasts. Lindsay turned her attention to the car's window crank handle. She twisted the little knob at the end of the handle and heard Mrs. Stokely firmly announce that "Animals do not ride in my 1979 Buick LeSabe-ruh."

"Of course not, Mrs. Stokely." Lindsay reached for the door handle. "I'll just walk him home."

"You will do no such thing." Mrs. Stokely sighed. "The mutt may ride with us, but he has to stay on the floor."

"Yes, ma'am." Lindsay opened her door.

Her tummy fluttered when Ren smiled at her and said, "Deb told me it was your painting. She said there are others. I'd love to know more about it. Maybe we could have coffee sometime. When you're feeling better, of course."

Would Lindsay faint again if they had coffee? No. It was the shock, the surprise of seeing the woman she'd painted standing right in front of her. She could have coffee with her, couldn't she? Lindsay wasn't so sure. It would help if it was Irish coffee.

Ren raised her eyebrows ever so slightly as if to say, Well?

"You also bought one of Mrs. Stokely's paintings," Lindsay blurted.

A look of confusion flashed across Ren's face but quickly morphed into another breathtaking smile. "I'd love to have coffee with both of you, then."

"It's a date," Mrs. Stokely said. "Two p.m. tomorrow at my house. 189 West Center Street. Don't be late."

Lindsay leaned over and snapped her fingers. "Get in and stay, Barksy." She turned to Ren. "I swear I don't usually leave my dog in public places. Thanks for taking care of him for me." Another wave of humiliation washed over her when she noticed just how much coffee she'd spilled on herself. Pretty much the entire cup had soaked through her shirt and bra. She imagined a parallel universe where the Mistmobile's thrusters lit up and lifted them straight into the air like a helicopter, then shot off at light speed to another galaxy called Anywhere Else.

Ren's hair would blow back, and she'd block her eyes from the sun as she watched them go, never to be seen or heard from again. Ren would recount the strange events, but with time, her memories would fade, and she'd eventually sell the paintings she'd bought that day.

The town of Salt Creek would realize a superhero had lived amongst them for years. Mrs. Stokely and her Mistmobile would live in infamy. Sadly, the car remained firmly in park.

Sir Barksalot didn't like being relegated to the floor. He barked and pawed at Lindsay's leg. Ren got down on one knee and scratched his ears. "His name is Barksy?"

Since the thrusters hadn't kicked in, Lindsay would have to come up with an excuse so she wouldn't have to join them for coffee.

Of course, that wouldn't be hard, considering the huge bump on her head. "His full name is Sir Barksalot. You know, because he—"

"Barks a lot?" Ren said with a grin.

Mrs. Stokely laughed and patted Lindsay's knee. "No explanation needed, dear."

"Right." Lindsay rubbed her forehead. "I'm not myself today."

Ren stood and put her hand on the door to close it. "Put some ice on that bump, and I guess I'll see you both tomorrow?"

"You've made a commitment, so it seems there would be nothing to guess about, is there, dear?"

"No, ma'am, I don't believe there is." Ren looked at Lindsay. "Like you said, it's a date."

"Good. What's my address?" Mrs. Stokely put the car in reverse and waited for Ren to answer.

"189 West Center," Ren said without diverting her gaze.

"A woman who listens. I like you already. It's the red brick house on the corner."

Ren barely got the door closed before Mrs. Stokely hit the gas and reversed without looking behind her. Lindsay turned and shared a look of half-faux panic as she gave Ren a small wave good-bye. It was fine if Ren was the last person she saw before she died on the way to the clinic. Saffron Firemist dying in the Mistmobile after seeing her one true love for the first time? It seemed like an epic ending. She'd take it.

❖

As it happened, Lindsay did not die in a fiery crash. After they dropped Barksy off at Lindsay's house, Mrs. Stokely took her to the clinic as promised. Lindsay insisted Mrs. Stokely not wait with her. The retired teacher still did occasional private tutoring at the library and had a student waiting.

Lindsay waited in the lobby until Mrs. Stokely drove away, then walked the few blocks back to her car. The clinic was packed, and she'd spend at least an hour sitting on a hard chair while her chest burned and her head ached. Besides, she'd be fine, and she sure as hell wasn't going to explain what had made her faint.

While she was a supporter of truth-telling at the doctor's office, this particular clinic was run by Dr. Jim, a kid who'd been three grades behind her in school. A kid who would've been voted more likely to Revolutionize the Bong Industry than Go to Medical School.

They'd called him Jimbo at his request. So no, she would not be telling this particular story to Jimbo, but she also knew that not giving any reason at all would mean they'd have to run tests. No, thanks. It was just a bump on her head, and the burns were superficial. Nothing she couldn't take care of on her own. Or with the help of Patty, who was parked in her driveway when she pulled in.

Lindsay stopped and unrolled her window.

"I knew you wouldn't go to the clinic. Get in," Patty said.

Lindsay ignored the request and pulled into the garage. Patty was right there when she got out of her car. "This is nuts, Linds. I could've helped you."

"What was I supposed to do? Decline the ride from Evil Knievel Stokely? And miss my chance to ride in a classic?" Lindsay dropped her purse on the kitchen counter. She needed a clean shirt and something for her headache.

"I'm not talking about the LeSabre, and you know it. You should be at urgent care. What if you have a concussion or something?"

"I don't."

"Okay, but will you at least tell me what that was all about? Did Ren say something to upset you? Was it the painting? Oh God, it was the painting, wasn't it?"

"She didn't have to say anything, Cakes." Lindsay covered her face with her hands. "God, one look and I knew."

"Okay, you've lost me."

Lindsay dropped her hands. "It's Roo. She's Roo. I felt it. I don't know how to describe it, but I just knew."

Patty blinked. No words, no movement. She just blinked. And then she blinked again.

Lindsay broke their gaze. She couldn't really blame Patty. She knew how it sounded. She opened one of the kitchen cupboards, slammed it shut, and opened another one. "That's what's on my mind at the moment, so no, I'm not really worried about a concussion." She turned back around. "What's nuts is, last night, I finally painted Roo, and today, a woman I'm certain is her walked into your gallery and bought one of my paintings—Timmy, of all paintings—right off the wall. What the hell is happening?"

Patty pointed at herself. "You're asking me?"

Lindsay laughed. "Right. Maybe I do have a concussion." She grabbed a bottle of aspirin out of the cupboard and checked the expiration date. "Damnit, it's old." She tossed the bottle in the trash.

"OMG. You're such a mom. You check the expiration dates?" Patty didn't wait for a reply before digging through her purse. "You never were prepared for emergencies." She pulled out a small vial and shook two pills into Lindsay's palm.

"The thing I wasn't prepared for was finding myself in a *Stranger Things* episode." Lindsay climbed the stairs to the second floor with Patty right behind her. She sat on the bed and took off her shirt.

Patty went into the master bathroom and started opening drawers and cupboards. "Aha!" She came out holding a bottle of aloe vera gel. "Lean back, and I'll squirt it on your chest, and don't you dare ask me what the expiration date is on this. It's fine."

Lindsay leaned back on her elbows. "Try not to make a mess. I just changed the sheets."

With her pinkie finger, Patty spread the aloe over the red patches. "I shouldn't have sold Timmy to her, but she wouldn't take no for an answer, and you know how hard it is for me to say no to a pretty lady."

"You say no to me all the time."

"Well, Linds, I have high standards when it comes to who I have sex with."

Lindsay plopped back on the bed and threw an arm over her eyes. "In your dreams."

"Only once. And it was a really long time ago. Like, ages."

Lindsay pushed her hand away. "Okay, get away from my boobs." She tried to suppress her laughter, but it broke through. She needed a good laugh after what had just happened, so she let it go.

"Nice bra," Patty said. "It's really a shame they didn't have to rip your shirt open and use those paddle thingies."

Lindsay covered her chest with her hands and laughed even harder.

"I mean, apart from the fact that your heart would've stopped beating. But I guarantee, those EMTs, be they male or female, would've thought to themselves, damn, that's a sexy bra."

Lindsay wiped the tears from her eyes and caught her breath. The laughter helped release some of the tension, but it didn't take away her confusion. It was all so humiliating. She didn't think she'd be able to show her face at You Mocha Me Faint for quite some time. Possibly not ever. "Am I going crazy, Cakes? I feel like I'm going crazy. The idea of Roo has never felt crazy to me. But this? This I didn't see coming."

The bed sank with the weight of Patty by Lindsay's side. "Maybe you're right. Maybe it's her, and you were always meant to meet again."

"Maybe."

"Linds?"

"Yeah?"

"How many times have we been out on the grass in this exact same position, staring up at the sky, wondering what else is out there?"

"Too many to count."

"And still no answers."

Lindsay turned onto her side. "Cakes?"

"Yeah?"

"You were there that day when I first remembered Roo."

Patty put up a finger. "Correction. I slept through those stupid past life CDs and dreamt about Emily Burton, that hottie from English class. Remember her? Also, peach schnapps? What were we thinking? We could have stolen anything in my dad's liquor cabinet. I still cringe every time I hear someone order a fuzzy navel."

"Which is exactly never, I bet."

"The point is, we were pretty tipsy, and my experience was, you know, more like on the unconscious side of the hypnosis spectrum."

"Seriously, Cakes? Those CDs cost ten dollars! What was I thinking, spending my hard-earned money on an experience you'd pass out for?"

"Terrible decision-making skills on your part, and not the first time either," Patty said. "Right up there with that time you insisted we take the Ouija board to the cemetery at two in the morning."

"Whoa. Hold up. I insisted? As in, me? You think that was my idea?"

"Uh, yeah. You were all, 'Cakes, look at this thing I found at the pawnshop.' And I was all, 'I don't know, Lindsay, this doesn't seem like the best idea. Maybe we should study instead.' Remember?"

"No. I definitely don't remember that pile of bullshizzle. What I do remember is that because of *your* stupid idea, we ended up scaring ourselves shitless."

Patty sighed. "Well, if it was my idea, and I'm certainly not copping to that, but if it was, I'm still paying the price."

"What do you mean?"

"To this day, I still can't look Brent Atkinson in the eye. Every time I see him, I wish he'd move out of town."

"Oh my God, that's right," Lindsay said with a laugh. "You jumped on his lap that night and peed your pants."

"And ruined that fab vintage skirt I'd found."

"Don't forget the combat boots you wore *with* that skirt."

"Yeah, I was like a walking billboard for Al's Penny and Pawn."

"No wonder he went out of business," Lindsay quipped.

"Oh, stop. My artsy look was hot," Patty said. "And FYI, Al had knee surgery and developed a blood clot in his leg that went to his heart. Don't you ever read the obituaries?"

Lindsay huffed. "Like I need more dead people in my life." She rolled onto her back again. "Maybe it was the schnapps that fucked with my head. I let Ben go all the way that night too."

"Ha! It would take a lot more than peach schnapps—" Patty threw a hand over her mouth. "Sorry. I know he's the father of our little Brookey. That's probably my fault too. I'm the one who called you a prude that day. I remember thinking I should apologize, but I don't think I ever did. And then, boom! You were pregnant."

"Relax, Cakes. I only regret that night when Brooke is slamming doors in my face. And not even then, not really. She's everything to me, although these days, it feels like she'd rather have another mother."

"No way. She's ten times better and more interested in you than we ever were in our parents. Plus, you're the best mom ever. And one day, Brooke is going to realize that. In fact, it'll probably hit her right when she's accepting the Nobel Peace Prize, and she'll get so choked up she won't be able to finish her speech. That's when her awesome wife, the hot Wimbledon champion, will step in and finish for her. And there you'll be, standing in between your two grandchildren, clapping and crying tears of joy. But no one will know you're a grandma because you'll still look so young."

Lindsay shook her head. "Oh, Cakes. You want everyone to be gay, don't you? Not that it would be a bad thing."

Patty shrugged. "The world would be a better place, in my not so humble opinion."

Lindsay rolled onto her side. "Agreed. You deserve the Nobel Prize for friendship. Now, let me spoon you so I can sleep off this massive headache."

Patty grabbed a pillow and fluffed it. "You know I'm always up for spooning. And naps. Preferably at the same time."

❖

Lindsay locked herself in her studio and pulled the blinds. After a short nap, she'd told Patty to go back to the gallery. Her need for a babysitter had passed, even if that babysitter was the person she trusted more than anyone in the world.

She told Patty she could use a bit of alone time to get her emotions under control before Brooke came home. It wasn't a lie, but it wasn't the whole truth, either. She was desperate to get back out to her studio and see the painting of Roo again.

Had she somehow made a connection between Ren and Roo that didn't really exist? She was running on very little sleep since she'd spent the previous night painting. Was it simply a lack of sleep combined with the intense emotional experience of painting Roo that had her in a vulnerable place?

Lindsay knew the difference between what she did for a living as a portrait painter and what she did painting Timmy and Roo. The process couldn't have been more different.

Lindsay's paying clients came to her through word of mouth, and for some reason—"Because you're amazing," Patty had said—word had really spread over the last few years. People from all over the country hired her to paint their portraits. For the most part, she required that they come to Salt Creek for sittings so she could be a constant presence in Brooke's life. She also saw things more clearly there, in her studio, at home. It was where she belonged. It was where she worked.

Occasionally, a prospective client would insist she work from a photograph. They were too busy or too important to meet her conditions. They couldn't possibly sit in person. It always amazed her how confidently they'd try to explain how she should do her job. Equally confident, Lindsay would explain that perspective and personality didn't come to her through a photograph. Yes, a great photographer captured those things in a moment, but the chances of it being the same moment that would inspire Lindsay were approximately zero.

She'd grown accustomed to good feedback. People said she had the ability to capture a person's essence. More than one stated that it felt as if they had been truly seen and that the canvas had come to life. For Lindsay, it was always a matter of trying to grab hold of the moment when someone didn't know she was watching. As implausible as it sounded, it happened every time.

Yes, people knowingly sat for paintings, but they tended to

forget that fact after a few hours. Some were anxious; others were overconfident. Some didn't seem to know why they were there at all. But the stillness of the studio was the same for everyone. The rich, the famous, the powerful. The gentle light and slightly warm temperature seemed to relax her subjects. It was a quiet place, with only the soft sound of Lindsay's voice and the occasional scratch of her pencil on sketch paper or the brush flicking against the canvas.

It took more time for some than others, but there was always a moment when they stopped shifting or making awkward jokes. Most were accomplished people. Busy people. Lindsay liked to imagine her studio as a place where, for the first time in a long time, they were forced to reflect on stillness. The moment they gave in to the stillness was the moment she sought to capture. It was something she'd never seen in a photograph.

When people commissioned portraits of lost loved ones, she'd interview the client and sift through as many photographs as she could get her hands on. She'd seen more video footage of strangers than most people had seen of loved ones.

Lindsay had a soft spot for those clients. Her passion was to bring back the person's laughter, their voice, and cherished memories for the people they'd left behind. It wasn't easy, but she'd be damned if she would paint from a photo someone gave her without taking the time to honor who the person really was.

And then there was the way she painted Timmy. She didn't have anyone sitting for her. She didn't have photographs. She didn't even have her own dreams to reference like she did with Roo. But somehow, every time Lindsay painted Timmy, he looked the same. A young boy, maybe ten or eleven. Straight brown hair. Freckles across his nose. Rosy pink lips. He never smiled, even though she desperately wanted him to.

Sometimes she would paint him with a fury, and other times, it felt as if she was moving in slow motion. Either way, she would lose track of time and forget to do things like make dinner.

And now, there was this woman who'd kept her in the studio all night. The woman who stared back at her. Looked right through her. Made her feel something she couldn't yet describe. Painting her had felt different from the boy. Soft. Tender. Almost sensual. And now, that woman from long ago had a name in the here and now. A personality. A disturbing presence. She knew it was absurd to think Ren was Roo. Wishful musings. But that was the thing. Ren *was* Roo. Lindsay was sure of it.

She pulled the protective sheet off the painting, and with a gasp, she whispered, "My God, it's really her." It was the eyes. Something about the eyes. But it was more than that. Something she couldn't put into words.

It didn't make sense, but when had any of it ever made sense? The memories that weren't her own didn't make sense. The persistent dreams of Roo that felt so real she could practically taste and smell them didn't make sense. Her belief that Ren was the reincarnation of Roo didn't make sense. Even their damned names were confusing.

But those memories were a part of Lindsay and had been for years. She was helpless to stop them.

CHAPTER SIX

Ren closed her eyes and took in the sounds and smells of Salt Creek. Or more specifically, Deb's backyard. Was *backyard* the right word? Did people keep a horse and ducks and chickens in their backyards? Or was it considered a pasture at that point?

It smelled of wet grass, pine tar, and fire. She could hear Deb chasing Number Two around the house. He didn't want to go to bed. He said he wanted to stay on Ren's lap and sing more songs around the campfire. That's what the kids called it. Apparently, they loved to pitch a tent and sleep by the firepit in the summer. Deb said it saved her from having to do any actual camping, which meant less work for her. Ren was just content knowing Number Two wanted to snuggle with her.

The screen door slammed. Ren opened her eyes and saw Deb walking toward her with two glasses of wine. She'd changed into yoga pants and put on a long sweater over her T-shirt. Her high rubber boots were mismatched. One blue, one green.

Deb handed her a glass and pulled an Adirondack chair closer. "I chained Number Two to his bed. If you hear screaming, ignore it. He'll pass out eventually."

"Good thing I know you're joking."

"Am I, though?" Deb stretched out and propped her feet up on the edge of the firepit. "How can you be sure?"

"Because you talk a big talk, but I know how much you love being a mom. Plus, I heard you singing that *Frozen* song to him earlier, and in my book, that makes you the queen mother of all mothers because good Lord, that is truly an awful song after sixty-eight thousand times." Ren scanned Deb's haphazard look and hid a grin behind her wine. "Nice boots, Mama."

Deb clicked them together. "Mismatching is all the rage in Paris. Just make sure the colors complement each other."

"You want me to run around Paris in mismatched boots?"

"No, I want you to give me my boots back, so I don't have to scrounge by the back door for whatever my lazy kids kicked off on their way to the fridge."

"Never. I love these boots. Besides, this is definitely a possession is nine-tenths of the law type situation."

"Because you're an attorney now?" Deb said with a smirk. "Fine. They probably stink anyway, but let's not talk about that. Let's talk about sex." Deb took a sip and settled into the chair.

Ren snorted. "Like I want to hear what you and Colby get up to."

"Oh, it's hot. And sweaty. And quick. And—" Deb started to giggle. "Oh God. I think talking about those boots would be more interesting."

Ren held up her glass. "Here's to *not* talking about our sex lives because mine wasn't much better with what's her name."

"Krazy Kerry?" Deb scoffed. "That bitch didn't know what she had."

"Thanks, babe. Although I think it's fair to say she never really had me. The better question is, does Colby know what he has? Maybe I should fill him in before it's too late."

"He has a wife who doesn't care if her shoes match."

"And he's damn lucky for that. It's sexy. And from what I hear, all the rage in Paris."

"Ha!" Deb pointed at Ren's feet. "Are you really going to wear my old boots every day while you're here? I still can't believe you stole them." She slapped her forehead. "Oh God. I just brought up boots again. Who have I become that I can't have a decent conversation about sex?"

Ren put a hand on her arm. "Sweetie, if you really need to tell me about the goings-on in your love chamber, then of course, I'll listen. But stop calling these *your* boots. I claimed them long ago, and the statute of limitations has clearly expired."

"See? This is why I wear mismatched shoes around you." Deb sighed. "If we're going to talk about me and Mr. C, we need some music. Alexa! Play some Marvin Gaye!" They both froze and waited for something to happen. When nothing did, Deb cupped a hand around her ear. "Do you hear any sexual healing happening?"

Ren leaned in and lowered her voice. "I'm not sure I know what that sounds like. Is it like regular sex, or is there more crying?"

"Crying?" Deb whispered. "The only time I've ever cried during sex was when Colby decided to perform a lap dance as foreplay, and those were tears of laughter." She took her hand from her ear and slapped it on the arm of the chair. "That woman is never there when I need her."

"Who?"

"Alexa. Colby probably has her in the garage reciting sexy poems while he works on his snowmobile."

Ren tapped her chin. "Hmm. I wonder how one would ask Alexa to recite a sexy poem. Are you like, 'Alexa, read *Song of Myself,* but read it extra sexy'? Also, maybe we need to think this one through. Is Colby really the sexy poem type?"

"He's more evolved than you'd think."

"I guess you're right. I mean, only an evolved man would think he could lap dance his way into his wife's masterpiece."

"Hey, Number Two was born nine months later. I may have laughed hysterically at first, but the fact that he'd even try was a total turn-on."

Ren laughed and put her hand up. "Okay, subject change. I have the floor. I want to talk about hot women. Tell me about the woman in the coffee shop. Is she your first fainter?"

"Are you kidding? That's a regular thing with me. I keep smelling salts in my purse because sometimes, the scent of my cookies overwhelms the senses, and people drop like flies."

Ren shook her head and shouted, "Alexa, how do you smack the smartass out of your former friend?" She waited and turned toward the detached garage. "Alexa!"

"Soda Pop, stop shouting. We don't actually have Alexa."

"What? You just asked her—" Ren gave Deb's foot a little kick. "You're such a dork sometimes."

She laughed. "Oh, please. Imagine the chaos if my kids had the ability to shop on command. Alexa, order some Skittles!"

"Alexa, I ran out of Lucky Charms. Order five cases, please."

Deb raised her voice an octave. "Alexa, like, I've run out of mascara, and like, I want the best kind. Is that, like, Sephora or MAC?"

"Oh, let me do Number Two," Ren said. "Awexka, I need five hundwed and two bananas, and a million fwoot snacks. And no socks. I don't wike socks."

Deb pointed at Ren. "You killed it. Except he would order two million fruit snacks, but you absolutely killed it. Now do me."

Ren cleared her throat. "Alexa, I need two packs of cigarettes I won't ever smoke but need to have close by so I know they're there if I want them. No, Alexa, I don't smoke, but that's not the point. Yeah, don't ask, Alexa. It's a thing, okay? Just order the cheapest kind. Pall Malls or whatever. You know what I'm saying, Alexa? Okay, good. Thank you for having my back, Alexa. If you need any baked goods, maybe my sticky buns or my famous muffin, just let me know, k? I got you."

Deb leaned in and whispered, "You are a horrible person and also, my kids still don't know I ever smoked, and I'd like to keep it that way."

"Deal." Ren made a zipping motion across her lips. "Now tell me about the fainter."

Deb leaned back and narrowed her eyes. "Alexa, why is Ren asking about the fainter, aka Lindsay Hall? Aka Corey's best friend's mom."

"I was just wondering if she's okay. It was a pretty hard fall with the hot coffee and all."

"Uh-huh." Deb crossed her arms defiantly. "You think I didn't see whose painting you bought? What gives, Soda Pop?"

Ren didn't want to say it out loud. It would sound arrogant. "I don't know," she said. "It seemed like she went down after she saw me. Like, our eyes locked and then, boom."

It was a quiet laugh that came out of Deb at first, but it soon turned into a full-on belly laugh. "Boom?" She bent over and wheezed, she was laughing so hard. "You're cute, Ren, but not that cute."

"Okay, yuk it up. I'm just saying, it seemed like—"

"You made a woman faint at the sight of you? No, I get it. I mean, I get light-headed every time you roll into town too." Deb bent over again in a fit of laughter. "You know they have to staff up the urgent care clinic when they hear you're coming? No, really. They bring in extra staff from Fairview just to meet the demand."

Ren rolled her eyes. "Could you please tell me a little bit about her? I'm having coffee with her and the lady who took her to the doctor tomorrow."

"Mrs. Stokely? Oh God. Don't be late."

"I plan to be five minutes early. She seemed like a stickler for time."

"Mrs. Stokely is a mixed bag. She'd do anything for me, but at the same time, she has no problem letting me know if there's even one crumb left on the table she sits at, she...what? Why are you looking at me like that?"

"Has Mrs. Stokely ever fainted in your shop? Because I made it pretty clear I'd like to know more about the fainter, not Mrs. Stokely."

"I told you what there is to tell, Casanova. She's an artist. Kind of a big deal artist. Corey's best friend's mom. Nice girl. Got divorced last year. Anything else, you're going to have to figure out on your own."

❖

Lindsay stood on the sidewalk at 189 West Center. It seemed funny that after all these years, the woman who'd encouraged her art so fiercely had remained a mystery to her. As she walked up the cobbled path toward the perfectly manicured rosebushes that flanked an oversized front door, Lindsay realized that walking over the threshold of her former teacher's home would be a first. Mrs. Stokely was nothing if not extremely private.

Sure, she'd stood on the doorstep many a time. There was the trick or treating every year when Mrs. Stokely reminded the children of good oral hygiene and handed out toothbrushes. When Christmas caroling came around, Mrs. Stokely watched politely with a tight smile. And then there was the candy at least three generations had sold to raise funds for their field trips, marching band uniforms, and in Brooke's case, a show choir trip to Europe. Eager to find the one thing in a box of candy that wasn't actually candy, Mrs. Stokely always bought two packs of the raisin and nut bars.

It was amazing how fast seventeen years could go by. Lindsay's thoughts turned to Brooke walking this same path to sell whatever fundraising novelty the choir had going that week to fund their trip.

The only reason Lindsay was there now was because her excuses for not going seemed silly compared to the regret she'd feel one day if she hadn't responded positively to the invitation. Even if it was originally Ren's invitation, Mrs. Stokely was not someone who looked favorably upon a poorly thought-out excuse. Lindsay told herself the fact that Ren would be there was irrelevant.

She'd dressed up just enough to avoid a disapproving look from her hostess. She told herself it had nothing to do with impressing Ren. Mrs. Stokely didn't care for the faded, ripped jeans fad. Black jeans, black boots, and a gray V-neck sweater would make the grade. At the last minute, she'd thrown a black and white houndstooth scarf around her neck to shake things up a bit.

"I see you survived the Batmobile yesterday."

Lindsay's breath caught, and her heart rate quickened at the sound of Ren's voice behind her. She was slow to turn and make eye contact. If she'd had the presence of mind to think about it at all, she would have hoped it came across as being a bit shy, coy even. When their eyes met, she tried not to react. She tried to remain stoic and in control of her emotions, but when Ren flashed that smile that surely disrupted the town's power grid, Lindsay felt her knees go weak and her throat dry up.

So much for Ren's presence being irrelevant. But Lindsay was determined to not let it show this time. She wouldn't faint. She wouldn't break out in a cold sweat, even if she did want to rip the scarf from her neck so she could breathe. No, she would smile and reply in a calm voice. "I call it the Mistmobile. Batman's got nothing on Mrs. Stokely."

Ren gave her a curious look. "Mistmobile?"

"It's just, you know, the color of the car. It's called Saffron Firemist, so we've always. Just. You know." She just let it end there. Not a sentence exactly. Not a statement or proclamation either, since those would be sentences. Lindsay had simply placed a random assortment of words together. On the upside, she was still conscious, so that was something.

She leaned against the door. She wasn't going to faint, but she didn't feel steady on her feet either. Not with Ren standing there looking so amazing in tight jeans, a white T-shirt, and a cropped tan jacket. She didn't know whether to warn Ren about her jeans or stare at them for hours. Slivers of skin were visible through the subtle rips on the faded denim. She swallowed hard before she made eye contact again. "I should probably warn you..."

The door opened, and Lindsay stumbled back until Mrs. Stokely caught her and swiftly pushed her upright. "What in the world is wrong with you, dear? Do we need to find an old fainting couch and follow you around with it?" Mrs. Stokely might have been pushing eighty, but she was surprisingly quick to react.

"So sorry." Lindsay kept hold of her shoulders. "I hope I didn't hurt you."

"Don't you worry about that. I come from sturdy stock. But you'll hear from my lawyer if it turns out I pulled a groin muscle."

Mrs. Stokely turned and went back into the house. Lindsay grimaced at Ren, who seemed to be holding in laughter. "It's not funny."

Mrs. Stokely turned back around. "I'm just teasing about the lawyer. My groin muscle has been giving me trouble for years. Now close the door before I lose all my heat."

Heat? There was barely a chill in the air. Lindsay hadn't even turned on the heat in her house yet. Why in the world had she worn a sweater?

Ren had obviously thought things through by layering. She'd be cool as a cucumber while Lindsay sweated to the oldies she could hear playing on Mrs. Stokely's radio.

"Well, what are you waiting for?" Mrs. Stokely opened the door wider and made a grandiose wave with her hand. "Get in here."

Ren gave Lindsay a smile. "After you."

Her voice. Her smile. Her entire being seemed to pull Lindsay in like a magnet. Resistance seemed futile. Lindsay would be assimilated into the Ren Collective. Maybe the fainting couch wasn't such a bad idea after all.

"Good to see you, Mrs. Stokely." Lindsay stepped into the foyer. "Thank you for taking care of me yesterday."

Mrs. Stokely took a close look at Lindsay's eyes. "What did the doctor say?"

"Yes," Ren interjected. "Tell us how you're doing."

They stood close to one another in the small foyer. Ren's shoulder brushed hers. It was clear no one had any intention of moving until the question had been answered. "I, um…well. I'm doing well. Everything's fine. Just a few superficial burns. A little aloe went a long way." She gave Ren a nervous smile, and damnit, did her eyes have to fall to those lips? She quickly looked away.

"That's good, dear. Very good."

Fortunately, Mrs. Stokely seemed satisfied enough with her answer to not inquire any further. Lindsay attempted to keep a sigh of relief from escaping. The last thing she wanted to do was admit she hadn't actually seen a doctor. Or a nurse. Or even a receptionist. She could tell by the scrutiny Ren's jeans were receiving that Mrs. Stokely's hatred for current fashion trends had saved the day.

"I have a sewing machine in the back room," she said. "I'd be happy to patch up those holes for you, dear."

"Oh," Ren said. "That's very kind of you, but I kind of like the holes. I have to dress up every day for work, so this is a nice change."

"I appreciate an attempt to separate work and pleasure." Mrs. Stokely turned and went into the kitchen. "But you swung the pendulum a bit too far in the other direction, if you ask me."

Lindsay grabbed Ren's hand and tried hard to not laugh. "Oh my God," she whispered through her silent giggles.

Ren whispered back, "Did I just get admonished?"

Lindsay's brain caught up with her heart, and she pulled away. It felt like such a natural thing to grab Ren's hand. A sign of solidarity against the unsolicited opinions of a woman who meant well but had lost most of her tact over the years.

"Mrs. Stokely was a teacher, my teacher, actually," Lindsay said. "She still likes to school everyone."

Ren leaned in closer. "I hope she makes good coffee."

"Oh. Um, don't get your hopes up."

They continued to stand a few feet from the door while they waited. It gave Lindsay the opportunity to look around, and what she saw didn't surprise her. It was as if time stood still. It was apparent that Mrs. Stokely had purchased good quality furnishings with the belief that she'd only have to spend the money once, just like she had with the 1979 Buick LeSabre.

A sitting room sat to the right of the front door. It was one step down and had a perfectly manicured and maintained shag carpet in the shade of a martini olive. Straight ahead, she could see into the door of a kitchen with all the latest 1970s appliances. The standing mixer matched the dishwasher and the oven. Both were a subtle shade of sunshine yellow, a refreshing contrast to the dark cabinets. Lindsay found herself wondering if Mrs. Stokely had a microwave. Because that was a mission-critical thing to wonder on that afternoon of all afternoons.

What Mrs. Stokely probably didn't know—though she'd perhaps always assumed it—was that her color scheme of avocado green, orange, and bright yellow was right back in style. Even the dramatic floral wallpaper by the kitchen table would be considered hip today.

"This place is kinda groovy," Ren said under her breath.

Groovy. Hip. Retro. Who would have thought those words could be used to describe anything related to Mrs. Stokely? Okay, maybe that last one. And who would have thought Ren's breath would smell like sunshine after a rainstorm? Okay, maybe just spearmint, but Lindsay had to resist the urge to rest her nose on Ren's lips so she could really get a good whiff. Her thoughts turned to Roo's smoky kiss, even though Ren looked nothing like her.

"Am I going to meet my maker before you girls think to offer some help?"

They both rushed into the sitting room and reached for the serving tray before Mrs. Stokely had to bend down to place it on the coffee table. They bumped shoulders but managed to not spill the coffee that had already been poured into three small cups, those tiny teacups that came with old sets of dishes. Lindsay knew because her grandmother had some. She associated them with instant coffee. And not just any instant coffee but decaffeinated instant coffee. Sanka, to be exact. She assumed the chances that Mrs. Stokely would serve the same would be slim. Just in case, she thanked God the cups were small. And then, as she reached for the cream, she bumped Ren again.

"First, fainting and now bumbling around like a bull in a china shop," Mrs. Stokely said. "I'm concerned about you, Lindsay Hall."

Ren raised her hand. "My bad."

Mrs. Stokely raised an eyebrow. "Your what? Oh, never mind. We'd be here all day. I think I have a boot polishing kit in the garage. I'd be happy to lend it to you, dear."

Lindsay gave Ren an almost imperceptible nod, letting her know she should save herself some pain and just accept the offer. Ren widened her eyes in response. "Oh, of course! I'd really appreciate that." She glanced down at Lindsay's boots. "And maybe Miss Fainty Pants here could teach me how to polish a boot since I've never had the pleasure."

Mrs. Stokely slapped her knee and let out a big ol' belly laugh. "Miss Fainty Pants. That's a good one." She continued to giggle while she held up a small bowl full of sugar cubes. Ren looked all too pleased with herself until Mrs. Stokely said, "And you can be Sister Holey Pants of the Not So Immaculate Order." Mrs. Stokely slapped her knee again and laughed even harder at her own joke.

Lindsay tried not to smirk while she stirred milk into her coffee, then offered it to Ren. "A little milk, Sister?"

Mrs. Stokely laughed again and said, "I'm so glad you girls stopped by. I haven't laughed this hard in years."

Or ever, Lindsay thought to herself. *Jovial* wasn't a word anyone in town would use to describe Mrs. Stokely. *Stoic* and *stern* were the more likely choices. It was all very curious. Even the way she'd just used the term *stopped by*, as if she hadn't set up the time and place yesterday.

"Thank you for inviting us," Ren said. "I've really been looking forward to hearing more about your work." She turned to Lindsay. "Both of you."

The lightheartedness of the moment turned into panic. Those gorgeous brown eyes were on Lindsay, scanning her from head to toe. She needed to say something. "I'm a portrait painter."

"Where did you study?"

"Study?" Lindsay's throat felt dry, and the damned scarf around her neck needed to come off.

"She's a natural," Mrs. Stokely said. "A rare talent."

Lindsay wrapped her fingers around the knot and untied the scarf. "I didn't study anywhere." She toyed with the scarf for a moment, rubbing the fabric between her fingers. "I mean, uh, you know. Not formally."

"So you were born with an innate gift."

"I suppose I was."

"Well, your work is exceptional," Ren said.

Wasn't it funny how the act of removing a piece of clothing could become something entirely different when someone was watching? Even a scarf. Lindsay pulled on one end while Ren looked on. She could've taken it off over her head with both hands. It would've been quicker. But she found herself wishing the scarf were fifty feet long so Ren wouldn't look away. Maybe she could take off an earring too. Then the other. Maybe pull the sweltering sweater over her head. Or even better, ask Ren to do it for her.

With the sweater gone, it wouldn't make sense to leave her bra on. She could turn her back to Ren and let her unhook it. Maybe she wouldn't turn back around right away. Maybe she'd wait to see where Ren's hands went. Ren, who stared while the scarf broke free and fell onto her lap.

She heard Mrs. Stokely say something, but she couldn't make it out. Mrs. Stokely cleared her throat and asked a bit more loudly than normal, "Are you all right, dear?"

Had all the air left the room? Because Lindsay could barely breathe. "A little warm, maybe."

Mrs. Stokely got up and adjusted the thermostat. "Forgive me. These old bones get cold."

Ren removed her jacket. "Would a cold cloth help?"

"No, I'll be fine." Lindsay didn't need a cold cloth. She needed to get control of her thoughts. It was so hard, though. Even harder now that Ren had taken her jacket off.

A fire raged inside Lindsay. The closer she was to Ren, the hotter it burned. Sitting on the sofa together had been a bad idea. She'd have to remember that if they ever saw each other again. Sit. Far. Away.

Mrs. Stokely handed her a glass of ice water. She took a sip and pressed the glass to her cheek. Fainting, stumbling, stuttering, overheating. What was next, spontaneous combustion? An unassisted orgasm? Her eyes shuddered closed at the thought.

Ren patted Lindsay's knee and turned her attention away. "How about you, Mrs. Stokely? When did you start painting those wonderful landscapes?"

"Oh, years ago. It's always been a hobby of mine, but I started taking it seriously when someone close to me passed away. I could lose myself in a painting for hours, which meant there were fewer hours in the day to grieve. It became my therapy."

Lindsay breathed a sigh of relief. Mrs. Stokely would surely go on for some time before the conversation came back around to

Lindsay's work. She sat back on the sofa and sipped the cold water while trying to keep her eyes off Ren.

❖

Ren gave Mrs. Stokely a final wave and waited until she'd closed her front door to say, "I think I won her over."

"Won her over? I think she fell madly in love with you." Lindsay tied her scarf to her purse.

Ren switched the tiny suitcase that held Mrs. Stokely's shoe polishing supplies to her other hand so she could walk a little closer to her new friend. "Well, I do have that effect on women."

"Women of a certain age or women in general?"

Lindsay had a quick wit. Ren liked that about her. She set the suitcase down and put her jacket back on. "It really was overly warm in there."

Lindsay scoffed. "Yeah, like a dry sauna."

Ren slowed her pace and let Lindsay get a little bit ahead. There was something about the way Lindsay looked at her, even from the very first moment before she'd fainted. Ren knew Lindsay would turn around. She was sure of it. And she was just as sure that when Lindsay did turn to find out what the holdup was, Ren would see that look again.

She waited for it, unable to move until Lindsay stopped and turned. She needed to see it again to know for sure. And there it was. Pain, sadness, uncertainty. Why would anyone look at a stranger with such emotion in their eyes?

It had happened a few times while they sat on Mrs. Stokely's green sofa. Ren caught her staring. If anyone was making eyes at anyone, it was Lindsay. But it wasn't the kind of look Ren would want from such an intriguing, beautiful, talented woman. It wasn't a flirty look or a come-hither look. In fact, if Ren hadn't known better, she would've thought she'd done something terrible and had a lot of making up to do. A lot of trust to rebuild. A lot of wounds to heal. But they barely knew each other.

"Are you okay?" Lindsay bent and picked up the little suitcase.

When their eyes met again, Ren asked, "Are you?"

Lindsay hadn't just turned. She'd come back for Ren. Picked up her suitcase. And the question hung in the air for what felt like an eternity. Why couldn't Lindsay say she was fine or not fine or somewhere in between?

Without an answer, Ren felt compelled to pull this beautiful stranger into her arms. Those hands were slow to return the hug. Hesitant. But once Lindsay's arms wrapped around her, Ren found herself in a warm embrace she had no desire to escape.

It was Lindsay who let go first. The blush across her chest and neck were the first things Ren noticed. Then she realized Lindsay still had a firm grip on her forearms.

"I'm not sure why I did that," Ren confessed. "I guess you looked like you needed a hug."

Lindsay's grip loosened. "You were right."

"I hope it helped." Their stance was far too intimate. Their gaze too full of emotion. Ren felt something she couldn't define. Concern? No, it was bigger than that. She was quite capable of feeling concern for a stranger in distress. This was different.

"I think you're the only person in the whole world who..." Lindsay shook her head. "I'm sorry. I shouldn't."

"Shouldn't what?" Ren wanted to touch her face. Cup her cheeks and urge her gaze upward, but she only did that with girlfriends. Lovers. Lindsay was neither. And yet, she found Lindsay's chin and lifted it until their eyes met. "Tell me."

An obnoxious car horn startled them. Instant anger rose in Ren. She wanted to tell the asshole who had honked their horn to fuck the hell off, but this wasn't the city. Whoever it was, she'd probably run into them again, and that would be embarrassing.

Lindsay took two steps back. "I hate it when he does that."

A teenage girl jumped out of the passenger seat of the truck. "Mom! I need you to give me and Corey a ride to—" She stopped when she saw Ren. "Oh, hi."

"Brooke, this is Ren Christopher," Lindsay said. "Deb's good friend from New York."

Ren offered her hand. "Nice to meet you, Brooke."

"Likewise." Brooke gestured over her shoulder. "This is my dad, Ben."

Ben came around from the driver's side of the truck. "Miss Christopher. Good to see you again."

"You've met?" Lindsay looked to both of them.

"We met on the road," Ren said. "Officer Hall was kind enough to give me a warning instead of what I imagine would've been a very expensive speeding ticket."

Ben leaned against his truck and crossed his ankles and arms as if settling in for a pleasant conversation. The look on Lindsay's face said that was the last thing she wanted. "I saved you over two hundred bucks," he said. "I think that means you owe me one of Deb's cinnamon rolls."

Ren couldn't tell if he was flirting again, but she did a casual sidestep and put her arm around Lindsay. "We were on our way to Deb's right now."

"I thought you already had coffee with old Mrs....I mean, Mrs. Stokely," Brooke said.

Ren cupped a hand around her mouth. "Sweet lady. Well, not exactly sweet. More like—"

"Hostile toward anyone younger than her? Yeah, I know," Brooke said. "But you'll have to get coffee later. I need my mom right now."

Ben shrugged. "I guess old Dad is just chopped liver over here."

"Ew. I don't even know what that means, but it's disgusting, Dad."

Lindsay stepped forward. "It means, why can't your dad take you, honey? What's this about?"

"It needs to be a woman." Brooke put up a hand. "That's all I'm going to say."

"I'm out." Ben pushed off his truck. "Love you, Brookey."

"Love you, Dad." Brooke turned back to her mom. "Okay, seriously, Dad drives me crazy sometimes. He's so nosy."

"Everybody seems nosy when you're...how old are you?" Ren guessed she was tall for her age since Lindsay couldn't possibly have a daughter as old as Brooke looked.

"Seventeen. Still can't drive because of my dad, or I wouldn't be begging for rides."

"Brooke, Ren doesn't need to hear about your woes," Lindsay said. "Do you need tampons or something? You know your dad has no problem buying those."

"Really, Mom? You obviously don't know Dad very well. But you do know when my period is. Same time every stupid month." She let out a big, overly dramatic sigh and said, "It's Corey. She needs to get something in Lake City, but she's been grounded from driving for two weeks. Bad grade on a math test or something."

"I'll drive you," Ren said. "I've hardly seen Corey since I got here, so this is the perfect opportunity. She'll be a captive audience in my car, which means I can grill her on her latest boyfriend."

"He's a loser," Brooke said. "But yeah, she *loves* to talk about him."

Ren realized she probably shouldn't have made the offer without conferring with Brooke's mother first. "Are you okay with this, Lindsay?"

"It's fine. It's good. I mean, for you and Corey to have some time together."

Ren felt a strange need to say good-bye appropriately. Or inappropriately. She didn't kiss someone she barely knew good-bye. She didn't caress their cheek and study their face in case she never saw them again. "I'll see you again soon," she said in hopes that the feeling would go away.

"See you soon." Lindsay pointed at Brooke. "Make good choices."

"Really?" Brooked huffed. "In front of strangers?"

"Honey, Ren's not a stranger," Lindsay said over her shoulder. She got in her car and waved before driving away.

Ren couldn't suppress the huge grin that popped out, hard as she tried. Lindsay didn't think of her as a stranger. Was she swooning? She was swooning. "See you soon, Lindsay Hall!"

Brooke furrowed her brow. "You already said that."

"Which part?" Ren's eyes were on Lindsay's car until it turned the corner.

"*See you soon*. You said it twice."

Ren turned to Brooke. She had no idea what this kid of Lindsay's was getting at, and she felt too happy to care. "It's called a pleasantry," she said. "You should try it sometime." She opened the car door and motioned with her head. "Let's go."

CHAPTER SEVEN

Corey chose to sit in the back seat of the convertible. She seemed quiet. Not the bubbly girl Ren knew. Brooke, on the other hand, hadn't stopped asking questions. Was Ren one of Lindsay's clients? How long was she in town for? How fast had she driven in the car?

Ren downplayed that one and said eighty.

Brooke was full of answers to unasked questions too. Her dad probably wouldn't want Ren to know that he'd recently had surgery on a super gross ingrown toenail. Ren didn't really want to know that either.

"You should really let my mom paint you," Brooke said.

Paint me? "Didn't you just tell me your mom has a waiting list? Besides, I don't need a portrait of myself. Although I do love that painting I bought of the boy."

"She sold you one of Timmy?" Brooke clapped. "Oh, good! Maybe that means I can go on the Europe trip with the school choir. You should totally do it, though. My mom's really good. She gets the details right."

Ren gave her a side-eye. "Can't I just buy some raffle tickets or something?"

Brooke giggled. "Not for the trip, silly. But now that you mention it, the fundraiser we're starting next week is going to be gourmet popcorn. Who doesn't love gourmet popcorn, right?"

"You'll sell the heck out of gourmet popcorn. Put me down for three. No, make it five. Popcorn is my weakness." Ren knew she wouldn't take popcorn to Paris, but that was hardly the point. Besides, it probably wouldn't last two days in Deb's house.

Brooke did a fist pump. "Yes!"

Ren glanced at Corey in the rearview mirror. "How's it going back there?"

Corey gave her a nod. "Fine."

Ren looked at Brooke with a raised eyebrow and whispered, "Boy trouble?"

"Understatement of the year," Brooke whispered back.

Ren had her suspicions as they pulled into town. She hoped it wasn't the kind of trouble she was thinking of. "Where am I going?"

Corey piped up. "That strip mall over there. The one with the dance shop."

"Need something for dance class?"

"Uh, yeah. We might grab a few things from the drugstore too."

"Uh-huh." Ren parked her car in between the two stores. It was obvious the girls wanted to go in alone. "Maybe I'll get a bottle of wine from the liquor store. What's your mom's favorite?"

Corey and Brooke answered simultaneously. "Red."

"She means my mom, Brooke."

"Oh, right. Sorry." Brooke got out of the car and pulled the seat forward so Corey could get out too.

"No worries." Ren gave Brooke a smile. "Maybe I'll get a bottle for her too, and she can tell me about the painting I bought."

"His name is Timmy." Brooke closed the car door. "That's all we know. Well, that and he keeps my mom up at night."

Ren went in the other direction toward the liquor store but kept her eye on the girls. They walked past the dance store and went in the drugstore first.

"Red" hadn't given her much to go on, but she found a decent Zin to bring to dinner and a Pinot Noir for Lindsay, if the opportunity ever presented itself. She'd been waiting in the car for several minutes when the girls came out of the drugstore and walked straight to the car.

They got in the car, and Brooke said, "Will you take us to my house?"

Ren wanted to ask why they hadn't gone to the dance store, but maybe it was best to let it go. She wasn't Corey's mother, after all.

❖

Lindsay set two wineglasses on the kitchen table and sat across from Patty. "You didn't have to close the gallery early for me."

"Are you kidding? I'd take any old reason to close up early on the slower days." Patty reached across the table and squeezed Lindsay's hand. "Besides, you sounded a little broken up."

"I'm not broken up. Just confused about what to do. Maybe this will help." She held up her glass. "Cheers."

"Cheers, babe. Now, tell me what you're so confused about, as if I can't guess."

"Can we just chill with the wine for a minute first?"

"I'm always up for chilling with wine. Tell me about Mrs. Stokely's place. Did it smell like mothballs?"

"You'd love it," Lindsay said. "Very retro. In fact, I would guess that she hasn't changed a thing in forty years. And get this, it's all in great condition."

"Wow," Patty said with a look of awe. "Just like the 1979 Buick LeSabe-ruh."

"I guess it pays to not have any kids. Then your sh-stuff doesn't get ruined."

"Sh-stuff?" Patty lifted her glass again. "Here's to us swearing like normal human beings. And here's to me never having kids because I like my shit."

"If you say so." Lindsay took an extra large sip.

"Now, about that new girl in town. And slow down. The last time you drank wine like that, I had to hold your hair back."

"Bullshit. You did not." Lindsay set the glass down. But Patty was right. Getting drunk wouldn't help. She crossed her arms and laid her head on her hands with a dramatic sigh. "Do I tell Ren? Do I not tell her?"

"Are you nuts?"

"Okay. Do I go see a psychiatrist?"

"Well, I've been suggesting that for years, but no one listens to me," Patty said with a wink.

Lindsay lifted her head. "Ha, ha. Take me seriously, please."

"Okay. My advice, don't tell her. She'll be out of your life soon enough, and this way, there won't be another person out there who knows…" Patty stopped. "I mean, not that more people knowing about your past life would be a bad thing."

Lindsay rolled her eyes. "You're a terrible liar, Cakes."

"Sweetie, you know I've always supported you on your past life stuff. But this I'm not sure about. It's a little too convenient, isn't it? I mean, your long-lost love from another lifetime just happens to visit your hometown? And even if it is true, picture yourself telling her. You think she's just going to be like, 'Great! Let's ride off into the sunset!' 'Cause I promise you, that's not going to happen."

"What about the painting? Why would I paint Roo for the first time the very night before Ren arrived?"

"Why do those two things have to be connected? So you had an urge to finally paint Roo. It's about time, don't you think? It really doesn't seem like a big deal."

Lindsay stiffened. "No big deal? Is that really what you think?"

"Okay. I'm sorry I said that. It just seems like there are a lot of possibilities. You haven't so much as glanced at someone romantically since the divorce. Maybe you're ready now. Don't you think it's possible that you want it to be her because you want that kind of love in your life?"

"Of course I know that's possible. It just doesn't *feel* like that's what's happening, you know?"

"And she might be Roo. And whether she is or isn't, I don't see how telling her will do you any favors. Either way, I'm here for you. Tell me what I can do to help."

"If I knew, I wouldn't be drinking wine." She took another sip. She knew it all seemed too convenient. Roo was supposed to stay in her dreams, not show up on her doorstep.

Brooke burst through the front door with Corey in tow. They headed straight for Brooke's room. "Hey!" Lindsay shouted. "You didn't close the front door." She got up to close it. "It's like I raised her in a…oh, hi."

Ren stepped inside. "Hi."

"Hi," Lindsay said again. "I mean, I guess I said that already." She felt a blush crawl up her chest, and she tried to tame her grin, but there was no stopping it. "Come in." She felt a little bit giddy and wasn't sure if it was the wine or if seeing that beautiful face again had her feeling unsteady on her feet.

"They wanted to come here first," Ren said. "But I thought I'd stick around in case Corey decides she wants to go home."

There was a soberness in Ren's tone that Lindsay didn't like. "Is something wrong?"

"I think so, but it's not my place to say."

Brooke came back down the hall looking sullen. She leaned against the wall and folded her arms. "We have to wait a few minutes."

Patty came into the living room. "For what?"

"It might be nothing," Brooke said. "Just give it a minute, okay?"

Patty looked at Lindsay. "Am I the only one having déjà vu?"

Brooke put up her hands. "Please, Aunt Patty. Just give it a minute."

Lindsay glanced down the hallway. The bathroom light was on, but the door was closed. Déjà vu indeed. She corralled everyone into the kitchen. "Let's give her some space."

Patty sat at the kitchen table with her hands clasped against her forehead and started whispering to herself.

"Cakes? Are you okay?"

"I'm praying."

"But you're not religious, Aunt Patty."

Patty flopped back against her chair. "You're right. God didn't listen to me the first time, either. No offense, Brookey."

"No, I get it," Brooke said. "My life as I know it is probably over. All of our plans to travel Europe together and share a dorm at college and then an apartment in the city, just poof, and it's gone.

Mom, I need a glass of wine so I can drown my sorrows." Brooke's forehead hit the table with a dramatic thud. "I'd like the 1998 merlot, please."

Lindsay gave Patty a questioning look. "It's not a thing," Patty said. "She means the purple Gatorade."

Corey came into the kitchen and leaned against the doorway. Lindsay took a step toward her. "Honey, we're all here for you."

Corey wiped the tears from her cheeks. "I know." She held up the pee stick. "And it's all good. See?"

Brooke screamed with delight. She picked Corey up and spun her around. Everyone breathed a big sigh of relief. Patty looked at the ceiling and whispered as she made something that looked like the sign of the cross, but Lindsay couldn't be sure. "Okay, girls, quiet down now. We have to talk." Lindsay turned her attention to Corey. "Sweetie, I have to make one correction. It's not *all good* because there's still the matter of you having had unprotected sex."

Brooke got a look of disgust on her face. "Ew."

"That's good, Brookey. I like that face," Patty said. "Keep that face, and no boy will go near you for fear they'll get puked on." She winked. "Good strategy."

Ren stepped forward. "How can I help, Corey?"

Corey fell into Ren's arms. "You already did."

Lindsay put her hand on Corey's back while Ren held her. She had an overwhelming desire to wrap herself around both of them and assure them that everything would be okay. She pulled away and went to the sink. She needed to keep herself together for Corey. She needed to have full use of her voice and her brain, not be a jumbled blob of feelings she couldn't control.

"Mom? Patty? Ren?"

Lindsay turned back around. Brooke had such a serious look on her face, she almost expected her to tell them she had a pregnancy scare too. "Yes, honey?"

"I'm calling a safe zone. For Corey."

"Oh God." Patty shook her head. "Don't fall for it, Corey."

"What I mean is, Corey doesn't want to tell her parents about this, and I think we should all respect that."

"Honey, that's not a safe zone. That's a secret zone," Lindsay said.

"But her dad hates this kid. Like, with a passion hates him."

Ren put up her hand. "I have a question. What's a safe zone?"

"I'd be happy to explain it to you," Patty said. "You see, tater tots are meant to be eaten with ketchup—"

"Cakes." Lindsay didn't want to hurt Patty's feelings any more than she already had, but she couldn't let her derail the conversation.

Patty put up a finger and whispered, "There's only one way. One."

Lindsay motioned to one of the barstools. "Corey, come and sit down." She waved Ren over. "You too." Once everyone was gathered around the island, she said, "Corey, I think you're putting Ren in an awkward position by asking her to keep something this big from your mom. It could put a strain on their friendship, and I know you don't want that."

Corey shook her head. "No, I don't."

"And I know you're close to your mom," Lindsay said. "And if this happened to Brooke, I would definitely want to be there for her, so she didn't feel all alone." Lindsay reached across the island and grabbed Corey's hand. "Let your mom help you with this. Maybe she'll agree that it's best not to tell your dad as long as you handle it together."

Corey nodded. "Okay. I'll tell her tonight."

"Good." Lindsay got a wink from Ren. Brooke came around the island and gave her a hug, then hugged Corey.

Patty wasn't so quick to forgive, and Corey had noticed. Lindsay tried to tell Patty with her eyes that she needed to step up, but she didn't get the message before Corey said, "Are you mad at me, Patty?"

"Honey, I'm disappointed. You need to own your sexuality. Be the powerful, in-charge woman that I know you are. And in the meantime, tell me who had sex with you and didn't wear a condom, so I don't hurt the wrong boy."

"Aunt Patty!" Brooke said with a gasp. "Is that how you felt when Mom got pregnant with me? Were you mad at my mom and dad?"

Patty started to answer, but Lindsay intervened. "Honey, yes. Everyone was pretty furious at both of us because we were so young, but then you came into the world, and everyone fell in love with you, and no one could be mad at anyone anymore. Including Patty."

"Well, to be honest, it did take a few years before..." Patty stopped mid-sentence and tilted her head at Lindsay. "What? Okay, fine. Enough with the slicing your throat open, Linds. Find a new way to tell me to shut the hell up, would ya? Maybe a gentle swaying of your hips or something."

"She could twerk," Brooke suggested. "That way, it's fun for everyone in the room."

Ren held up her hand. "I second that."

Patty's hand shot up. "Corey, get your hand in the air so it's unanimous."

Corey raised her hand. "Enter it into the record that henceforth, Lindsay can only tell Patty to shut the hell up by twerking."

Patty stood and raised her hands to the ceiling. "I'm free! I'm Julie Andrews in *The Sound of Music* free! I can say anything I want, anytime I want because we all know Lindsay can't twerk to save her mother effing life!"

Ren burst out laughing. Corey and Brooke started twerking at each other and saying, "Shut up. No, you shut up."

Lindsay joined in with the laughter. "Note to self...learn how to twerk."

❖

"Can I get you a glass of wine?" Lindsay motioned with her head at the girls, who'd moved to the family room. "I think it might be a little while before Corey's ready to face her mom."

"I hope it's not an inconvenience," Ren said. Of course, Lindsay was unaware that Ren had told Corey she could take her time. She was in no hurry. Being in Lindsay's presence felt comfortable. Warm. Hot, if she didn't stop thinking about Lindsay putting on a little twerk show for an audience of one later. But the look on Lindsay's face when she turned and saw Patty getting twerk lessons from the girls let her know that it most likely wasn't in the cards.

"Let's, um…" Lindsay opened the door to the backyard. "I can't watch that."

"Lead the way." Ren followed her to a wooden swing that hung from a large oak tree. It was a good-sized swing, and Lindsay crammed herself all the way to one side. Had Ren sat on the opposite end, there would have been three feet between them. She chose to sit a little closer.

Lindsay crossed her legs and gently pushed the swing with one foot. By the looks of the single drag mark in the grass, she sat right where she always did. The wine stain on the armrest told her it probably wasn't where Brooke made a habit of sitting.

Ren felt a strange sense of honor, as if she'd been allowed into a special place. A thinking place. A dreaming place. A taking-stock-of-one's-life place. A quiet escape from all of the have-tos and must-dos.

"What a day," Lindsay said, breaking the silence.

"What a day." Ren smiled. "You know, it kind of felt like we were having a cup of instant Folger's with Alice in the *Brady Bunch* house."

"If Alice were thirty years older and felt the need to sew up your very cool jeans."

Ren sighed. "A girl just tries to keep up with the trends."

Lindsay pulled her phone out of her back pocket. "I need to learn how to distress my jeans."

"You buy them that way."

"Yeah, but I have a closet full of old jeans. Let's YouTube it."

Ren found her excitement adorable. "Okay. I'm here for it." She leaned in so their shoulders were touching.

"Okay, but we can't go down a YouTube rabbit hole. It's frightening where a person can end up." Lindsay put up her index finger. "One video. That's it."

Ren hardly ever watched videos on YouTube that didn't have something to do with her profession, but she was very interested in this rabbit hole business. Especially if it meant she could sit close to Lindsay for a little while longer.

Lindsay hit pause on the video after they'd watched most of it. "I'm so doing that to some of my old jeans. It'll be fun!"

Ren tried for a casual tone and pointed at another video. "Do you mind if we watch that one?"

"Oh, that one's hilarious." Lindsay hit the play button.

Twenty minutes later, they'd watched cats riding Roombas, bot fly extractions, parrots having full-on conversations with each other, and Taylor Swift's latest video.

Lindsay put her phone away and said, "I think after all of that, you're not only prepared for Mrs. Stokely, you're prepared for anything that comes your way."

"Yes," Ren said. "I now feel completely confident in my ability to extract a bot fly from my own body with detailed commentary from my parrots while my cat cleans the house, and we all sing along to Taylor Swift. If the need ever arises."

"Not so fast," Lindsay said. "You forgot about the jeans."

"Right. Yeah, I think I should just let Dr. Pimple Popper remove the bot fly and buy the jeans when I go to see her in LA. The cat and birds will have to fend for themselves while I'm gone. Frisky knows how to use the Roomba. It'll be fine."

"And that time, you left out Taylor Swift," Lindsay said.

"Oh, Dr. Pimple Popper is a total Swiftie. She'll pull the bot fly out of my armpit while we sing along to 'Shake It Off.'"

Lindsay tucked her phone back in her pocket. "You had to make it worse with the armpit thing, didn't you?"

"Well, it's definitely not the worst place a bot fly could decide to call home."

"True." Lindsay folded her arms. "I'm still going to protect my armpits for the next twenty-four hours, just in case."

Ren laughed. She turned to Lindsay and put her leg on the swing and her arm on the backrest. She wanted to reach over and run her fingers through Lindsay's hair. She wanted to have her close again like they'd been in front of Mrs. Stokely's house before Ben and Brooke drove up.

"It's getting chilly." Lindsay looked at her. "You're not really dressed for it, what with all the rips in your jeans."

"Yeah, I'm not burning up over here at all."

Lindsay's eyes darted back to hers. Those always questioning eyes. Ren wanted to answer all her questions. She wanted to start by saying, *yes, Lindsay, that was me letting you know that I've been burning up since I met you*, but Lindsay turned away.

Ren decided it was best to lighten the moment. "Ripped jeans or not, I think I won Mrs. Stokely over so well, you should definitely not be surprised if she takes a pair of her husband's old jeans and tries to duplicate the look."

"Mrs. Stokely never had a husband," Lindsay said. "But it would certainly make my day to see her roll up to You Mocha Me Feel *Young* in her 1979 Buick LeSabre and step out of the car lookin' all fly in ripped jeans and a white tee."

Ren laughed. "Oh my God. So it's not just me who takes great pleasure in teasing Deb about the name she chose for her coffee shop?"

"I call it You Mocha Me Faint now." They stared at each other for a split second, then broke into a fit of laughter.

Patty stepped outside and shouted, "Since this isn't a serious conversation, may I join you?" She didn't wait for permission, and when she got to the swing, she turned around and said, "Keep swinging. I got this." She waited for the swing to hit her butt and squeezed in between them.

It was a tight fit, but Ren didn't move her leg or her arm that was now wrapped around Patty. She sped up the pace by pushing hard with her foot. Maybe she could give Patty a little case of motion sickness so she'd go back in the house. Not that she didn't like Patty, but she wanted to get to know Lindsay.

Patty gave Ren a side-eye. "You're really hot and all, but I could use a little breathing room here."

"Sorry." Ren put her leg down and slid over a bit. She noticed that Patty stayed right where she was, glued to Lindsay.

"What a day," Patty said.

"What a day," Ren and Lindsay replied in unison.

Patty tucked her fingers behind her ears. "In stereo. Cool. Say it again."

Ren hid her amusement. Patty was funny and cute but not her type. Lindsay with the sassy teenage daughter and the eyes of a philosopher was a different story. She liked that Lindsay appeared to be a deep thinker. And her talent as an artist was very impressive. She'd always been a sucker for artists. And then there was the way Lindsay seemed to come a bit unraveled by Ren's proximity. Of course, if she was honest with herself, she also came a bit undone.

Patty had put a sudden end to all of that. and Ren wanted it back. She leaned forward enough to catch a glimpse of Lindsay. Patty blocked her view and said, "Do you believe in past lives?"

"What?" Ren shook her head in confusion. "I mean, what?"

"You know, the belief that after we die, we're reborn as someone else. Because I'm super into that, so if we're going to be friends, you need to be cool with it."

"Um." Ren noticed Lindsay shoot her friend a glare. "I don't really—"

"It's cool," Patty said. "We can still be friends, but I'll probably have to bring you over to the dark side."

"Dark side of what?"

"Oh. Not a *Star Wars* fan?" Patty tapped her chin. "This could be a *real* problem."

"I get the reference," Ren said. "I'm just not sure what you're referring to."

"Past lives. Lived before this life." Patty turned on the swing so they were face-to-face. "I know it's a weird thing to believe in, but aren't all religions full of weird, otherworldly stuff? And no one thinks anything of it, but say the words *past lives*, and people tend to think you're off your rocker, you know?"

Ren was at a loss for words. What was all of this nonsense that seemed to come out of nowhere? And why the hell did Patty have to come out there and stomp all over what could've been a great conversation with Lindsay? Ren found herself annoyed by the whole thing.

"I don't know if that or any other belief about preexistence is a real thing or not," she said. "What I do believe is that it's not relevant to who we are and what we do today. It doesn't explain anything or absolve us of bad decisions."

"Oh." Patty looked at Lindsay, who'd turned away. It was obvious they both felt annoyed by the change of topic. She turned back to Ren and said, "So you've never met someone you feel like you knew before?"

"Sure, but that doesn't mean I really did. At least, not in a past life. But if you need to believe you were royalty in ancient Egypt with a staff of three hundred, then by all means, don't let me stop you. It's not my place to tell you how to live."

"Well, if that's the case, I've really come down the ladder in status," Patty said. "How the hell did I go from being Cleopatra to living in Salt Creek?" She tapped her chin. "And when did I start liking girls?" She leaned forward and timed her exit from the swing, then hopped off. "Your conversations are too deep for me. I'm out, ladies."

"See you soon, Cleo." Ren grinned. "Maybe in the next life, we'll all be slaves to Skynet."

"Ha! I get dibs on being Linda Hamilton's slave girl."

Ren turned to Lindsay. "She threw in a *Star Wars* reference, so I thought I'd terminate…okay, then." Ren knew how to read a room. Or a swing, as it were. Lindsay didn't look the least bit amused. In fact, she seemed guarded, with her arms folded tightly across her chest.

"Patty's not crazy," Lindsay said.

"I didn't say she was." Lindsay went to stand, but Ren grabbed her arm. "Hey, where are you going?"

"Who knows what bad advice Patty's doling out like candy in there? I should go back in."

"Okay, but can I ask you something first? It's actually why I wanted to speak with you privately."

Lindsay gave her a nod. "Something about Mrs. Stokely?"

"No. Something about us."

"Okay." She turned on the swing so they were face-to-face.

"Have we ever met before? Maybe years ago, when I would

come here with Deb on the weekends?" Ren realized she was still hanging on to Lindsay's arm. She let go.

Lindsay continued to stare. It was that look again. That penetrating, questioning look. "Why would you ask that?"

Lindsay's softer, fragile tone almost made Ren regret that she'd asked the question when so much else was going on. "I don't know why. It's just a feeling. I feel like we've met somewhere before."

Lindsay shot off the swing. "I don't think so. I'm pretty sure I'd remember you."

Ren got up and followed her toward the house. She grabbed Lindsay's arm again to stop her. "Can I see your studio? I mean, I did pay a small fortune for that painting of the boy. I'd love to see what else you're working on." Ren cringed inside. Was a guilt trip really the best she could do?

"I mostly do commissioned work. Portraits." Lindsay folded her arms again. "Why did you buy that painting when you knew nothing about the artist?"

"I don't have to know the winery to like the wine." She pondered the question a moment further. "It spoke to me. It drew me in. I felt it." She reached for Lindsay's hand, brought it to her mouth, and kissed it. Lindsay relaxed under her touch, but her breaths became shallower as her eyes focused on their joined hands. Ren didn't need any more proof that she wasn't alone in this feeling of connection and attraction.

Ren raised a hand to Lindsay's cheek. "You're so beautiful," she whispered.

Lindsay's gaze dropped from Ren's eyes to her lips. "Come with me." She took Ren's hand and led her through the trees behind the swing.

"Where are we going?" Ren didn't really care. She loved the feel of Lindsay's hand in hers. She felt practically giddy at the thought of whatever might happen next.

Ren glanced back at the house. They were well out of view due to the small grove. Would they kiss back here? Would time stop so they could forget about Corey's pregnancy scare and Patty's nonsensical musings?

"Ren? Are you out here?"

Lindsay stopped and turned. "Corey," she whispered.

Ren didn't want to go. She *wanted* whatever would happen next, even if her brain was screaming rational thoughts like, "Don't get involved. Especially not now. Right before you go to Paris. Deb needs you to be here for Corey right now. Remember how you were going to avoid drama?" And then, of course, there was the overriding thought: "Doesn't this beautiful woman standing in front of you have great legs, and wouldn't those legs feel good wrapped around your hips?"

Okay, so that last thought wasn't so rational. It was the God's honest truth but not so rational. When it came to Lindsay, Ren didn't feel rational at all. She took a step back. "I should go see what she needs."

Lindsay held her stare for a moment, then gave her a nod. Ren wanted to tell her that the disappointment was mutual. "Can I have a rain check?" Lindsay smiled, which made Ren smile. "I mean, no pressure or anything, but this is a moment I want back."

Corey came through the trees. Ren turned to her. "Hey. I was just saying good-bye to—" She turned, but Lindsay was gone. Ren kept her eyes on the darkness. "Are you ready to go home?"

"I can't put it off forever," Corey said. "But Lindsay's right. I need my mom right now, even if she grounds me for three years."

A light became visible through the trees from what looked like a little cottage. "That's where she paints," Corey said. "I've only been in there once, and that was only because she wanted me to stop asking what it was like inside. I was so totally over it once I saw it. It's just paints and easels and stuff. Was she taking you back there?"

"I'm not sure." Ren forced a smile and put her arm around Corey. "Let's get you home."

❖

Patty burst into the studio out of breath. "What's wrong? Are you okay?"

Lindsay was far from okay. She'd hardly slept the night before because she couldn't shut it all out. The betrayal she felt because of Patty's actions. The anger she felt because of Ren's response, coupled with the strongest attraction she'd ever experienced for another person. All of it had kept her tossing and turning in the night. "Do I look okay, Cakes?"

"I don't know. Do you have internal bleeding or something else I can't see because you used the emergency code, so I rushed back here."

"This is you rushing? You live five minutes away, and it's going on twenty since I texted you. Maybe we need to change the emergency code from *Ruh Ro Raggy* to something more serious, like *Get the hell over here, Velma.*"

"Oh God. I had such a crush on her growing up. The glasses and the brains totally did it for me."

"Okay, scratch that. I need you to focus on me. The emergency code stays the same."

"Fine. But just for the record, I was mid-poop when the code came through, and you can't rush these things, or you get hemorrhoids. And I don't know if you've ever googled hemorrhoids, but it's not pretty."

Lindsay slapped her forehead. "Oh my God. Sometimes, it feels like I'm living in a *Three Stooges* episode." She pulled a stool closer and motioned for Patty to sit. "Cakes, why in the world would you say all of that past life stuff to Ren?"

Patty put up a finger. "First of all, you're welcome. And number two—"

"Okay, stop." Lindsay took a deep breath so she wouldn't lose her temper. "Why should I be grateful that you told Ren my business?"

"Oh! Is that what I did? Because what I thought I did was take one for the team. At least we know now that you bringing up the whole Roo is Ren and Ren is Roo thing would be a mistake."

"So you were trying to protect me?"

"When it comes to this, you're fragile, Linds. You are defiant about it and stand by what you know to be true. But it would break your heart if you bared your soul and she scoffed at it. And now we know what the likely outcome would be. So, yes, I was trying to keep you from getting hurt."

Lindsay reached for Patty's hand. The anger she'd felt dissipated. "I was so ready to yell at you for doing that, but I should've known your heart was in the right place."

"It always is when it comes to you." Patty stood and opened her arms. "Let's hug it out. Oh, wow." She let go of Lindsay and focused on the painting of Roo. "Her eyes are amazing, Linds."

"Her eyes are everything." Lindsay covered the painting back up. "She'll be gone soon enough."

"Will she? Or will she be like the boy?"

"This is different. Don't look at me that way."

Patty put up her hands in defense. "I didn't say a thing."

She didn't have to. Skepticism was oozing out of every pore. Of course it was. How many times had Lindsay said she'd stop painting the boy only to paint him again? And again. And again. And now, she was certain Ren was Roo. *Her* Roo. Would she start painting her too?

"I'll be glad when Ren is on the other side of the ocean." She didn't even convince herself with that statement, but she needed the conversation to end. She opened the door and motioned for Patty to walk outside first, then locked the door behind them. "Have you eaten? I'm starving."

"I could eat a pink poodle." Patty scrunched her nose. "Ew. Why does that sound so much worse than eating a horse?"

"And specifically, pink. You're so weird, Cakes."

"Some people dye their dog's fur bright colors." Patty gasped as if she'd had an epiphany. "Hey, can I borrow Sir Barksalot for a few hours?"

"Oh my God, yes! Please dye him pink. It will kill Ben."

Patty stopped. "I was kidding, but damn, girl. Is there no bottom to your dog custody revenge?"

Lindsay shrugged. "No. I'm sure I could go lower."

❖

At Ren's suggestion, she and Deb went outside and sat by the firepit. Deb had been strong and supportive during the conversation, but Ren could tell what she really wanted to do was scream at her daughter for being so irresponsible. If they were far enough away from the house, maybe Deb could let off a little steam without the kids hearing.

Ren patted her leg. "You did good in there."

Deb put her hand out. "Hold my hand?"

"Of course." She covered Deb's hand with both of hers.

"If I can't tell Colby about this, I need someone to lean on, and babe, you're it."

"I got you." Ren wrapped her arms around Deb.

"Corey has responsibility here too. Six conversations," Deb said. "Six times we talked about safe sex and birth control. I told her we could go to the doctor together when she was ready. How many times does it take before your kid actually listens to you? Ten? Fifteen? Fifty? 'Cause it sure ain't six."

Ren knew she didn't expect a response from her childless best friend regarding the nuances of child-rearing, but she thought she'd give it a try anyway. "I never listened to my mother. In one ear and out the other."

Deb giggled under her breath. "Remember when I said I needed someone to lean on? Yeah, scratch that."

"Nope. You can't take it back," Ren said. "Two footprints in the sand."

Deb giggled again. She rested her head on the back of the chair and looked at the sky. "You're terrible at consoling, but God, you make me laugh."

Ren tucked her hands in her coat pockets. "So what's the plan?"

"Kill that kid who had unprotected sex with my daughter with my bare hands. Death by asphyxiation."

Ren gave her a nod. "Yeah, I'd probably cut his balls off before he took his last breath and whisper in his ear, 'Next time, use a condom, fucker.'"

"Wow. Thanks for making mine sound tame."

Ren shrugged. "I've got your back."

"I know you do, Ren. You always have. And if we're being honest, I never listened to my mother either."

"No one does. If my mom had known half of the shit I did in high school, I never would've seen the light of day."

"Ditto," Deb said. "For some reason, I thought it would be different for me. I was going to be the super cool mom whose kids weren't afraid to talk about anything. So much for that plan."

"Eh, you're super cool in my book. Like, way, way cool."

Deb put out her fist. "Word."

"Brooke called this kid a loser. Why would a smart girl like Corey date a loser?"

"Colby and I have wondered the same thing, but the harder we tried to talk some sense into her, the more she wanted to defy us. So we backed off, worried that she'd run off with him. The kid is handsome, and he knows it. Always wears a cocky grin. But his grades are terrible, and he ditches classes on the regular."

"I guess he thinks he'll get by on his looks."

"He'll probably have to." Deb covered her face with her hands. "Oh my God, what if she'd really been pregnant?"

"What's this kid's name again?"

"Leo."

"Leo the loser. Loser Leo. I like it."

Deb laughed. "So much for a drama-free vacay in sleepy Salt Creek."

"Hey, it could be worse. You and Corey could both find out you're pregnant at the same time."

Deb's eyes lit up. "Oh, that would *really* Jerry Springer this shit." She turned and grabbed Ren's hand. "Seriously, though, thank you for being you. For always finding a way to make me laugh, for loving Corey, for having my back. I'm not glad this happened, but if it was going to, I'm glad you're were here to go through it with me."

"Hey, that's what we do," Ren said. "If I was willing to help you talk Professor Rutland off the ledge freshman year when you accidentally turned in that paper with Professor Fuckface written on the top, I figure I'm all in on the being here for you."

"Oh my God. You're never going to let me live that down, are you?"

"Nope. Never. It's a top twenty Deb moment. Okay, maybe top thirty. There've been so many."

"You think you're so funny." Deb kicked Ren's boot and reached over and squeezed her leg. "Lucky me, Soda Pop. Lucky me."

❖

Lindsay's bedroom door squeaked open a crack. She'd never bothered to fix the squeak since it was an early warning system for her busybody daughter.

"Mom, are you awake?"

"That all depends on what time it is."

"Six thirty."

"Then no, I'm not awake." The bed dipped. Brooke cuddled up behind her. She heard a sniffle, so she rolled over. "Honey?" Brooke's face was blotchy, her eyes swollen. "What's wrong, baby?" Brooke buried her face in Lindsay's chest and started to cry. "Oh, honey."

Brooke cried for a moment, then lifted her head. "At first, I was mad at Corey for being such an idiot, but now I feel guilty because I was so bummed about how that baby would affect my life."

Lindsay kissed her forehead. "Number one, high five for thinking Corey was an idiot but not saying it out loud. And number two, it's totally normal to get a little self-centered when someone else's actions affect you. And you're right, it would have been a big change for your future, just like it was for Patty when I got pregnant with you. But you know what?"

"What?"

Lindsay had to smile. Lately, Brooke had been acting like she already knew everything about everything. All of the answers to the universe had magically been laid at her feet, and she wasn't shy about letting her parents know how clueless they were. Advice from her mother? Hell, no, she didn't need that anymore. Except maybe she still did. "I'm proud of you, honey. You were there for your best friend the same way Patty was there for me."

Brooke looked up at her with the saddest eyes. It reminded Lindsay of when Brooke was young and would skin her knee or have a bad day at school.

"What's wrong?"

"Did you ever regret keeping me?"

Lindsay kissed Brooke's forehead again and ran her hand over her hair. She'd always told Brooke that the truth was better than a firm denial because it showed that you were brave enough to face the consequences of your actions. And maybe just being honest was enough, and there wouldn't have to be any big consequences. That's how the "safe zone" became a thing. She wanted Brooke to always feel safe when admitting her mistakes.

Lindsay didn't want to sugarcoat her answer. She took a deep breath and said, "Sometimes, I felt overwhelmed and like I was drowning under the weight of such a big responsibility at that age. It was all on me and your dad to make sure you stayed healthy and safe and clean and that you were never hungry. Sometimes, I would hold you and cry because I didn't feel strong enough or smart enough to raise you. But then you'd smile at me or cuddle up to me like you are right now, and my heart would fill up with so much joy, there wasn't any room for regrets. And the first time you said *Mama*, my heart exploded. I remember I ran for the camera so I could catch the moment and keep it forever. It's in your baby album if you want to see it."

"You took a picture of me saying my first word? Why didn't you just record it?"

"All we had back then were cheap flip phones. If I'd had a smartphone, I would've recorded all of the firsts and taken a million pictures. You were such a cute, sweet kid."

Brooke sat up and wiped the tears from her cheeks. "I'm sorry I've been a jerk lately. I'll try not to be so lame with you and Dad." She leaned over and kissed Lindsay's cheek. "Love you, Mom."

Lindsay hadn't heard those words in a while. From anyone. Ben had stopped saying it long before they'd ended it officially, and Brooke had found it hard to say anything kind to either of them once they separated. The words washed over Lindsay like a warm wave. "Love you too, honey."

CHAPTER EIGHT

Before getting a few things at the grocery store, Lindsay decided to check in on Deb at You Mocha Me Crazy and get a much-needed coffee. She stopped short when she saw Ren behind the counter. She was tempted to turn around and sneak out before being spotted.

Were they going to kiss the other night, or had she taken Ren's hand to lead her back to the studio just to show her some work? Would clothes have been ripped off, or would they have stood there trading art commentary?

Lindsay was afraid to know the answer. Afraid that she might actually have had sex with a stranger if they hadn't been interrupted. She turned to leave, but Ren shouted, "Tall Americano, extra hot!"

Too late. Lindsay turned back around and raised her hand. "That's me."

"I happen to agree," Ren said with a grin.

Lindsay was sure she blushed from head to toe. "How do you know my drink? And more importantly, why are you behind the counter? And most important of all, can you make a good cup of coffee?"

"I can only think of one person who can shoot off questions faster than you, and that's your daughter."

It was really nerves kicking in, but Lindsay shrugged. "I guess she gets all of her good traits from me."

Ren's eyes widened as if she'd spotted a ghost hovering over Lindsay's shoulder. "Shit!"

Lindsay spun around to see what kind of monster or zombie was about to attack. No one was there. "You scared the hell out of me."

Ren pointed at the door. "Is that a bus full of high school kids headed our way?"

"Oh. Yeah, it's probably the away team for the football game tonight. The word is getting around about Deb's baked goods. Next thing you know...why do you look so scared?" She glanced around. She hadn't yet noticed that they were completely alone. "Where's Deb?"

"She wanted to take Corey away for the night, but her employee called in sick," Ren said. "I told her I'd cover for her until closing, but it's been years since I was a barista, and I'm so freaking slow, there's no way I can serve an entire football team."

"Yeah. Looks like you picked the wrong day to stop drinking," Lindsay joked.

"You're not kidding. Why isn't the dumb name turning them off? Go away, boys! No mocha in here, just crazy."

The door opened, and a large group of boys took over the space. Lindsay rushed behind the counter and whispered, "Maybe they won't want coffee. Do you have chocolate milk? They'll probably want chocolate milk."

Ren turned to her so they were nose to nose. "Don't leave me."

"What am I supposed to do? I don't know how to make coffee in those fancy machines."

"I thought you said they'd want chocolate milk."

"I was just trying to make you feel better."

"You do. So please stay."

Lindsay's heart skipped a beat. She wanted to tell Ren that she made her feel all kinds of things, but *better* wasn't one of them. Confused, turned on, sad that she'd never be able to tell her the truth, or at least the truth as Lindsay saw it. She'd never be able to tell her about an amazing woman named Roo and the love they'd shared. "I'll stay," she whispered, even though running away felt like the better option.

Ren put an apron on her. "Pretend you know exactly what you're doing and push the chocolate milk."

Lindsay tied on the black apron with the You Mocha Me Crazy logo stitched in white and shouted, "Chocolate milk is half-price today, guys!"

❖

Ren got down on one knee and stuffed a bag of cash into the safe cemented into the floor, a remnant Deb had decided to keep from the old drugstore. She got back up and took off her apron. "We did it."

"And we lived to tell the tale." Lindsay untied her apron and tossed it in the laundry bag along with several dirty towels.

"Barely," Ren said. "I'm dead on my feet, but I'm also starving."

"It's gone beyond starving for me. I'm in the 'take me to the Icey Shack and let me order one of everything' phase, including the deep-fried MoonPie they recently added to the menu."

Ren threw on her jacket and grabbed her purse. "I love that place. Do they still sell those chocolate-dipped Creamsicles? They're the best on a hot summer day." She followed Lindsay out the front door and locked it behind her.

"They do. I may have to get one of those, even though it's a chilly night in October, and hot chocolate would be the appropriate choice."

"Well, you're getting one of everything, right?"

"Nah, you're buying, so I'll go easy on you," Lindsay said.

That made Ren smile. She'd had such a great time working with Lindsay that she didn't really want the night to end. "I guess buying you dinner is the least I can do, but let's go somewhere nicer. I'd love a glass of wine right about now, and I don't think the Icey Shack offers merlot."

"They should make a merlotsicle. I bet that would be delicious."

"You're a genius," Ren said. "Please suggest it the next time you frequent their fine establishment, but in the meantime, I saw a place in Lake City that looked nice. Have you ever been to Reuben's?"

"I haven't, but…" Lindsay took her phone out. "I should check on Brooke before I say yes to anything out of town."

"Of course." Ren wanted to suggest that Brooke whip up some macaroni and cheese for herself and let her mom have a night of fun, but that seemed intrusive, given they barely knew each other.

"Hey, honey," Lindsay said. "Yes, it went fine. No, we didn't burn Deb's place down." She winked at Ren and turned away.

Ren found herself swooning over what was probably a very innocent wink. She couldn't help herself. Lindsay Hall was beautiful and fascinating and filled with a warmth and intensity that Ren was definitely not immune to. If she could get her out of town, away from all of the prying eyes and interruptions, maybe they could get to know each other a little better. That's all Ren wanted. Just a little more insight into Lindsay's personality. And maybe her body, if things went well. Assuming she was into women. It felt like she was. Ren was certain her gaydar was not giving her a false positive.

Ren mentally undressed Lindsay while she was on the phone and admired her naked body from afar. When Lindsay ended the call, Ren mentally dressed her back up in her jeans and black cardigan. She forgot about Lindsay's panties, so the tight jeans slid over her bare ass. She didn't worry about the bra or T-shirt either. She just mentally slipped her cardigan back on and only buttoned two of the buttons, which left plenty of cleavage for Ren to admire.

"All good," Lindsay said. "Ren?"

"Excellent." She mentally buttoned the cardigan all the way up and said, "Let's go." She unlocked her car with the key fob and tried to get it together before she got in, so she didn't blush her way to Lake City.

As Ren drove out of Salt Creek, Lindsay said, "I think Ben is on duty tonight. Next time, he won't be as kind."

"You think I can't talk my way out of another ticket? Just watch me." She shrugged and slowed down a bit. "Fine. I'll drive at a reasonable speed. The last thing I need is a court date right before I leave for Paris."

"Not too slow. We're starving, remember?"

"So ten miles over the speed limit?"

"Perfect."

Lindsay felt a bit tipsy after half a glass of wine. The chef needed to hurry up with that mushroom truffle ravioli before she said something stupid like, *Remember that past life thing Patty mentioned? Yeah, about that...*

Ren had let her hair down and fluffed it before they got out of the car. Earlier, Lindsay had noticed that the boots Ren usually wore had been replaced with a pair of black Chucks. They looked great with the yoga pants and long V-neck tee that were in full view now that the apron was gone. Lindsay's attraction to women had definitely come out to play since Ren had been in town. She couldn't help but wonder about those boots, though. "You're not wearing the boots."

"Yeah, I didn't want to spill coffee on them."

"I don't think you could hurt those boots," Lindsay said. "Anything you do to them at this point will just add more character."

Ren laughed. "You're probably right, but I love them so much. In fact, will you keep them in Salt Creek for me? Just tuck them in the back of your closet or something?"

"I'd be happy to, but why not have Deb keep them?"

"Well, the thing is, I stole them from her several years ago, and if I left them in her house, she might reclaim them. She's kind of a bitch that way."

"Deb doesn't have a bitchy bone in her body, but I get it. You want to hang on to your ill-gotten gains."

"She doesn't, does she? It amazes me sometimes how much the people in this town love her. It's always been that way. Back when we were in college and we'd come to Salt Creek, everywhere we went, people were hugging her and wishing her well. I was always in awe of that."

"Her dad was that way too," Lindsay said. "Being the only

pharmacist in town, he knew everyone. It was a sad day when they closed the drugstore."

"Deb will do right by it. They'll just come in for a different kind of medicine."

Lindsay smiled. "Deb should've named it Love and Coffee. You pay for the coffee, but the love she spreads is free."

Ren's eyes lit up. "I love that name. Do you think that's why Mrs. Stokely goes there? After yesterday, we both know it's not for the excellent coffee."

"Two things," Lindsay said. "Everyone in town, including Mrs. Stokely, wants Deb's place to be a success, so they're supporting her in whatever way they can. Also, I think it's a good place for her to sit and socialize with whoever comes through the door. Keeps her from being too lonely."

"Tell me more about her. Why does she go by Mrs. if she never married?"

"All of her students called her that, so I think she just went with it instead of correcting them. It's probably the only time that ever happened." Lindsay took another sip of wine even though she probably shouldn't have. Ren had her elbows on the table and her chin resting in her hands as if she was hanging on every word. She felt tempted to bring up a more serious topic of conversation. After all, she might never have Ren's undivided attention again.

"Her house seemed like it had been furnished for two," Ren said. "There were two rockers in front of the TV, and both cushions were worn on the edges."

"Okay, private detective. What else did you notice?" Lindsay didn't care for the crunchy breadsticks the restaurant gave in lieu of bread, but she took a bite so her stomach wouldn't cave in on itself. She took another bite to soak up some of the wine so she wouldn't tell Ren how gorgeous she looked in old-school Italian restaurant lighting.

"Two TV trays tucked in the corner," Ren said. "Two crocheted afghans neatly folded and hung over the back of the rockers. Two champagne glasses in the hutch. She doesn't seem the type to live in sin, which means..." Ren gasped loudly. "She's gay!"

"That's my guess, detective."

"Who all knows?"

"It was an open secret. Sort of. Mrs. Stokely doesn't know we all knew her cousin Millie wasn't really her cousin. I mean, if they were together, I sure hope she wasn't her cousin. I guess everyone accepted it as long as she kept up her end and didn't reveal anything publicly. I mean, could you imagine an out lesbian being allowed to teach young kids back then?"

"Wouldn't happen. We were classified as deviants. Did you know Millie?"

"Not well," Lindsay said. "She wasn't from Salt Creek. All I know is that she was older than Mrs. Stokely by about fifteen years, so the older widowers in town had their eye on her. I remember she had graying hair and wore those polyester pantsuits that were so popular in the 70s. By the time I met her, the look was back in style. Cooler than anyone else in town."

"Maybe she influenced the decorating style in their home. It seemed pretty hip too. What happened to Millie?"

"She passed away years ago. MS, I think."

"How sad that they couldn't live their lives out in the open," Ren said. "Mrs. Stokely must've been devastated when Millie passed. Can you imagine having to hide that kind of pain from everyone?"

"I know. It's so sad. She's a strong woman, but you have to wonder if losing her lover and never being able to talk about her made her harsh. I wish she knew she didn't have to hide anymore."

"One would hope," Ren said. "God, the hell our community went through for so long. All of the hiding. All of the lies and heartache. It makes me furious to think that the same bigotry still exists."

"I guess you're right. There are no guarantees that everyone who knows Mrs. Stokely would accept her if she decided to come out."

"And how utterly sad is that?" Ren shook her head. "Sorry. I tend to get worked up when talking about this stuff."

"It's okay. I get it." Lindsay couldn't explain further. She couldn't talk about the dreams she'd had that were full of pain and heartache. The dreams she'd wake up from in a cold sweat. Roo screaming and crying as she was pulled from Katie's arms. The words *I love you* said over and over as she faded farther and farther away.

"It's real life," Lindsay said. "And you nailed it. If anyone told straight people that they weren't allowed to post pics of them kissing each other, they'd riot in the streets. But two men posting an engagement pic or a wedding kiss? Well, that deserves a snide comment or two...hundred."

"Poor Mrs. Stokely and Millie. I bet it was hard."

Lindsay could tell Ren was trying to hold back her emotions. She leaned across the table and patted her hand. "Hey. Maybe we should go visit her again. I'm sure she'd really love that."

Ren's expression brightened. "We should. And I'll even wear better jeans."

"So it's a date?" Lindsay found herself warming up to the idea of spending more time with Ren. Well, she had already been plenty warm. Maybe she could stop overthinking it and just enjoy their time together. It would be short-lived anyway. She might as well make the most of it.

"I don't know, is it?" Ren asked in a serious tone. She started twirling her coaster. "I guess I should ask if you date women."

"Are you asking if I'm bisexual? Because maybe you should've asked that question before you almost kissed me the other night. You know, right before you bailed?"

Ren demurred. "Not gonna let that go, huh?"

Lindsay kept a teasing tone in her voice. If they were going to build a friendship, something like that should be put on the table so they both knew where they stood. "In answer to your question, I've never been with a woman, but I'm bi. I've always been attracted to women. Just never had the chance to date one before Ben, and then, well, Brooke happened."

Ren rested her chin in her hand again and stared long enough that she had to look away.

Lindsay felt a blush work its way up her chest. "Why are you staring?"

"I'm just wondering what would've happened if I hadn't bailed."

Lindsay dropped her gaze for a moment. Butterflies filled her stomach. She looked at Ren again, and before she could stop herself, she asked, "What did you want to happen?"

Ren let her eyes do the talking. They wandered down to Lindsay's chest and lingered. "If you really want to know, I'll show you."

"Sorry for the delay, ladies." Their server set their plates on the table. "Anything else I can get you?"

Ren grinned. "No, I think we've got it from here." She picked up her spoon and spun some spaghetti on her fork. "I'm so hungry, it could be Chef Boyardee Beefaroni, and I wouldn't care."

The light comment sent a wave of relief through Lindsay. They could both move on without her having to respond in kind to that very sexy statement, even though the answer was yes, please. She picked up her fork and said, "I probably shouldn't tell you this because it's embarrassing, but Brooke pretty much grew up on SpaghettiOs, tuna sandwiches, and Kraft macaroni and cheese."

"So did most of America. And hey, she's lucky she got the good mac and cheese."

"Oh, I raised a mac and cheese snob," Lindsay said. "It's Kraft or nothing."

"Smart kid."

"I'm not sure it ever got a reaction quite like your pasta just did." She laughed at the speed with which they were eating. "You realize we're stuffing our faces right now, right?"

"This is how hardworking women eat." Ren gave her a wink and crammed half a meatball in her mouth.

❖

Ren felt giddy. Lindsay Hall was everything she didn't know she was looking for. Smart, thoughtful, with a depth of character she found fascinating but also a lighter side she got to see when they'd unexpectedly played coffee shop together.

And then there were the physical aspects she couldn't keep her mind off of. The way she tucked her hair behind her ears when she felt nervous or shy. How one eyebrow arched a little bit more than the other, making her look as if she was questioning everything you said. Her soulful eyes and her high cheekbones always had some pink to them.

Lindsay never talked over her. She chose her words carefully and sometimes used as few as possible. That was a nice change from her ex, who insisted on rehashing everything until Ren was too tired to argue anymore and just gave up.

So many positives, except one. Lindsay lived in Salt Creek.

As they exited the restaurant, Lindsay patted her tummy. "I'm so full."

"Too full for ice cream?" She spotted a little place across the street. "I doubt they have merlotsicles, but maybe a dipped cone or something?"

"I'm never too full for ice cream," Lindsay said with a tone Ren took to mean, "Is anyone ever too full for ice cream?" She took Ren's arm. "Let's walk."

Ren bent her arm in hopes Lindsay would keep her hand there. "I want to clarify something."

"You've never eaten Beefaroni in your whole life?"

Ren laughed. "Only once at a friend's house. Little eight-year-old me wasn't that impressed."

"I bet little eight-year-old you was adorable."

"Ah. Well, my parents might dispute that statement. I was a handful." They stopped at the crosswalk.

"My parents divorced while I was still in high school," Lindsay said.

"Are they in Salt Creek?"

"No. My dad moved to California, and my mom took off not long after I found out I was pregnant."

Ren was taken aback. "She abandoned you?"

"At that point, I was pregnant and engaged to Ben, so she probably considered me an adult. I was a month out of high school.

Not exactly grown-up, but I think she was just biding her time until I graduated. She wanted to go and live her life the same way my dad had. And when I got pregnant, I think she panicked because she didn't want to get saddled with another kid."

"And where is she now?"

"Right now, I honestly don't know. She'll show up for a few days and talk about her latest boyfriend and play with Brooke, and then she disappears again." Lindsay shrugged.

"And Ben's parents?"

"They've been amazing grandparents. I'm no longer their favorite person since I divorced their son, not that I ever was. But Brooke is their entire world, and that's all that matters. They helped us out a lot when we were young, and I'll always love them for that."

Ren noticed her shiver. "Are you cold?"

She rubbed her arms as if to warm them up. "I should've worn a warmer sweater."

Ren didn't want her to be cold, but she felt ecstatic that she had a reason to move in closer. She took over the arm-rubbing for a few seconds and opened her leather jacket and wrapped it around Lindsay too. It didn't go very far, but that didn't matter. Their bodies were touching. Their cheeks were touching. And Lindsay's arms were wrapped around her waist. "We can't eat ice cream out here," Ren said. "Let's go inside."

Lindsay didn't move. She snuggled in closer and said, "Do you always think of others first?"

"Just my date. Everyone else can freeze to death." She kept one arm wrapped around Lindsay's shoulders and led her inside.

She didn't react to being called Ren's date. They ordered a brownie sundae to share. They both hummed their approval on the first bite.

"About that thing I wanted to clarify," Ren said.

"Oh, right." Lindsay put up a finger. "Hold on." She took another big spoonful, expertly distributing ice cream, brownie, and hot fudge in equal portions on her spoon. She closed her eyes and seemed to be lost in a state of ice cream nirvana. "Mmm. This may be the brownie sundae against which all other brownie sundaes will henceforth be judged." She put her spoon down. "Okay, I'm ready."

Ren laughed. "You're kind of adorable when you have chocolate on your chin."

She grabbed a napkin. "First the ravioli with the not stopping for air and now the ice cream. You're going to think I have no table manners."

"Does it matter what I think?"

She went still. "Of course it does."

"Why?"

"All the normal reasons."

"I don't know, you seem to live life on your own terms," Ren said. "Do you really care what anyone thinks of you?"

She seemed stumped. Her eyes searched Ren's. "You're not just anyone."

Ren smiled. She liked that answer. "The thing I wanted to clarify: it's that kiss that almost happened. I wanted to make sure you knew that I didn't bail because I'd changed my mind. I could've asked Corey to wait for me inside. I just figured it probably wasn't the best timing. I also thought that if something did happen between us, I wouldn't want us to be interrupted. Would you?"

Again with the searching eyes. God, she was sexy when she got that intense look in her eyes. Ren reached across the table and let their fingertips touch. It didn't matter that they barely knew each other. Ren wanted her, and with Deb out of town, it seemed like the perfect opportunity.

"No, I wouldn't," Lindsay said.

Ren leaned in closer and ran her fingers under the sleeve of Lindsay's sweater and caressed her wrist. "See, the thing is, you fascinate me, Lindsay. You make my heart beat a little faster. You know?"

She nodded and whispered, "Yes."

Ren felt goose bumps raise up on her skin. "So you feel it too? This thing between us?"

"I've always…"

"What? Say what you're thinking."

"What I meant to say is…" She shook her head. "I'm not sure what I meant to say."

Ren took her hand and gave it a gentle squeeze. "Sorry if I'm being too direct. I'm very attracted to you, and I thought you should know that I think you're beautiful and sexy and so desirable, I can't believe I didn't kiss you when I had the chance."

Lindsay held her gaze for a moment and said, "It's not too late. Wanna go somewhere?"

❖

The short ride to the hotel was a quiet one. Lindsay hardly took her eyes off Ren while she drove. Whether or not she was doing the right thing didn't seem to matter anymore. Whether or not she came out of it unscathed was no longer a worry. Ren had come into her life for a reason. And maybe that reason wasn't so they could have sex, but who was to say it wasn't?

Of course it wasn't, but Lindsay was all in. And by all in, she meant she'd say everything she was thinking except the past life stuff, because she knew Patty was right. But everything else, she'd say it.

Ren parked the car and unbuckled her seat belt. Lindsay did the same and said, "I'm not even nervous." She turned and looked out the side window at the Fairfield Inn, aka the place she'd have sex with a woman for the first time. The first time she'd have sex with Ren. She turned back and in a bold, intimate way, ran her thumb over Ren's bottom lip. "This is going to be good, isn't it?"

Ren took Lindsay's hand and kissed it. "You have no idea."

❖

Lindsay couldn't catch her breath. Ren had her up against the wall and was devouring her neck, causing shocks of electricity to crash through her body. "Oh my God," she whispered through bated breaths. "Your lips. Your tongue. Your—"

Ren worked her way to her cheek. "Where do you want my tongue?"

She gently kissed Lindsay's cheek until she answered, "Everywhere."

Ren kissed her with a force that made her knees almost buckle. The passion she could stir with just her lips was astounding. She broke away from the kiss and pressed her entire body against Lindsay. She had one hand in her hair and the other gripping her waist.

She caressed Lindsay's ear with her tongue and whispered, "Are you as wet as I am?"

They still had their clothes on, but Lindsay could feel the moisture building between her legs. She moaned. "Let's just say it won't take much."

"Is that usually the case?"

"Oh God, no."

Ren pulled back and met her gaze. "You're so fucking sexy."

Lindsay leaned back and rested her head against the wall in hopes Ren would devour her neck again. "Can you talk while you kiss? I need those lips on my body."

When she had sensual dreams about Roo, Lindsay imagined her lips would feel this soft against her skin, her tongue this warm, her touch this tender. Ren gripped her hips while she took her time, kissing every inch of her neck. Her tongue dipped lower, following the line of Lindsay's collarbone, and she moaned her approval.

Ren took her time. Lindsay loved that. She wanted this feeling to last forever. She also wanted to grab Ren's hand and push it into her panties. Her body and mind were at war with each other. *Go slow. No, fuck me now. Take your time. Take me now.*

Ren held her close and worked on loosening the buttons on her cardigan. Lindsay wondered if those long slender fingers would soon be inside her. Or would she use her left hand? Either way, the anticipation was killing her.

Ren pushed her cardigan off and let it fall to the floor. "I've undressed you in my head already."

Their eyes met, and time slowed. She took Ren's hand and

put their palms together, then intertwined their fingers. If they stopped right now, it would be enough. She'd experienced more all-consuming bliss in the last few minutes than she ever had in her marriage. *Say it. Say everything.* "I'm so happy to have this moment with you."

"You make it sound like that's all we have. A moment."

"Isn't it? You're going to Paris."

Ren brought their joined hands to her lips. "What if we make every moment we have together something we'll never forget."

"There's zero chance I'll ever forget you."

Ren smiled. "I feel the same way."

Lindsay ran her finger along Ren's hairline and tucked a stray piece behind her ear. "Now that we have that cleared up, why don't you undress me for real?"

❖

Lindsay responded to every flick of Ren's fingers. It was such a turn-on to hear her groans of pleasure, feel her fingernails digging into Ren's shoulders. The vibration of Lindsay's lips on her ear as she whispered profanities mixed with approval, the scent of her glistening skin and the sweat on her brow...all of it was making Ren crazy.

They were on their knees facing each other, a deliberate decision on Ren's part. It was hot and sexy and so intimate being eye to eye.

Ren's fingers were deep inside her, pushing and flicking. When she thought Lindsay might have had enough, she moved faster and deeper. The moan her actions elicited delighted her no end.

As much as she wanted to stay where she was, it was time for more. Ren carefully pulled out and, with a featherlight touch, made small circles around Lindsay's swollen clit. God, she looked beautiful like this, panting for air, hair damp with sweat, eyes partly closed. "You're gorgeous," she whispered. "Stay right here."

Ren got behind her. She wrapped her arm around her waist and whispered, "I've got you."

Lindsay relaxed against her and covered Ren's hand with her own. "I know you do. I trust you."

Ren wrapped both arms around her and dipped her right hand lower into her wet folds. Lindsay whimpered at the touch. "Oh God, yes," she whispered. She took Ren's other hand and guided it to her breast.

Ren wanted Lindsay's orgasm to build slowly, so she kept her touch light at first, just circling her clit instead of putting direct pressure on it. "How does that feel?"

Lindsay nodded. "Uh-huh."

Was she speechless? Ren smiled at the thought and applied a little more pressure. Lindsay arched her back and bucked harder. "Don't stop," she demanded. "Don't stop."

Ren lightly sank her teeth into Lindsay's shoulder and let her tongue circle her skin with the same rhythm that her finger circled her clit. Lindsay's back arched. She reached behind and grabbed Ren's hair. "Fuck," she whispered. "Fuck, I'm coming. Oh God. Oh!" Her whole body tensed in Ren's arms. She fell forward onto her hands and knees and said, "Oh my fucking God."

Ren had to agree with the sentiment, considering her new view. She ran her hands over Lindsay's backside and gripped her hips. God, how good it would feel to take her like this. "You're so sexy, Lindsay. I wish you could see yourself."

"I want you inside me," Lindsay said.

"Again?"

"God, yes. Fuck me again."

Ren ran the back of her index finger between Lindsey's legs. Since she was already so wet, she didn't need to ease her way in. She drove two fingers in, and Lindsay's response was a loud, "Yes! Oh God, yes!"

So Lindsay liked it hard. This was very valuable information. Ren positioned herself with one hand on Lindsay's shoulder and added a third finger. Lindsay responded to every thrust with a moan or a word of encouragement. Ren bent over and sank her teeth into Lindsay's ass and sucked until she left a mark. She sensed Lindsay was losing her strength, so she slowed down. "Had enough?"

"I'll never get enough of you, but yeah." She dropped onto her stomach, looking rather sated.

Ren wanted to lie on top of her, but she was still catching her breath. She snuggled in next to her and threw a leg over her ass, then moved the damp hair from her face. Lindsay's eyes were wide open and searching. Ren caressed her hair and ran her fingernails over her backside. Lindsay continued to stare. Ren leaned in and kissed her forehead and her cheek. "You okay?"

"I'm the best I've ever been in my whole life."

Ren grinned. "That good, huh?"

Lindsay got up on her elbows and leaned in for a kiss. "I think you should pay the seventy-eight dollars I owe to the potty mouth jar."

Ren laughed. "You don't even know how much I'd pay to hear you scream *fuck* again."

"Lots of dollars?"

Ren ran her fingers into Lindsay's hair and pulled her in for a kiss. "So many."

❖

Lindsay buttoned her cardigan over her white T-shirt and looked in the mirror. Her world, as she knew it, would never be the same. She wondered if the dreams would stop, if Roo would drift into the background because Ren was here now. Or if the dreams did continue, would they feel the same? Have the same depth? Make her feel the same joy and loss and everything in between? And the biggest question of all, what was Ren feeling?

Lindsay opened the bathroom door and found Ren just outside, leaning against the wall. "I was just about to knock and ask if you're okay."

"I'm fine. Better than fine."

Ren smoothed down her hair. "You're so beautiful."

Lindsay leaned into the touch. It hadn't even been ten minutes since they'd been wrapped around each other, skin on skin, lips on lips, yet Lindsay found herself missing it already. Ren looked amazing in whatever she wore, but now that Lindsay had seen her naked, there was no going back. She wanted more of that body. She wanted to take her time exploring it. She wanted to know what it felt like to have her fingers buried inside Ren. She wanted to taste her. She wanted to hear her moans of pleasure and feel her body tense and see her hips buck. And she wanted that to happen at least a thousand times. Maybe more. She hadn't really done the math yet.

But what did Ren want? Lindsay was too afraid to ask. This whole thing might have just been sex to her. A good ol' romp in the hay. A spectacular romp, but just a romp nonetheless. Ren's eyes weren't telling her anything. "I'm sorry we have to rush back," Lindsay said. "Brooke isn't used to me—"

"Dating?"

Lindsay hesitated. "Is that what we're doing?"

Ren caressed her cheek with the back of her hand. "I know it's been a while for you, but dinner, wine, dessert, you holding my arm while we walked, and ending up in bed all add up to a pretty fabulous date."

Lindsay took her hand and kissed her palm. "What are you doing this weekend?"

Ren grinned as she ran her fingers into Lindsay's hair and pulled her closer. "I like where your head is at." She leaned in for a kiss.

Lindsay didn't want a peck. She cupped Ren's cheeks and deepened the kiss. She would never get enough of Ren's lips or that talented tongue that she could only imagine would feel like heaven on other parts of her body.

Ren whimpered and pushed her against the wall. She kissed her deeply again and said, "Either we leave now or we stay the whole night, because you're killin' me here, Linds."

Lindsay needed to get back before Brooke panicked and called Ben because Mom hadn't come home. She felt guilty that she hadn't had time to reciprocate. "Sorry," she whispered. "I wish we could stay so I could—"

Ren put her finger on Lindsay's lips. "Shh. Don't be sorry. Just tell me that this won't be the last time."

Lindsay took Ren's finger into her mouth and let her tongue

roll around it, then sucked it in farther. Ren let out a little gasp and said, "Okay. I like that answer."

❖

They held hands most of the way home. Lindsay stared at Ren most of the way too. She couldn't believe what had just happened. Shouldn't she feel guilty for leaving her kid to fend for herself while she had mind-blowing sex in a hotel room? She felt elated and satiated and so relaxed it seemed like her voice had dropped an octave. A sense of guilt was nowhere to be found.

Ren pulled into Lindsay's driveway and put the car in park. She turned and shook her head as if she couldn't believe what had happened either. "Wow," she whispered.

"What a night," Lindsay said.

"What a night." She took Lindsay's hand and held it to her lips. She gently kissed each knuckle.

"I know," Lindsay said. "I don't want to leave you, either." Apparently, she was still in "say everything you're feeling" mode. Well, not everything. She wasn't going to tell Ren that it felt as if she'd found a home in her arms. Or that Ren's touch was everything missing from her life. Or that her kiss seemed to soothe wounds Lindsay didn't even know she had.

Ren held her stare but didn't reply. Lindsay wanted to pull her hand away and take back the words, because what if that wasn't what Ren was feeling at all? What if the sigh was a precursor to her giving the "let them down easy" speech?

Lindsay fought the urge to run and leaned in. A kiss would tell her exactly where Ren's mind was. She closed her eyes and waited for Ren to meet her halfway. And there were those soft lips she'd grown to adore. The fire between them ignited again. A jolt of electricity shot through Lindsay's body when their tongues collided. She desperately wanted to crawl onto Ren's lap, put the seat down, and make mad love to her right there in the driveway, but she knew Brooke was in the house. She slowed down the kiss and pulled back.

Ren touched her cheek. "You sure know how to leave a girl wanting more."

Lindsay smiled and said, "See you soon."

"See you soon."

Lindsay got out and watched Ren drive away. Whatever happened next, this would be a night she would never forget.

CHAPTER NINE

L indsay rolled her eyes as Patty started another round of pacing in her studio. She'd only get about three steps in before she had to turn around. It was making Lindsay dizzy.

"I can't believe this," Patty said again, this time with both arms in the air.

"Hey, watch it. You're going to break something." Lindsay opened her minifridge. "Want a beer?"

Patty tapped her watch. "It's ten o'clock in the morning. Don't you have something stronger?"

"I thought you liked to wait until noon. I have an airplane bottle of Jack that I could mix with your Diet Coke. It's that or a Sam Adams."

Patty put out her hand. "Just the Coke, smarty-pants."

Lindsay shrugged and handed her the soda. "I kinda wish you were more of a day drinker right now."

Patty continued pacing, then made an abrupt stop. "You had sex with her. You actually had sex with her." She threw a hand up. "Oh. My. God."

"Hey! You're spilling Coke everywhere. Drink it or lose it."

"I can't believe you, Linds. After that promise you made years ago?" Patty tapped her chest with her finger. "It was supposed to be me, Linds. Me."

"You're my best friend, Cakes. My...I don't know, my soul sister, my Pattycakes, Brooke's godmother, the Rachel to my Monica, the best friend I could ever ask for. You get me like no one else. You're the most important person in my life next to Brooke. You are both the loves of my life, and I couldn't bear to lose you. That's who you are to me."

Patty slumped on a stool and dramatically covered her eyes with her hands. "Don't touch me. Just let me get through this…this betrayal."

Lindsay tried not to laugh while she waited. She loved Patty, and part of loving Patty was loving her dramatic tendencies. She opened the fridge and got a Diet Coke for herself. She took a sip and said, "Can I ask—"

"Shut up."

Lindsay closed her mouth and waited. She looked at her watch and waited. "Cakes. Come on."

Patty pulled her hands away from her face. "You can't even give me five minutes to mourn the loss of us ever bucking? Really, Linds? Not even five minutes?"

"Bucking?"

"Yes, swear jar lady. It's what I would say in front of Brooke, like, oh buck, I burned the toast, or, oh buck, I drove right past the school and ended up at the Icey Shack."

Lindsay lifted an eyebrow. "What was that?"

"It only happened once when she absolutely did not want to go to school because of that kid who called her chicken legs."

"That was in the third grade."

Patty pointed her finger. "Which is why you're going to give me a pass."

"You weren't in the safe zone, Cakes. And you absconded with my daughter so you wouldn't have to order the Mega Banana Split and eat it all alone. Did you call the school and pretend to be me too?"

"Okay, number one—"

"No," Lindsay said. "No numbers. Just tell me how many times you impersonated me and took Brooke to the movies or bowling or—"

"Ice skating," Patty blurted. "I taught Brookey how to ice skate, okay? No bowling or movies. Just ice skating. And she got pretty good too. Besides, who needs to go to third grade when there's a little Masshole in the class."

"Masshole? You're talking about a third-grader, Cakers." Lindsay giggled under her breath. "Now, would you please sit down?"

"Fine. But I'm not over this Ren thing."

"That's what we need to talk about." Lindsay made a large circling motion with her hand. "Cone of truth here, okay?"

"If this is anything like the safe zone, I'm out." She went to stand. She got about halfway up into a standing position and froze. "Aren't you going to stop me? Grab my arm or something. Don't leave me hanging like this."

Lindsay rolled her eyes and gave her arm a gentle yank. "Okay, I'm just going to jump right in. I need to know if you're *really* telling me you've been secretly pining away for me all these years."

"You said I'd be the first to know."

"Cakes, that's not what I'm asking."

"I know, I know." Patty leaned forward and put her elbows on her knees. "I've actually been thinking about that. I never thought I was crushing on you. Not since high school. And then this Ren-Roo thing happened." She paused and took a deep breath. "I guess I got kind of jealous."

Lindsay put her hand on Patty's knee. "I can see that, hon. I'm just trying to understand why."

"So am I. But the short answer is, no, I'm not pining away for you. I'm just worried I'm going to lose you."

"Lose me? Why would you lose me?"

"Because it's always been me and you. Joined at the hip. Then this chick shows up."

Lindsay grabbed her hands. "Okay, listen to me, Cakes. This is Ren we're talking about, not some rando I found in a bar."

"I know. I know. It was like you were having sex with the woman of your dreams. Like, literally."

"Not exactly literally. She isn't Roo."

"You said she *is* Roo."

"She is, but not..." Lindsay sighed. "I'm confusing myself

now." Patty got up and started pacing again. "Oh God," Lindsay whispered to herself. At least this time Patty had her arms folded and wasn't holding a can of soda.

"Lindsay, look at me. If you really believe Ren is the reincarnation of Roo, you're going to tell her, right?"

Lindsay didn't answer.

"Lindsay?"

"You're the one who said there was no point in telling her the truth."

"That was before you slept with her," Patty said. "Things are a little different now, don't you think?"

Lindsay didn't know what to think. "Are they? I mean, she's moving to Paris. It's not like we're going to have some long-term, long-distance thing."

"You're lying to yourself, Linds. Don't you see that even if you have a two-week fling or whatever, you're going to fall madly in love with her? And you can't be in love with someone who doesn't know the truth. *Your* truth. It would kill you to keep that buried inside."

"You want to know my truth, Cakes? The truth is that no one, not Roo, not Ren, not anyone else, will ever replace you." Her phone dinged. "Hold on." She opened the text from Ren. It said, *Do we have to wait until the weekend?*

Lindsay grinned and typed a reply.

Patty put her hands on her hips. "It's her, isn't it?" She grabbed for the phone.

"Stop!" Lindsay pulled it away. "Yes, it's her."

"I say this out of love, Linds. You need to tell her about Roo. If she accepts it, great. You'll work things out. If she doesn't, at least you won't be too far in. Tell her before it's too late to let go."

❖

"Brookey?" Lindsay knocked on Brooke's bedroom door and opened it. "Can I come in?"

Brooke didn't look up from her phone. "You're already in."

Lindsay sat on the edge of the bed. "Have you talked to Corey?"

"So you're gay now?"

Taken aback, Lindsay furrowed her brow. "What?"

"Gay, Mom. As in, kissing women in the driveway. Do you think I'm blind?"

"I guess I didn't consider that you'd be spying from the window." Brooke moved to get up, but Lindsay stopped her. "Okay, wait. That wasn't totally fair. I didn't know that what happened last night was going to happen. But I've always been attracted to women, Brooke. I just married your dad so young, and I would never have cheated on him."

Brooke blinked a few times and seemed to consider that. "Still. You're an adult, Mom. You don't get to go around randomly kissing people. I mean, are we all about to die from an asteroid or something? Is that why everyone's sleeping with whoever they want because maybe I want in on that. Maybe I'd like to get with…" She pursed her lips. "Forget it. I don't care anymore." Sir Barksalot climbed the little steps Brooke had at the end of her bed and snuggled next to her. "At least I know that Barksy isn't sleeping around."

"Honey, I'm not sleeping around. I know your world feels a little bit upside down right now, but that's not what's going on."

Lindsay got on the bed next to her and put a pillow on her lap. She patted it. "Take out your hair tie." Brooke huffed, but she complied. Lindsay started the head massage at her hairline, massaging in a small, circular motion on her forehead. It was working. Brooke's eyes were closed, and her breathing had slowed. Lindsay hated to see her so stressed out, but Brooke had always been a worrier. She could come up with a worst-case scenario for any situation in the blink of an eye. Give her a few minutes, and she'd have a top ten list.

Just when Lindsay thought Brooke had dozed off, she opened her eyes. "Did you like kissing a girl?"

"I liked kissing that particular girl."

"What do you mean?"

"Honey, Ren is someone very special. I haven't talked about her in a while, but do you remember me telling you about Roo?"

"The woman in your dreams."

"Yes. The woman in my dreams. And do you remember when I explained to you my belief in past lives?"

Brooke nodded. "Yeah."

"Honey, I think Ren might be Roo. Not think, I *know* Ren is Roo."

Brooke rolled onto her back and met Lindsay's gaze. "You mean Roo was reborn as Ren?"

"It sounds crazy, but I know in my gut that she's Roo."

"Is that why you kissed her?"

"I feel connected to her in the same way I feel connected to Roo. Plus, I think she's pretty cute." Lindsay winked, trying to keep things light.

"Mom, she's not cute. She's totally hot." Brooke looked at her intently and seemed to be taking it all in. "When you told me about Roo before, you never said you were girlfriends."

"I know, honey." Lindsay traced her facial features with a finger. "A mom is entitled to some privacy too."

"I guess so." Brooke grinned. "Does this mean I'm going to have two mommies?"

Lindsay's eyes widened. "Okay, slow down, honey. It was only a kiss."

"Please, Mom. Spare me the gross details. I'm already freaked out enough about Corey touching Leo's...oh my God, I can't even say it."

"Good. Because you know Leo's hmm-hmm isn't worth talking about."

"Mom!"

Lindsay dug her fingers into Brooke's sides and tickled her. "You're the one who brought it up. Get her, Barksy!"

Barsky jumped up and barked. He spun in a circle and barked again.

"Okay, stop!" Brooke grabbed her hands. "If Ren makes you happy, I'm cool with it, okay?"

Lindsay leaned over and kissed her forehead. "That's all I want for you too, honey. Lots and lots of happy."

❖

Ren waited until the talkative customer left the coffee shop before she turned to Deb and said, "You wanted to talk about something?"

"Yes. What are you thinking trying to seduce a woman right before you leave town?"

"You make it sound like I failed."

Deb slapped her hands over her ears. "Oh God. Don't tell me about it. I won't be able to face her."

"And by that you mean you'd like details?"

"God, no." Deb moved in closer. "Just the highlights. I'm kinda busy."

Ren laughed. "It was a highlight from start to finish. And yes, I made sure she finished."

"Oh, well, at least there's that. Now if I hear any rumors, at least they'll include the fact that Deb's best friend is good in bed."

"And really, what else is there? In fact, I think I'll put it on my gravestone. Right under my DOB/DOD: *She was good in bed*."

"And your gravestone will go viral," Deb said. "In fact, I'll take the photo and post it so I can benefit from your death."

"Done."

"Just promise me you won't spend every waking moment with her until you leave. I need some Ren time too."

Ren bumped her shoulder. "Aww. Of course. That's why I came here." Ren meant it, but as soon as the words left her mouth, she knew that there was even more to love about Salt Creek now.

Ren decided to walk to Mrs. Stokely's house. The air was crisp and clear with a slight breeze. Chilly enough for a coat but refreshing at the same time. When she rounded the corner onto Center Street, she saw Lindsay ahead. Ren slowed her pace so she could look for as long as possible. Lindsay had a scarf around her neck similar to the one she'd worn on their first visit to Mrs. Stokely's house. This one was a pink and white buffalo check. It looked cute with her oversized cable sweater and dark skinny jeans. The pink beanie on her head was too adorable for words, and Ren couldn't wait for her to turn around and catch her eye so that even if the right words escaped her, her eyes would tell the story of how much last night meant to her. And how time felt as if it had been going backward all morning. And that the permanent smile on her face was all Lindsay's fault.

Lindsay. Sexy, enigmatic, passionate Lindsay.

Ren remembered every moan, every thrust against her fingers, every aching request for more. More touch, more tongue, more skin on her skin. Lindsay gave all of herself without hesitation. No holding back. No questioning looks. Just trust. And lust.

Lindsay turned, and Ren grinned from ear to ear. "You look pretty in pink." The beanie had matching fingerless gloves. Ren imagined how much fun it would be to remove this outfit from Lindsay's body. She'd do it slowly, one finger at a time.

Lindsay got closer and looked her up and down. "Did you dress up for me?"

"If I said I dressed up for Mrs. Stokely, would you believe me?"

"After the last visit? Yes."

It was a lie, though. Ren had spent the morning throwing clothes around her room. She'd brought a few nice outfits with the intention of never wearing them. That was before she met Lindsay.

She'd decided to stick with jeans so her outfit wouldn't be such an obvious cry for attention. Her ankle boots were black. It was probably the tucked-in silk shirt Lindsay had commented on, a shade of blue that reminded Ren of cotton candy. She wore a black puffer vest that would be removed once they were inside Mrs. Stokely's roaster oven of a house.

Lindsay grabbed Ren's vest with both hands and pulled her closer. "I think you wore this sexy outfit for me. And after last night, I'd say you're two for two."

Ren put her hands on Lindsay's hips. "Last night was amazing. I need more of last night. You know, right after I get out of detention for kissing you good night."

"Wait. How did you get in trouble?"

"Brooke told Corey, who told Deb."

"We might as well be in high school. Sorry my kid's such a blabbermouth."

"I'm not sorry about anything. Are you?"

"About last night?" Lindsay shook her head. "No. When can we do it again?"

"What was your favorite part about being with a woman?"

"Not just any woman. I was with you, Ren. And I have lots of favorite parts."

"Please tell me."

"Here on the street? In front of Mrs. Stokely's house?" Lindsay grabbed her forearm and pulled her closer. She leaned in and whispered, "I loved how turned on you got just looking at me. How in tune you were with what I was feeling. How wet you made me. How you felt inside me."

Ren swooned. Lindsay had been on her mind all morning. She couldn't wait to see her again. Touch her. Tell her how incredible last night was. Tell her how desperately she wanted to do it again. No one—not Deb, nor anyone else—could keep her from seeing Lindsay. How she wanted to make love to her at midnight and again at six a.m. Hand-feed her breakfast in bed. Lick maple syrup off her nipples. And whipped cream. Definitely whipped cream.

Lindsay cleared her throat and whispered, "You're staring at my boobs."

"Right, um…sorry. I was imagining…anyway, hi." Ren breathed out that last word as if it were a sigh of relief.

"Hi." Lindsay motioned with her head toward the house. "Maybe we could sneak into the garage and fool around in the Mistmobile."

Ren bit her lip. Oh, the things they could get up to in the back seat of Mrs. Stokely's car. "I should be so lucky."

Lindsay bounced on her heels. "How is it even possible that I could feel this excited to have coffee with Mrs. Stokely?"

"It's the anticipation. You can almost smell the mountain-grown aroma wafting from the kitchen. The instant crystals tingling your nostrils, tempting your taste buds."

The door creaked open, and Mrs. Stokely shouted, "The coffee's brewing. Better get in here."

They hurried down the path to her front door. "Brewing?" Lindsay whispered.

"Maybe we're wrong about it being instant."

"I think she's probably using the word loosely." Lindsay raised her voice to a normal volume. Or perhaps a bit louder than normal given the audience. "Hi, Mrs. Stokely."

"Come in. But don't make yourselves at home. Just semi-comfortable."

Ren tried to cover up the snort that snuck out with a light cough. She took off her vest and waited for Lindsay to take off her hat and scarf, then put them on a chair. While Mrs. Stokely was in the kitchen, she took the time to really look around for any evidence of the mysterious Millie. There were a few old, tattered black-and-white photos hanging in frames on the wall. Parents and grandparents, Ren imagined. Maybe an aunt and uncle or two. Nothing of a woman with graying hair dressed in a fabulous pantsuit.

"Psst." Lindsay pointed at a small oval frame on an end table next to a basket of yarn and crochet hooks. Ren recognized the pile of multicolored squares that would eventually become a beautiful blanket that would hang over the back of a rocking chair or be placed on the end of a bed. Her own grandmother used to sew something very similar while watching her favorite soap opera—her "story" as she called it—*The Light of Day.*

Ren picked up the frame. "Millie?" she whispered. Lindsay nodded. Sure enough, Millie had on a yellow pantsuit with matching pumps. Large plastic jewelry adorned her neck and ears. She was stylish for her time, no doubt. Ren turned the frame over, hoping to find an inscription. It simply said *M. 1977.*

"That's my cousin Millie." They both turned and found Mrs. Stokely standing with a tray, watching them.

Ren set the photo down. "I didn't mean to pry." She took the tray and set it on the coffee table.

"It would appear otherwise." Mrs. Stokely slumped into her chair. "I'm feeling a bit tired today. You two go ahead and serve yourselves." She picked up the photo of Millie and ran her thumbs over the narrow gold frame. "It's her birthday today."

"Oh," Lindsay said. "I hope we're not intruding."

Mrs. Stokely waved her comment off. "If you hadn't stopped by, I'd have no one to tell that it's her birthday today."

Ren leaned over and admired the photo again. "She's beautiful. And she wore that pantsuit like a boss."

"Like a boss?" Mrs. Stokely asked. "Well, I suppose that's because she was. She was the school principal."

"No, I meant she wore it really well," Ren said. "She's fabulous."

"She was indeed." Mrs. Stokely looked at the photo again. "Millie loved all of the latest fashions. Her pant legs were so wide it was like ironing a tablecloth. I was more on the conservative side. Pedal pushers and skirts were my style. Now comfort is all I care about. Millie would roll over in her grave if she knew I wore old lady shoes with Velcro straps."

Ren sat next to Lindsay on the sofa. Mrs. Stokely seemed to have drifted into thoughts of Millie, so she whispered, "Let's give Millie a birthday party."

Lindsay raised her eyebrows. "Right now?"

Ren winked, then pulled her phone out of her pocket and sent a text to Deb.

"I see you took my advice," Mrs. Stokely said, her eyes on Ren.

"Advice?" Ren put her phone back in her pocket in hopes she wouldn't get reprimanded for using it during their visit. Manners and all that.

"You look smart today. Pretty instead of lazy. Well, I shouldn't say lazy. Anyone with that many holes in their pants probably works too hard."

Mrs. Stokely had a hearty laugh that Ren could appreciate, even if the laugh was at her expense. "Thank you, Mrs. Stokely. Would Millie approve?"

"She would indeed. And she'd probably ask where you bought those fancy boots. I swear it's like night and day. What'd you do? Hire one of those expensive stylists from New York?"

Ren nudged Lindsay's knee. She needed to get in on this conversation so Ren could look at Deb's reply. "Oh," Lindsay said. "We haven't even poured the coffee."

"Millie used to make the best coffee," Mrs. Stokely said. "Isn't it funny how everything tastes so much better when someone else makes it for you? Of course, Millie would splurge on high-quality coffee as if she owned shares in Maxwell House." Mrs. Stokely shook her head and laughed under her breath. "Sweet, sassy Millie."

One could safely assume that Mrs. Stokely wasn't one to throw things away. She'd had the same car and furniture for forty years. That gave Ren an idea. "Mrs. Stokely, did you happen to keep any of Millie's outfits?"

"A few things. Maybe a closet full. It's been so long I really can't remember what I saved and what I didn't."

Lindsay caught right on and said, "I'd love to see some of those fabulous clothes. If it's not too much trouble."

"Why would you want to see a bunch of old clothes? Are you trying to pull a trick on me, Lindsay Hall?" She shook her finger at them. "I know how you young people are, always wanting to sell things on the eBay."

Ren was about to cut in so she could quell Mrs. Stokely's suspicions, but Lindsay put a hand on Ren's knee and said, "You know me, Mrs. Stokely. I would never try to trick you into doing anything."

"That may be true, but fancy dresser over here, she has my radar up so high I can hear Russians snoring in their sleep." Mrs. Stokely leaned forward. "Is this outfit supposed to charm me? Make me blind to your trickery?"

Okay, this wasn't going well at all. Ren wondered if it was too late to stop Deb from stopping by. "This is how I normally dress. Like I said yesterday, the old boots I stole…I mean, borrowed, from Deb are strictly for Salt Creek."

"That doesn't make a lick of sense, but I'm glad to hear you have some taste."

Mrs. Stokely got up from her chair. "If you're in town for long, you should probably take heed of the fact that people around here don't know how to keep to their own affairs. Always butting into people's business."

She hobbled toward the hall that Ren assumed led to the bedrooms. They followed her to a closed door at the end of the hall.

She put her hand on the door and paused. "You'll probably notice that she was special to me. We were as close as sisters, and this was her room." She opened the door. "You two go ahead. I'll wait out here."

Ren had assumed Mrs. Stokely would pull an old suitcase out from under a bed or grab a few things from the back of the closet that she'd held on to over the years. It was clear from the look of surprise on Lindsay's face that neither of them had expected to find an entire room dedicated to Millie.

The room didn't smell stale. There wasn't a thick layer of dust like one would expect to find in a room that had been closed up, never to be used again. This room looked pristine. There were even fresh vacuum marks in the avocado green carpet.

A double bed sat against the far wall, flanked by two windows. A loud floral print bedspread in shades of greens and blues covered the bed. There was a dent in one of the pillows, though the bed was still made.

They explored the room in silence, giving it the reverence it deserved. Framed photographs of Mrs. Stokely and Millie covered the walls. In every photo, they'd found a way to touch each other without *really* touching each other. A hand on a shoulder. Hips touching. Heads leaned in to one another.

In her prime, Mrs. Stokely had been just as beautiful as Millie. She wore pretty summer dresses and colorful shorts with fitted tops. Her jewelry was more subdued than Millie's. A small gold cross hung from her neck in most of the photos. Knowing what to look for, Ren took a closer look and yes, there they were. Thin gold bands that they wore on their middle fingers instead of their ring fingers. Ren quietly pointed it out.

Lindsay's eyes widened in surprise. "She still wears it."

Ren's heart broke for both of them. She went to the door. "Mrs. Stokely? Will you come in and sit with us? Since it's Millie's birthday, I think it would be nice to hear a story or two about her, and if she's out there, maybe she'll know that she hasn't been forgotten."

"She's out there, silly girl." Mrs. Stokely sat on the end of the bed, and sure enough, the narrow gold band was still on her finger.

Ren sat on one side of her and Lindsay on the other. Ren didn't dare take Mrs. Stokely's hand, though she wanted to. The trust hadn't been built yet, but Ren hoped she could change that with what she was about to say. "This room is a lovely tribute to a beautiful woman and a life well lived. She was lucky to have you."

"Oh, I was the lucky one." Mrs. Stokely patted Ren's knee. "But I thank you for saying so."

Ren took a chance and covered Mrs. Stokely's hand with her own. "Mrs. Stokely, did you know that I'm a lesbian? I'm only announcing it because I want you to know that you can trust me. You can also trust Lindsay because last night, we kissed for the first time. Well, we did more than kiss, but I don't want to get too graphic."

Mrs. Stokely turned her stiff neck and raised her eyebrows at Lindsay. "Is that so?"

Lindsay leaned in and said, "Brooke saw the kiss, and you know what that means."

Mrs. Stokely glanced at her watch. "You say it happened last night? Well, it's too late, dear. Even the mayor has been informed of your misdeed, but that's not the worst of your troubles."

"No?"

"Heavens no. It's Patty. She's had her eye on you for years. Better not tell her, or you'll be in a heap o' trouble."

Lindsay gasped. "You knew that?"

"Oh, please," Mrs. Stokely said with a huff. "That girl may know fine art, but she most certainly doesn't know the fine art of subtlety."

"I bet you and Millie were experts," Ren said.

It was a risky thing to say, and it caused Mrs. Stokely to go still. Then, with a slow turn of her head, she eyed Ren. The three of them sat in silence at the end of the bed. Ren wondered if she should break the silence with a joke, but she couldn't think of a single thing to say. Luckily, Lindsay saved the day by putting her arm around

Mrs. Stokely's shoulders. "You're right about Patty. She wears her heart on her sleeve."

"Millie and I didn't have that luxury. Back then, the people of this town weren't so accepting." She stood and went to the side of the bed and lingered there for a moment. She opened a drawer in the nightstand and pulled out an old photograph. "We said our vows to each other right here in this room, just the two of us." She wiped a tear with the back of her finger. "I remember thinking, why does this magnificent woman want to be bound to little ol' me when she could have anyone? I didn't question it for too long, though. I jumped in with both feet, and boy, did we have a life together." She handed the photo over to them. Lindsay took it, and she and Ren admired it together.

Mrs. Stokely and Millie had somehow managed to take a selfie on their wedding day. They both wore white veils and simple white dresses. The photo had indeed been taken in this very room where time stood still, even down to a perfume bottle that hadn't moved from the dresser.

Lindsay sat by Mrs. Stokely and wrapped her arms around her. "What a beautiful wedding day. You both looked stunning." She grabbed a tissue from the box on the nightstand. It was the last one. Mrs. Stokely had surely cried many tears on that bed over the years.

She tucked the photo back in the drawer and closed it. "We took the film to the city to be developed. Couldn't risk doing it here where everyone knew us as cousins. I wanted to have one where we were kissing, but Millie said even the city folk might cause us some trouble."

"Where is Millie buried? I'd love to visit her with you someday," Lindsay said.

"After she passed, her family came and took her away. I imagine she's buried up in Maine somewhere." She patted her chest with her hand. "But she's always right here with me."

The doorbell rang. "I'll get it," Ren said.

Ren barely held it together as she went to the door. She wanted to cry for Millie and Mrs. Stokely. She wanted to cry with her and let her know that it was safe to declare her love for her wife now. No one would hurt her. No one would try to besmirch Millie's memory or the life they had together.

Ren opened the door and took the box from Deb, then kissed her cheek and whispered, "Have I told you lately that I'm so lucky to have you in my life?"

Deb kissed her back. "Don't ever forget it, Soda Pop. Gotta run. Number Two is in the car screaming his head off about how his shirt isn't purple enough."

"Buy twelve purple shirts, then when one fades…"

Deb hurried back up the sidewalk. "If I did that, he'd say he wants blue shirts. Trust me, there's no winning here."

"You're a winner in my book," Ren shouted. She took a peek inside the box and whispered, "Perfect."

❖

Lindsay chided herself for not having this conversation much sooner with Mrs. Stokely. After a life of total secrecy, she shouldn't have had to bear the weight of her loss all alone. But they were here now, and she promised herself she'd do all she could to make sure Mrs. Stokely felt safe both celebrating and mourning the life she had with Millie.

Ren came back in the room carrying a cake box. "Don't look, Mrs. Stokely. It's a surprise."

"What are you up to, dear?"

Mrs. Stokely tried to look, but Lindsay blocked her way. "My goodness, don't you ever listen?" she said, repeating Mrs. Stokely's famous line from her teaching days.

Mrs. Stokely seemed unimpressed. "Nice try. But you didn't get the tone right. I'm a mite surprised, frankly, given how often you heard it."

Ren sported a huge grin when she turned around, birthday cake in hand. "Oh, wow," Lindsay exclaimed. It was a round cake, frosted white with pink roses with Millie's name written in yellow. She stood and pulled Mrs. Stokely up with her.

"Okay," Ren said. "I'm not singing alone." She started singing the birthday song, and Lindsay joined in.

Mrs. Stokely threw her hands over her mouth. Her eyes teared up as she blew a kiss to the ceiling. "Happy birthday, dear Millie..." She couldn't finish the song, but Ren and Lindsay finished it for her.

They stayed in that room for over an hour, eating birthday cake and listening to stories about Millie and Mrs. Stokely's life together. Apparently, Millie had been named principal at another school in the district. When Mrs. Stokely met the older, stately woman, as she described her, it was love at first sight.

They danced around each other for a few months. Every once in a while, Mrs. Stokely would have a moment of boldness and flirt. Not very effectively, she said. Until one day, Millie showed up in her classroom after the kids had all gone to the lunchroom. Mrs. Stokely was wiping down the chalkboard when she felt a presence behind her. She turned and saw that Millie had crammed her tall frame into one of those little desks. She must've done it as the kids were shuffling out because Mrs. Stokely hadn't heard a thing. She said Millie greeted her formally, saying, "Good afternoon, Miss Stokely. I thought maybe we could stop being so afraid and say what's on our minds."

Well, Mrs. Stokely said she was shaking in her red patent leather pumps because how could she possibly say what was on her mind when the only things on her mind lately were scandalous thoughts? Luckily, Millie said, "How about if I start?"

Mrs. Stokely said she gave a fervent nod. And then, Millie said the words that she would never forget as long as she lived. She said, "Miss Stokely, if you're waiting for an invitation, I've given you several. But if you need one more..."

Millie never finished that sentence. She eased back out of that little desk and sauntered out the door. Mrs. Stokely said she gathered up her things and dropped half of them trying to chase Millie down the hall. Papers flew everywhere. Her shoe came off. She snagged her pantyhose. But she managed to catch up to Millie in the parking lot, and even though she was breathless, she managed to say, "I don't need another invitation."

She said Millie proceeded to put on her very stylish, oversized sunglasses and say, "Good. I didn't want to have to hit you over the head with it, but I would have. For you, Miss Stokely, I would have."

Ren seemed as engrossed in Mrs. Stokely's storytelling as Lindsay was. It reminded her of a time in class when, instead of listening to Mrs. Stokely talk about a certain book they were reading, she sketched it. Her drawings were rudimentary at that point, but she was pretty sure that was the first time Mrs. Stokely had noticed her talent and commented on it.

As they tidied up the bedroom and stacked forks and plates, Lindsay noticed that the tired, bereft woman they'd met at the door was gone. It was as if a light had been turned back on inside Mrs. Stokely. Her eyes shone brighter, her skin had more color, and she seemed to have a new spring in her step. Could it be that the simple act most people took for granted—that of freely expressing love for another person—could change someone's demeanor this much? Of course it could, Lindsay thought.

Mrs. Stokely went to close the bedroom door but stopped. "I think I'll leave this door open from now on." She grinned and then waved to hurry them along. "I'll pack up some of that cake for Brooke. What do you say, Lindsay?"

"She'd love it, Mrs. Stokely."

"Oh, that's too stuffy, don't you think? Now that you two little detectives have made my business your business, I think it's appropriate for you to call me Joyce." She patted Lindsay on the back and smiled as widely as Lindsay had ever seen. "And don't make a fuss about it, or I'll change my mind."

They waited by the door while Mrs. Stokely busied herself in the kitchen. Ren leaned in and stole a kiss. "I couldn't help myself," she whispered.

Lindsay felt so proud of what they'd done, and it was all because of Ren. "You're amazing with her, you know that?"

Ren shrugged. "I think you're still her favorite, but I've moved up a few rungs on the ladder that leads to Mrs. Stokely's heart."

Lindsay whispered, "I really enjoyed last night. I don't know if I told you that."

"I think you got that message across in a pretty big way." Ren made an explosion with her hands.

Lindsay grabbed her. "Don't embarrass me in front of Mrs. Stokely."

"I told you to call me Joyce. And you should know my hearing is quite excellent, girls." Mrs. Stokely walked up and handed her the box the cake had arrived in. "Here you go. I kept a piece for myself. But I'm sure Brooke would enjoy some of that." She turned her attention to Ren. "My dear, you simply made my day. Millie would've loved your spirit."

"Well, I certainly love her style, and I loved hearing about her even more. I'm so glad we were able to celebrate her birthday with you." Ren risked leaning in for a side hug.

Mrs. Stokely reciprocated wholeheartedly by putting her arm around Ren's waist and giving her a good squeeze. "I hope to see you both sooner rather than later."

"You will, Mrs., I mean, Joyce. Take care," Lindsay said with a wave.

When they were far enough away from the house, Lindsay said, "I can't call her Joyce. It would be like calling God's wife Joyce instead of Mrs. God or whatever."

Ren put up a finger. "Could we get back to how much you enjoyed last night?"

Lindsay took her arm and leaned in. "I'd love to do it again, but I told Brooke I'd stay home with her tonight."

Ren sighed. "Yeah, I should be there for Deb tonight too."

"Don't want to piss off the best friends any more than we already have."

"Patty?"

"Yeah," Lindsay said. "She assumed that if I ever, you know, was with a woman, it would be with her."

"Ah. Yeah, that's a tough one. I had a crush on Deb for about fifteen minutes in college, and when I finally got over it, she still needed me to lust after her. Apparently, it fed her ego."

"We probably shouldn't have this conversation in front of Mrs. Stokely's house." Lindsay opened her car door and put the cake on the passenger seat.

"But it was just getting good."

"Don't worry," Lindsay said. "I'll stroke your ego another time." She got in and started the engine. As she started to back up, she leaned out the window and said, "Actually, if you're nice, I'll stroke more than your ego."

CHAPTER TEN

O h my God, you're like a lovesick puppy." Deb plopped on the sofa next to Ren. "Sending flirty texts to a certain artist?"

"It was a meme, thank you very much." Ren put her phone down. "How's Corey? You were so busy asking sex questions this morning, I forgot to ask."

"You weren't very forthcoming. How am I supposed to live out my lesbian sex fantasies vicariously through you?"

In the sexiest narrator voice she could muster, Ren said, "There they were at the Icey Shack, sharing a chocolate sundae, when the windows began to steam up around them."

Deb elbowed her in the side. "Nope, you've ruined it now. It's no longer sexy."

"But I ate a banana split off her bare stomach."

"Bullshit."

Deb stared at her until Ren shrugged. "Fine, it's bullshit. No banana splits were involved. Now, tell me where you took Corey."

"I just wanted to get her away from everyone so she'd talk to me. We kept getting interrupted by the kids and phone calls and texts from her boyfriend, so I took her phone away, and we shopped like the bad bitches we are. I know that might seem like a reward for her bad behavior, but everything we bought was for me."

"Oh, that's just cruel. Like, super mean." Ren folded her arms as if she was about to pout. "I don't know if we can be friends anymore," she said with a wink. "How did it go?"

"She's such a smart kid, Ren. I've always said that she's wise beyond her years, but she told me that when this hot guy started paying attention to her, it was like a hole opened up in the back of her head, and her brain drained out. The good news, however, is that this pregnancy scare woke her up. Or at least, I hope it did."

"Thank God. Is there anything I can do to help?"

"You can sit here with me for fifteen more minutes, and then you can get the hell outta my sight."

"What? Why?"

"Because there's a girl out there waiting for you." Deb tilted her head. "This is serious, isn't it?"

"Don't sound so surprised. After years of suffering, I've suddenly realized that smart, beautiful women are now my type."

"Well, it's about time!" Deb plopped back on the sofa and rested her stocking feet on Ren's thigh. "Wanna give me a nice foot massage? Number Two tries hard, but he loses interest so fast."

"Oh, I live for such pleasures." Ren took a foot and pushed on Deb's arches with her thumbs. "It would have to be a long-distance thing with me and Lindsay. I'm not sure how well that would work."

"Wait. You're really *that* serious about her? After one night?"

"Didn't you tell me that you knew you'd marry Colby after your first kiss?"

"I was young and stupid. He drove a muscle car. What did I know? You, however, are older and wiser and should know better than to fall in love on the first date."

"I've never fallen in love with anyone on the first date. Ever. I'm just thinking out loud about the what-ifs."

It wasn't Ren's style to fall so quickly for someone. In fact, Krazy Kerry had to do some persuading to even get Ren to say they were exclusive. She obviously should have listened to her initial instincts.

Lindsay was different. Special. Yes, her life was complicated, but whose wasn't? For the right person, they could work anything out.

Deb nudged Ren with her foot. "If you fall for someone who

lives in Salt Creek, you damn well better move here. Especially when that someone has a damn kid."

"A damn kid who's going off to college."

"You realize the girls are looking at Williams, right? It's, like, forty-five minutes from here. Pretty sure a two-hour drive to Logan and a quick jaunt to Paris aren't what Lindsay or Brooke have in mind for Brooke's freshman year. Oh, and never mind that she has a whole year of high school left."

"Oh." Ren knew it wasn't realistic to think Lindsay would end up being her girlfriend, but she hadn't really thought through the particulars of just how impractical a relationship would be. "Has anyone ever told you you're a buzzkill?"

"All the damn time, Soda Pop. I have a teenage daughter and an adolescent husband."

"I love it here," Ren said. "But what would I do for a living?"

"True. You're a terrible barista."

Ren gasped. "I ran that place like a finely tuned machine yesterday."

"A finely tuned chocolate milk factory, maybe."

Ren scrunched her nose. "Yeah, sorry. A bunch of guys from the football team descended on us, and Lindsay wisely suggested we push the chocolate milk because I'm so slow making the coffee."

"And you thanked her for that fine advice by going down on her?"

"Well, it was awfully good advice." Ren narrowed her eyes. "Are you fishing for details about last night?"

Deb shrugged. "Just wanna know what I'm missing out on by being straight and married."

"So much, Deb. You're missing out on so much."

Deb nudged Ren with her foot again. A little harder this time. "Don't tell me that. Just tell me if that's what you did."

Ren shook her head. "Nope. Not what we did. I'm saving that for next time, and Jesus, I can't wait. Like, seriously, I'm dying to—"

"Get in her pants again?" Deb threw her head back and laughed.

"*See* her again. But yes, that too."

"Aww, I'm happy for you, Soda Pop. I want you to settle down with someone who really loves you, and Lindsay's great. She'll also be a very lucky girl if she manages to snag you."

"Is that sappy talk?" Ren put her hand over her heart. "You mocha my heart sing, Deb Stewart."

"Okay, smartass." Deb waved her other foot in front of Ren's face. "Double time on this one."

❖

Ren zipped up the polyester jumpsuit and buckled the matching belt. She'd never considered orange to be one of her best colors, but damn, she looked snazzy. She slipped into Millie's orange flats and did a fist pump when they were a perfect fit. "Yes!"

She hung the white purse with the large yellow flower from her shoulder and picked up Millie's round sunglasses off the bathroom counter, then opened the door and sauntered down the hall. She rounded the corner into the living room to whoops and whistles from Lindsay. Mrs. Stokely leaped out of her chair and held out her hands. "You look fabulous, dear. Just fabulous." She had Ren turn in a circle. "And what a perfect fit. I don't even need to hem it for you."

The jumpsuit hugged Ren's ass like nobody's business, so she made a point of turning just right so Lindsay would have a good view. "What do you think, Linds? Could I walk the runways of Paris?"

"You can walk my runway anytime."

Ren took note of the seductive tone in Lindsay's voice. She'd address it later when they were alone. Possibly with her tongue.

"My Millie would approve," Mrs. Stokely said. "You've made my day by trying it on."

When Mrs. Stokely made the request that Ren try on her favorite outfit of Millie's, she wasn't so sure it was a good idea. Would it bring back too many memories? Would Mrs. Stokely burst into tears? So far, all she could do was clap and grin from ear to ear.

Mrs. Stokely motioned with her finger. "That zipper came in handy a time or two." She cupped her mouth with her hand and whispered, "Easy access."

Lindsay gasped. "Why, Mrs. Stokely!"

Ren and Mrs. Stokely responded in unison. "Joyce!"

"Oh, don't be such a prude. We were no different from you two. Couldn't keep our hands off each other. Millie especially liked it when I wore full skirts so she could...well, I'll let you use your imagination."

Oh, thank God. Ren loved seeing Mrs. Stokely's newfound freedom, but there were limits to what she wanted to hear.

"Do you still have those skirts?" Lindsay asked. "Could I try one on?"

Mrs. Stokely chuckled. "I think you have a little bit of devil in you, girl." She turned to walk down the hall to the bedrooms. "Follow me."

As she went by, Lindsay said to Ren, "I just meant I'd love to see them."

"Yeah, sure, girl," Ren teased. "Can't wait to see you in that skirt."

❖

Lindsay waited patiently while Mrs. Stokely perused every skirt she owned. Her bedroom had a different feel than Millie's. Frillier, with lace doilies and ruffled curtains. It smelled like her too. Kind of a powdery rose scent that she'd worn forever. Her classroom even smelled like it back in the day.

The skirt Mrs. Stokely held up was shorter than Lindsay imagined. Red and white horizontal stripes. Fitted halfway down then flared a bit with pleats. Cute but conservative.

"Millie was always the stylish one," Mrs. Stokely said. "I preferred a more classic look." She held up another hanger. "I always paired it with this red top and wrapped this little silk scarf around my neck." She grinned. "Please try it on, Lindsay. I'm sure it's just your size."

Lindsay took it into the bathroom and closed the door. The red top was short sleeved but high necked with a half zipper down the back. She got it zipped up and tucked it into the skirt. The waistband was a bit loose, but still, it looked great. She felt like she'd fit right in with the country club crowd. She just needed a cute pair of sandals.

"I have shoes for you too," Mrs. Stokely shouted through the door.

"Perfect." Lindsay tied the small, bandana-like scarf around her neck and opened the door. "What do you think?"

"Oh." Mrs. Stokely covered her heart with her hands. "You look almost as good as I did in it. You just need a cute little flip hairdo." She grabbed Lindsay's hand. "Put on my red sandals, and let's show Ren."

Lindsay tried to imitate Ren's model walk by swinging her hips as she walked into the living room. "How do I look?" She turned halfway around and looked over her shoulder. "Golf, anyone? Tennis? Maybe a quick round of croquet?"

Ren lowered her sunglasses. "Oh, Mama's got a new outfit. Do that turny thing again. Yeah, I love that skirt."

Mrs. Stokely beamed with delight. "I almost can't believe this is happening. We had such good times in those outfits, and here you girls are, wearing them again. Oh, isn't it just grand?"

Ren took her eyes off Lindsay long enough to witness the joy emanating from Mrs. Stokely. She swayed in place with her hands clasped as if she was soaking in the moment so she could hang on to it forever. She stopped mid-sway and said, "Hey, I have an idea. Let's go uptown and show you girls off. That's what we always did when we got a new outfit. We'd go up to Main Street and show it off. We'd walk from end to end, just to make sure everyone got a good look."

"You and Millie?" Ren asked.

"No, this was when we were kids, and we got a new Easter dress or a Christmas coat or a new pair of shoes. What do you say?"

Lindsay glanced at her bare legs and sandals. "Well, it's October."

"That's okay," Mrs. Stokely said. "We'll just go to that You Make-a-Me Crazy Place and get a drink and share a slice of that lemon cake."

Ren just happened to take a sip of coffee at the same time Mrs. Stokely put on her best Italian accent to pronounce the name of Deb's shop. Coffee spurted out of her mouth, but she managed to grab a napkin that got most of it. She didn't dare catch Lindsay's eye for fear they'd burst out into gut-busting laughter.

"In the 1979 Buick LeSabre?" Lindsay covered her mouth with her hand in an obvious attempt to control herself, then she gave Mrs. Stokely a thumbs-up. "I'm in."

"Nobody drives my car but me." Mrs. Stokely didn't waste any time. She grabbed her purse and headed for the garage.

Ren picked up Lindsay's jacket just in case there was a chill in the air. Their eyes met, and she said, "You make-a-me crazy when you wear that skirt."

"Shh," Lindsay said with a giggle. She took Ren's hand and led her to the garage. "I get shotgun."

❖

When they arrived at the coffee shop, Deb looked up from the table she'd been wiping and put her hands on her hips. "Well, what have we here? Hi, Mrs. Stokely."

"Hello, dear." Mrs. Stokely sat at the first table she could get to. Once she was settled, she pointed at Ren and Lindsay. "Just get a load of these two lookers."

"I am," Deb said. "Damn, girls. Where can I get a zip-up suit like that?"

"1977." Ren struck a pose. "You're so jealous right now. I can tell."

"Green," Deb said. "Like, Grinch green with jealousy. And Lindsay, where's your cocktail and tennis racket?"

"Don't forget my cigarette." Lindsay fake inhaled and blew the smoke back out.

"These were mine and Millie's clothes. We sure had some fun

in those outfits. The skirt hit a little lower on my leg than it does on Lindsay's, but you get the general idea."

"Those outfits are the bomb, Mrs. Stokely." Deb waved a hand at Ren. "Stop showing off your assets. I know you have a nice ass."

Ren pushed it out even farther. "And now, so will all of Salt Creek. By the way, these clothes may stand the test of time, but saying something is the bomb does not."

Deb cleared her throat. "Attention, everyone. The Cool Word Police is in da house, so please keep your *lits*, *as ifs*, and *yases* to yourself. Also, whatever you do, don't have a cow."

Mrs. Stokely stared at Deb with a confused look. "We're just having some fun. Me and the girls."

Deb winked at Ren. "Good for you. Now, you said one of these outfits belonged to Millie?"

"The zippy one. It was a little too flashy for me, but boy did I love it when Millie wore it." Mrs. Stokely got a look of panic. She cleared her throat and raised her voice. "We'll have a slice of that lemon cake if you've still got some. And three forks."

Deb leaned down and put her arm around Mrs. Stokely's shoulder. "You bet. And just so you know, you can be yourself here. This is my shop, and in my shop, everyone, no matter who they love, is welcome."

Mrs. Stokely smiled so big, her cheeks pinked up. "We sure are having a great time, aren't we? Sit down, girls. We'll be a little while."

Ren pulled a chair out for Lindsay and set her sunglasses on the table. She scooted another chair close and put her arm over the back of Lindsay's chair. "I feel so cool right now, I can hardly stand myself. I mean, look at the width on these bell bottoms." She crossed her leg and held up the fabric.

"I told you," Mrs. Stokely said. "Like ironing a tablecloth. But I never complained." She cranked her neck to look out the window. "Oh, damnation. Speaking of having a cow, Little Miss Vintage is going to have *two* when she finds out I've been keeping these clothes from her."

"Little Miss who?" Lindsay replied. Mrs. Stokely didn't have time to answer. Patty walked in the door and stopped dead in her tracks when she saw Lindsay and Ren.

Mrs. Stokely stood. "Tell me you sold a painting, dear." She winked at Lindsay a little too obviously and hobbled over to Patty. "How are you, dear? I was planning on stopping in sometime tomorrow. I've got a real pretty one for ya. It's small, but sometimes people like the small ones for a reading nook and whatnot."

Patty hadn't taken her eyes off Lindsay and Ren. "Is it Halloween?"

Mrs. Stokely huffed and sat in the closest chair. "I tried," she said under her breath.

"Hefner dates a tennis bunny?" Patty got a little closer. "Oh God, where did you find those outfits?"

"Hefner always wore a smoking jacket," Mrs. Stokely said. "Everyone knows that." She shook her head and tsk'd.

Deb brought out a slice of cake and three forks. She set it on Mrs. Stokely's table and sat next to her. Mrs. Stokely leaned in and whispered loud enough for Lindsay to hear, "This could get ugly. Do you have the cops on speed dial?"

Lindsay couldn't quite tell if Patty liked the outfits or hated them. "What's up, Cakes?" She patted the chair next to her. "Have a seat."

"Hey, Patty." Ren gave her a little wave.

Patty raised an eyebrow. "Seriously. It's not Halloween yet, so what's up?"

Lindsay gave her their special shut-the-hell-up look, but Patty just stared at her with a blank look. "Mrs. Stokely was kind enough to let us try on some of her and Millie's old clothes."

Patty gasped. "That's real vintage? Like, not from the Halloween store in Lake City?" She caressed Ren's shoulder. "Real Crimplene polyester. Oh my God, Mrs. Stokely. How have you been hiding this from me my whole life?"

"What'd I tell you, girls? The whole town will want to buy my heirlooms for pennies on the dollar. Well, that's not happening."

Patty shook her head. "No. I'll pay top dollar, Mrs. Stokely. Top. Dollar."

"Well, it'd be a step up for ya. That's for sure."

Deb waved. "Hey, Patty. Large iced coffee and a cherry bomb muffin with vanilla frosting?"

Patty hesitated. "I don't know what you're talking about. I'll have a small skinny mocha, no whip." She sat at Mrs. Stokely's table. "So, Mrs. Stokely, I'm thinking about ripping out that old false wall my grandpa put up in the store years ago. I've got a sculptor who wants me to sell some of his stuff, but I need more room."

"What are you telling me for? My paintings aren't that big, and I have a contract with you, young lady."

"No, it's not that," Patty said. "I'm just wondering if you remember what's behind there. I can't find anything in the old photo albums. I think that wall's been there since at least the 60s."

Mrs. Stokely gave her a nod. "At least."

Lindsay furrowed her brow. "Wait. The wall at the back of the gallery is fake?"

"Plywood," Patty said.

"It used to have shelves on it when it was the camera store," Deb shouted.

"That's right," Mrs. Stokely said. "We took our film there once or twice."

Patty rubbed her hands together. "I'm hoping to find a back office where my grandpa secretly ran a gambling ring or something just as nefarious. And money. I'm hoping for stacks of money. Maybe some moonshine and naked lady magazines."

Mrs. Stokely burst out laughing. "Oh, you'd make good use of those, I'm sure."

Patty's eyes almost popped out of her head. "Did you just make a lesbian joke, Mrs. Stokely?" She offered her fist. "Give me some sugar."

Mrs. Stokely huffed and reluctantly gave Patty a weak fist bump. "You act like I don't have a sense of humor." She tried to suppress a grin, but she couldn't hold back. "Oh, it feels good to laugh again."

"It's dressing rooms." Lindsay had no idea how she could

possibly know, but she was sure it was dressing rooms behind that wall.

Mrs. Stokely's smile faded. "Oh, dear. She's right."

"Dressing rooms?" Patty sank back in her chair. "Well, that's about as boring as it gets."

CHAPTER ELEVEN

Lindsay grabbed her clothes out of Mrs. Stokely's room and followed Ren down the hall to Millie's room. Ren seemed surprised as she closed the door behind them. She put her clothes on the bed and untied the scarf from her neck. "If I can't have you today, I at least want to see you."

Ren took a step closer. "Oh yeah?" She unzipped the jumpsuit so a little bit of cleavage showed. "How much do you want to see?"

Lindsay turned away and asked over her shoulder, "Do you know why shirts like this had a zipper back in the day?"

Ren unzipped the shirt and kissed Lindsay's neck. "I imagine it was so they could get them over those huge bouffant hairdos."

Lindsay lifted her arms. "It's hard to imagine putting that much work into a hairdo and then not washing it for days on end."

"It's even harder to imagine why they did it in the first place. Were men really that attracted to Marge Simpson hair?" Ren pulled the shirt over Lindsay's head and kissed her shoulder. She gripped her arms and sank her teeth in.

"Was that a growl?" Lindsay felt goose bumps all over her body from Ren's warm breath.

"I want you," Ren whispered.

Lindsay turned around and took a step back. "Undress for me. I want to know if your panties are as wet as mine." It wasn't like her to verbalize her desires so freely, but that was how Ren made her feel—free.

Ren slowly unzipped down to her panty line. "I guarantee

they're just as wet." She took her arms out of the sleeves and let the jumpsuit slip off her hips.

"Your nipples are so hard." Lindsay had no idea she could say things like that out loud, either.

"I really don't need to take off my bra. In fact, Mrs. Stokely is probably wondering what's taking so long."

All Lindsay could do was stare at the nipples barely visible through the thin material. She wanted to taste them. Suck on them. Roll her tongue around them. Squeeze them. "You're right. Maybe you should just..." The words came out softer and sultrier than expected. As if it had a life of its own, her hand lifted the short skirt and slid into her panties. She whimpered when her finger hit her clit. God, she was so turned on. And Ren was intently watching her every move. She slid her hand back out. Her fingers were glistening with her wetness. She held up her hand and waited for Ren's reaction.

"You're fucking amazing," Ren whispered. She pulled her bra down so her breasts were visible while she slid a hand into her panties. She took her time getting some wetness on her fingers. "I wish this was your hand," she whispered.

Lindsay lunged and grabbed Ren's hand through her panties. "Let me," she whispered. Ren took her hand out, and Lindsay slid hers in. Ren's pussy was so warm. So wet. So silky smooth, she wanted to stay there all day.

"Fuck." Ren pushed her panties all the way down and moved her hips in rhythm with Lindsay's fingers.

This was happening. Lindsay was going to have sex with a woman in Mrs. Stokely's house. "Spread your legs," she whispered. "I need to be inside you, if only for a minute."

Ren complied. Lindsay slid her hand lower. She wrapped her arm around Ren's waist to steady her and pushed in with one finger and then two. It felt exhilarating. Magical. Ren was hers at this moment. All hers.

Ren's hips bucked with every push, and it was clear she was trying hard to stifle her moans. "Fuck. Fuck."

Lindsay felt Ren tighten around her fingers. Should she keep going? Should she pull out and touch Ren's clit instead? She didn't have to wonder for long. Ren moved her hand from Lindsay's shoulder to her own clit and whispered, "Keep fucking me."

Lindsay kept up her pace and watched in awe as Ren threw her head back and bit her lip. God, she was so gorgeous. So soft and sexy.

Ren's expression tensed. Her breathing almost stopped, and then she came undone in Lindsay's arms. Lindsay held her while she came back down. She kissed her temple and kept her from falling to her knees. "That was the sexiest thing I've ever done or seen."

Ren grabbed her face. "Thank you. I really needed that." She pulled Lindsay into a hug. "You have no idea how badly I needed that."

"Do you think Mrs. Stokely heard anything?"

"God, I hope not." They giggled in each other's arms for a moment. Lindsay pulled back and looked her in the eye. "That thing you did when you pulled down your bra—sexiest fucking thing ever."

Ren ran her hands up Lindsay's thighs and under her skirt. She rubbed her clit through her panties. "I want to run my tongue all over you. Inside you."

"Brooke stays with her dad on Friday nights," Lindsay said.

"Does that mean we could have a sleepover?"

"You're so adorable," Lindsay said.

"Hey, I thought I was sexy as fuck."

Lindsay gave her a big nod. "That too. And beautiful and kind and—"

Ren laid a kiss on her that left her speechless. And breathless.

❖

"I don't kiss and tell." Lindsay took a sip of the hot coffee Patty had just brought to her studio.

Patty smirked. "Oh yeah? Since when, Linds? And you're welcome for the coffee. Deb says hi."

"Thank you for the coffee, Cakes. Heh, I just said coffee cakes. Where's the cake for my coffee, Cakes? Okay, I'll stop." Patty eyed the small cot she kept in the corner. "Hey, don't get too comfortable. I'm working here," Lindsay said.

Patty ignored the warning and spread out on the cot. "Trust me, there is absolutely nothing comfortable about this old camping cot."

"I needed something for Brooke to nap on while I was working. It's not supposed to be for an adult. At least, I don't think it is."

Patty's eyes popped open. "Hey, when Ren stood up in You Mocha Me Wet and showed off her ass, I think my mouth literally started to water. I mean, that jumpsuit thing was just so form-fitting."

Lindsay laughed. "You Mocha Me Wet. How apropos."

Patty shot up and put her feet on the floor. "Spill, or I walk out, and my shadow will never darken your doorstep again."

"So dramatic, Cakes."

"Have you told her about Roo yet?"

"No."

Patty shook her head. "Linds."

"I know, okay? I know." Lindsay set her coffee down and picked up a sketching pencil. "Can we change the subject now?" It never took long for Patty to come up with something else to talk about. Lindsay gave it about three seconds, tops.

"Is Mrs. Stokely finally out of the closet for real?"

Lindsay stopped sketching. "She's so happy, Cakes. You should've seen her smiling and laughing because she can finally talk about Millie. They were so in love. So devoted to each other."

Patty covered her heart with her hand. "Stop. You're going to make me cry."

"You should go visit her soon. I'm sure she'd love to show you Millie's room."

Patty sighed. "I had such a crush on Millie when I was little. She was this tall, sexy drink o' water who always looked like she should be dating Warren Beatty, and instead, she was Mrs. Stokely's lover. It's moments like these when my belief in a benevolent God soars through the roof." Patty tried to make the sign of the cross but got it backward and gave up.

"Have coffee at Mrs. Stokely's with us tomorrow, Cakes. We're kind of making it a thing until Ren leaves for Paris."

"I don't want to intrude on your little love affair. Unless, you know, you want to make it a threesome."

"In your dreams, Cakes."

"Well, it would be if you'd give me a little more than just, it was fly me to the moon good. I want all the wet details. Does she have a landing strip? A heart? Nothing at all?" Patty clasped her hands together and whispered, "Please be a heart, please be a heart."

"You're incorrigible, you know that, right?"

Patty stood and put her hands on her hips. "I'm happy for you, boo. I really am. But you have to tell her. Promise me you will."

"Why? Why do I have to tell her? Why can't we just have a nice little fling and then let her walk away into the sunset?"

"God, I love it when I get to teach you something. Paris is in the east. And number two, why should you let her go when you don't have to? In fact, if you fuck this up, I'm going to be so mad at you because it's damn hard to find someone like Ren, and you went and claimed her before I could."

"I don't think it works that way."

"You don't know. We might have hit it off."

"I didn't claim her, Cakes. I didn't mean for any of this to happen. It just did."

Patty waved the comment off. "I'm kidding. She's not my type at all. Too pretty. Too smart. My type day drinks and wears other people's family reunion T-shirts. Who the hell are the Everetts?"

Lindsay tossed an empty beer bottle in the trash can. "Ha ha. That was from the other night. And I wasn't going to let a perfectly good painting T-shirt that someone left in the park go to waste."

"So that's where we are? You take Sir Barksalot for a walk and scrounge trash cans along the way? Personally, I prefer the 'country club wife who sleeps around with other women' look."

"I looked pretty cute in that outfit, didn't I?"

"The cutest." Patty sighed. "I think my work here is done. On to the next tragedy."

"Say you'll go visit Mrs. Stokely sometime."

"Maybe we'll go for a ride in the Buick and find a different view for her to paint. Something sans that black and white cow she loves so much."

"You're an angel, Cakes. I'd be lost without you."

Patty leaned down to kiss Lindsay's cheek, then pulled back and sniffed. "Did you wash that shirt before you put it on? It smells like the Everetts went hard on reunion day."

Lindsay gave her a shove. "Of course I did. Now, get outta here."

Patty snickered. "That wall in the gallery is coming down on Saturday. Be there at ten for the big reveal."

"I wouldn't miss it."

❖

Ren was so excited she could hardly stand it. Tonight, she'd be in Lindsay's bed where they could take it slow. Get to know each other's bodies better. Fall asleep and wake up together. She was on her way to the liquor store to buy a bottle of champagne when a truck pulled up and the driver unrolled their window. "Ms. Christopher."

Ren cringed at the sight of Lindsay's ex-husband. "Officer Hall."

"Can I take a minute of your time?"

"I was on my way into the liquor store."

"This won't take long." Ben pulled into a parking spot and got out of his truck. He dropped the tailgate and hopped on. "Have a seat. It's clean."

Ben's big red truck was obviously his pride and joy. Ren had never seen such a shiny clean truck before. She reluctantly walked over and sat next to him. "What's up?"

"I heard some things. Things involving you and my ex-wife."

"*Ex* being the operative word."

Ben chuckled. "You have no idea what you're getting into."

"And you're here to warn me off?"

"Just to let you in on a few facts."

His arrogant tone annoyed her. "I really don't think this is a good idea." She went to push off the tailgate, but Ben grabbed her arm.

"You're going to want to hear this."

She removed his hand. "You have thirty seconds." He was making her uncomfortable, but she was curious about what he had to say.

"Lindsay wholeheartedly believes that she has memories of a past life. Like, for real, lived another life, remembers it, remembers people from it."

Ren remembered Patty saying something about past lives, but Lindsay had never said a word about it.

"Flash forward to when you roll into town and bam! Lindsay can now live out her past life fantasy for real."

"I'm not sure I fully understand what you're saying here."

"Brooke told me that Lindsay believes you to be the reborn version of a woman named Roo. A woman…I don't like to use the word *obsessed*, but Lindsay's been preoccupied with this woman for a long time."

"I think we're done here." She wasn't clear on what any of this meant, but she didn't want to hear any more about Lindsay from him. He didn't try to stop her when she hopped off this time.

He did the same and closed the tailgate. "It was a shadow over our life. I just thought you should know," he said with fake concern in his voice.

"I don't know. You both seem to be doing just fine. Besides, I'm perfectly capable of making my own decisions. Thanks." Ren walked to her car and opened the door. She turned back toward Ben. "In my experience, when someone says 'I just thought you should know,' what they really mean is they thought they could piss you off. Nice try, but I'm still on my way to see Lindsay, and I'll be sure to relay your *concern* to her as well."

❖

The doormat said *Welcome You Are*. It had an outline of Yoda on it. Ren stared at it, annoyed at its wackiness. The whole thing felt weird. She considered turning around and marching right back down the walkway. To her car. To Deb's to get her things. Then to the airport. What would her life be like if she did that? How much would she think about Lindsay?

It wasn't like her to show up empty-handed, but it also wasn't like her to show up to the house of her supposed past life lover, which that same past life lover *failed to mention*. Champagne seemed a bit too celebratory for the occasion. As she rang the doorbell, she wondered if there was a flower that said, "Thanks a lot. It was great being played." She stuffed her hands in her coat pockets. The temperature had taken a sudden dive. She was pretty sure it wouldn't feel much different inside.

Sir Barksalot was living up to his name on the other side of the door. Lindsay opened it and said, "Hey!" She gave Ren a light kiss on the lips. "I've got something on the stove. Make yourself at home."

Fuck. She was so cute. So comfortable. Ren watched as she jogged back into the kitchen, looking adorable in her frayed, paint-covered overalls.

Ren closed the door behind her and bent down to give Sir Barksalot some attention so he'd stop barking. He gave her hand a good sniff and licked it, then trotted away. "Oh, so you're the love 'em and leave 'em type. I see how it is. I understand the inclination, Barks."

Lindsay came back into the foyer. "I lost track of time in the studio and didn't get a chance to change. Give me a few minutes, okay?"

"Oh my God. You realize you're one hundred percent Tom Cruise showing up for a date after a beach volleyball game, right?"

Lindsay scoffed. "I am not. First of all, this is my house, something Maverick couldn't say. And secondly, I'm pretty sure you'll prefer me, you know, clean."

Ren looked up from scratching behind Sir Barksalot's left ear. "Yeah? Why's that?"

"You're a smartass. Just give me ten, 'kay?"

"Take your time. Sir Barksalot and I have lots to catch up on. Last time I was here, he went on and on about that squirrel that taunts him on the back fence. He hit me up for some peanuts he could use to lure him down. I told him I couldn't be a part of that. Squirrels have a right to free speech. If squirrels aren't free, is anyone really free?"

Lindsay chuckled and shook her head. "I'll be right down. Don't unionize the squirrels while I'm gone."

Ren hated herself for acting so normal. She didn't even know why. Because she was holding back? Acting fake? Pretending nothing was wrong? What else was she supposed to do? She needed to figure out what she was feeling. And why it pissed her off. So what if Lindsay thought they had a past together? Ren couldn't deny their connection even if she didn't subscribe to the same fruit loopy idea.

Ren had been in this house before but hadn't really taken the time to look around. Much like Deb's house, it was a typical floor plan with the living room to the left of the front door and the dining room to the right. Stairs led up to the bedrooms, and the hallway led to a large open kitchen and family room. That much she did remember. Because that, Ren thought, is exactly the kind of thing a person should remember. The floorplan of a 1980's two-story? Yes. Hazy details of a past life? Not so much.

She went into the living room and took her coat off. The bookshelves that flanked the fireplace were orderly and held an assortment of books. The bottom shelf held at least a hundred children's books, and next to it was a well-worn rocking chair with a blanket folded over the back. She imagined Lindsay reading to Brooke in that chair. The thought made her smile.

She took a closer look at a few of the framed photos on the shelves. In all of them, Brooke was front and center. Lindsay looked so young. More like a babysitter than a mother. A child raising a child.

Ren took her time going down the hall. Lindsay's artwork lined the walls. Small sketches were interspersed with larger paintings.

The talent on those walls was so pure. So innate. Nothing felt forced or reworked. No matter what else happened, Ren was happy she'd purchased one of Lindsay's paintings. She'd cherish it. She promised herself she'd cherish her memories of Lindsay too, even though she knew where things would end up. Even without the hocus-pocus, it was never going to work. She was going to Paris. Free time wasn't a perk her new job offered. And besides, Lindsay had a life and a daughter in Salt Creek.

"I hope you like corn chowder."

Ren jumped at the sudden sound of Lindsay's voice. When she turned, she hoped her mouth wasn't hanging open. Lindsay had changed into leggings, a chunky sweater, and thick socks. The perfect outfit for a chilly October night. Her hair was piled on top of her head, and her face looked freshly washed. God, she was so beautiful. This look had her feeling all sorts of things. Not the least of which was a desire to snuggle up on the couch and watch a movie for the rest of their lives.

"Do you?" Lindsay asked.

"Do I what?"

"Like corn chowder?" Lindsay walked into the kitchen.

"Homemade? You didn't have to go to all this trouble," Ren said.

Lindsay stirred the soup and put the lid back on the pot. She walked over and gave Ren a light kiss on the lips. "It's from a mix, but if it counts for anything, I diced the potatoes."

"Oh, good. Because being an amazing artist and also a chef? That's, like, too good to be true."

"Ha. Brooke would laugh her butt off if she heard anyone call me a chef." She gestured with her thumb toward the oven. "Also, there's cornbread. Or I have oyster crackers if you'd prefer."

Ren sniffed the air. "Cornbread sounds great and smells great."

"Is everything okay? You seem a little out of sorts."

Lindsay had such kind eyes. Full of concern. Ren wasn't sure when she should bring up the conversation she'd had with Ben. Before dinner? After? Never? Could she carry on as if nothing had been said? Being with Lindsay in her home felt warm and comfortable. Familiar, even. It wasn't a struggle to picture a life with her. She could see it all so clearly, and although it might've been weird to think of it that way, it felt like a huge relief. It finally felt as if someone fit.

"I'm fine," Ren said.

Brooke bounded down the stairs and made a running start down the hallway, then slid on the hardwood floor until she bumped into the kitchen island. "Oh, hey, Ren."

She gave Ren an unexpected hug. "Hi. How was school?"

"Oh, you know. Everyone wants the inside scoop on the pregnancy that wasn't, but hey, I got an A on this stupid hard math test, which means my dad has to cough up twenty bucks tonight, which means I've finally got enough in the backpack-for-backpacking fund, so I won't have to trek around Europe looking all lame and shi...oot, I think I hear Dad out front. Gotta run."

Brooke stopped to give Lindsay a kiss on the cheek. "I'm taking Barksy."

"Don't forget his leash." Barksy jumped off the sofa and barked his way to the front door. "Barksy!" Lindsay shouted.

Ben came into the kitchen holding the pug. "His name is Bruno Mars. Not Sir whatever the hell you call him. And before you say it, I no longer live here, so I don't have to pay the potty mouth jar." He met Ren's gaze and gave her a nod. "We seem to be running into each other all over town."

Ren didn't feel the need to confirm his statement. Brooke's eyes darted between them. The silence was deafening until Brooke said, "Let's go, Dad."

Ren waited until she heard the front door shut before she said, "Bruno Mars?"

"Ben loves Bruno Mars. We never agreed on the name."

"Huh. I would've pegged him for a country music fan. Well, he's Sir Barksalot to me."

Seemingly unaffected by Ben's sarcastic comments, Lindsay went to the refrigerator. "How about something to drink? Some chardonnay? Diet Coke?" Lindsay took a carton of orange juice off the shelf and lightly shook it. "OJ? Chocolate milk?"

"I'd love a glass of chardonnay."

"Excellent choice. I'll have the same." Lindsay poured two glasses and held hers up. "Cheers."

In her head, Ren heard herself say, *Cheers, babe.* It would've been so easy to say the words out loud. So comfortable. So natural. But they had Paris hanging over their heads. Oh, and that minor thing Ben told her. She wondered how many people in town knew? Did all of Salt Creek think she was some reincarnated lost love? Yeah, it probably wasn't the right time for a term of endearment. Ren held up her glass. "Cheers."

She sat on a barstool and watched Lindsay get two bowls and two small plates out of the cupboard. She set a place in front of Ren and another to her right.

"We'll go casual tonight and eat right here if it's cool with you," Lindsay said.

"Sure." Ren took a large sip of wine while she tried to talk herself out of acting on her impulses. *Stay on the stool.*

Lindsay came up from behind and reached around her to set a spoon next to the bowl. Ren breathed in her scent. "You smell good."

Lindsay leaned down and nuzzled Ren's neck. "So do you."

She walked away before Ren could steal a kiss, then came back around with a butter knife and napkin. Ren wasn't about to let her get away untouched that time. She ran her hand under the sweater and caressed the small of Lindsay's back. "You're driving me crazy right now, you know that, right?" She slid her fingers under the waistband of the leggings and found bare skin. "No panties?"

"No panties and no bra."

Ren's mouth went dry. She had a sip of wine. And then another. Her eyes never left Lindsay's body. She bent over to take the cornbread out of the oven, and Ren's mind went right back to that night in the hotel room. She wanted to do that again, but what she wanted most was to taste Lindsay. She wanted to bury her face between Lindsay's legs and take her higher than she'd ever been before. She wanted to be inside her and licking her at the same time. She took another sip of wine, hoping she'd forget about Lindsay's stupid ex-husband and Paris and some dead woman who was named after a kangaroo. She stood. Fuck them all.

❖

Did it make Lindsay a bad mother that she couldn't have cared less if anyone walked into the kitchen and found her naked with Ren's head between her legs? If it did, so be it because this was a feeling Lindsay didn't want to end.

Ren's tongue felt magical. She knew exactly what she was doing, taking Lindsay to the edge and then backing off just enough to keep her from coming. It was as if they'd done this a thousand times before. Nothing felt foreign or awkward. Ren's request for Lindsay to sit on the island was met without hesitation. She felt free in Ren's presence. Free to drop all her walls and be both physically and emotionally naked. It felt insanely good, and Lindsay never wanted it to end.

Lindsay reached for her hand and intertwined their fingers. Ren gave her hand a squeeze and dipped her tongue inside her. Lindsay's body clenched as her orgasm built. Her hips bucked. The connection she felt with Ren was so strong, it felt as if her heart had doubled in size. She squeezed Ren's hand and closed her eyes as the orgasm ripped through her body.

Nothing else mattered. Not the past. Not the future. Just this moment, when she knew she'd always been in love with Ren Christopher.

❖

"Can I give you the first bite?" Lindsay held a spoonful of chowder close to Ren's mouth.

"Hmm." Ren gave her a nod and a thumbs up. "Delicious."

Lindsay leaned in for a kiss. "*You're* delicious. And my God, that tongue of yours. Holy smokes, you're good at that."

"Did you seriously just say holy smokes? Surely you mean Jeez Louise or Jiminy Christmas, right?"

"Too old fashioned for you? How about, oh my stars, that tongue of yours!"

"Oh yeah, that's better." Ren laughed.

Lindsay broke off a piece of cornbread and offered it. "Why aren't you eating?"

Ren ran her hands up Lindsay's thighs. "I'm just taking it all in. Everything I feel. Your beauty. All of the words that came out of that sexy mouth when you came. I definitely don't want to forget those."

Lindsay leaned forward on the barstool and until their lips almost touched. She pulled back and shook her head. "Sorry."

"What's wrong?" Ren held Lindsay's face. "Look at me. What just happened?"

"It's just that Patty's been telling me I really need to share something with you, but I haven't had the guts."

"Well, that sounds serious." Ren pulled her hands away. She assumed Lindsay was going to fill her in on their past life together. Ren wished it could wait until tomorrow or the next day. Or never. She wanted to enjoy the present for what it was. She wanted to sleep naked in Lindsay's bed. She wanted to wake up with her and make love again. Take a shower together. Cuddle on the sofa while they sipped coffee. It wasn't too much to ask, was it?

Lindsay stood and offered her hand. "Come with me."

The temperature had dropped even lower. Ren wrapped her arms around Lindsay from behind and waited while she unlocked the door to her studio. "I hope you have heat in there."

"I have a space heater. It warms up fast."

Ren nuzzled Lindsay's neck and breathed in her scent. "You smell so good." Her hand slid down Lindsay's stomach. The thin leggings meant Ren could feel her pussy perfectly. She ran her middle finger between her legs and back up again.

Lindsay jerked. "Do you want me to get this door open or not?" She turned and gave Ren a peck on the lips. "Welcome to my studio."

Ren stepped inside. The space was small, but there were two windows, so it didn't feel claustrophobic. Lindsay's supplies were well organized. Canvases were stacked upright in one corner, and there was a small cot set up with a blanket and pillow. Ren sat on the cot and tucked her chilled hands between her legs. "You have a great little setup here."

Lindsay cranked up the heater. "I'm sorry it's so cold. I should've just brought what I wanted to show you into the house."

"Nonsense. I've wanted to see where you paint. I'm kind of hoping the reason I'm out here is because you're ready to show me some of your work."

"You're in luck, then."

Ren rubbed her hands together. "Excellent. Let's do this."

Lindsay brought an easel forward. "This is the one I wanted to show you." She lifted the protective sheet and moved to the side.

"She's beautiful," Ren said. "I've seen a lot of portraits, and this is just, wow." She stood and took a closer look. "Linds, this is amazing."

"Thank you," Lindsay said. "That means a lot coming from someone who knows art."

Ren stepped back as far as she could to get a different perspective. "And trust me, I'm not just blowing smoke up your ass because I happen to love your ass. Who is she? A client?" Lindsay didn't answer, so Ren turned to her. "Linds?"

Lindsay pulled the sheet off another painting she'd been putting the final touches on. She stood back and said, "When I paint a portrait for a paying client, I have them sit for me. I study their gestures, their facial expressions. I take photos of them and blow up portions of their face so I get the details just right. I work hard to get a good likeness is what I'm saying."

"I can tell." Ren pushed her hair behind her ears and bent over so she could inspect the painting. "I'm guessing this guy is in his late forties. Has an abundance of confidence. Probably a great sense of humor too."

"He started his own tech company and sold it for fifty million. He's got a five-year-old daughter, so his arsenal of dad jokes is impressive."

Ren put her hand on Lindsay's waist. "You're so talented, Linds. I can see why you have a waiting list."

Lindsay stepped over to the painting of the woman. "Tell me about her."

Ren took another look. "She's vibrant. I can almost feel her enthusiasm. Her excitement for life. She looks like she's falling in love." She turned. "Am I right?" Lindsay seemed nervous. Afraid, almost. "Linds? Who is she?" And then Ren realized who the woman in the painting was.

"It's going to sound crazy, just like all of the time travel, parallel worlds, up is down, and down is up stuff that comes out of Hollywood," Lindsay said.

Ren put up her hands. "Wait. I need to tell you something. I should've told you right when I walked in the door."

"Told me what?"

"Ben told me some things."

Lindsay furrowed her brow. "Things? What things?"

"It doesn't matter. I don't care." She took a step and reached for Lindsay, but she backed away. Ren pointed at the painting. "Is that Roo?"

Lindsay stiffened. Her expression darkened. "He had no right."

"I know. He made it sound like he was telling me for my own good, but I think he had other motives."

"No shit. How long have you known?"

"He told me this afternoon. On my way here."

"Wow." Lindsay looked as if she'd just been slapped. "Just wow." She pushed past Ren and rushed out of the studio.

"Lindsay!" Ren went after her. "Lindsay, stop, and tell me if what he said is true."

Lindsay turned back. "Oh, I'm sorry. You're worried about the truth now?" She shook her head. "Why didn't you tell me you'd talked to Ben? Why did you just have sex with me, knowing full well that my ex-husband shared something that wasn't his to share?"

"I wanted…" Ren took a deep breath. "I wanted you."

"Oh. You wanted me. Seems perfectly reasonable. Sex first, transparency second."

Ren didn't know what to say.

"This is a big deal to me, Ren. It's had a huge effect on my life.

Yes, I believe I've lived before. In another time. With someone I loved."

"And why wouldn't you tell me? Instead, I've got Patty asking me random questions about past life crap."

"Crap? This is my life. Patty said those things because she wanted to gauge your reaction. I didn't ask her to do that, but that rarely stops Patty."

"So she wanted to know how I'd react to finding out you think I'm someone you knew before?"

Lindsay shook her head. "It's not just that I think you're someone I once knew. I *know* you are…were…Roo."

Ren didn't know what to say to make it okay for both of them. She couldn't pretend that it all made perfect sense to her. And it worried her that Lindsay seemed as caught up in the past as the present. Would she have to compete for Lindsay's attention? "I don't know what to say, Linds. I have a great time with you. I really like you—"

"A great time? That's what this has been about? Just sex? I think you should leave." Lindsay started toward the house.

"You didn't let me finish!" Ren shouted. "Shit."

Ren went back into the studio and shut the door. It was too cold to stand outside, and she didn't know how to fix this with Lindsay. She should've done the right thing and brought it up the minute Ben and Brooke left the house. But, no. She'd wanted Lindsay again. That was priority one. Could she be a bigger asshole? Not likely.

She heard the back door slam shut again, but she couldn't see anyone. And then, she spotted her jacket sitting on the doorstep. "Great. That's just great."

❖

It was too cold to be outside, but Ren didn't want the kids to see her tears. They had enough going on in their lives. She borrowed one of Deb's heavy winter coats and a grabbed a beanie out of the communal box of winter hats, then snuck out the back door.

She opened the gas valve and lit the fire pit. It would keep her feet warm while she tried to pull herself together. She'd fallen hard for Lindsay. Harder than she even realized until it seemed like it was over. Was it over? Ren didn't know for sure.

The screen door slammed. Ren thought it might be Deb walking toward her. She found herself hoping it was Lindsay. She stood and was about to call to her when Corey said, "Ren? I thought you had a date with Lindsay."

Corey came into view when she got close enough to the fire. "You shouldn't be out here, Corey. It's too cold."

"I brought a blanket for us." Corey pulled the two-seater Adirondack chair closer to the fire and patted the spot next to her. Ren sat, and Corey wrapped the blanket around them. She snuggled in close and rested her head on Ren's shoulder. "Brooke's really happy about you two. She said her mom lights up when you're around."

"Eh, maybe not so much tonight."

Corey looked at her intently. "Oh, crap. What did you do?"

She ran her hand over Corey's hair. "Do you ever wish you could turn back time about five minutes and get a do-over?"

"Um, you realize who you're talking to, right? I'm the girl who gets the 'made horrible choices when a cute boy winked at me' award."

"Sorry," Ren said. "I don't mean to steal your thunder."

Corey laughed. "Thanks. It's been fun wearing the stupidest girl on earth crown, but I'd gladly hand it over to you."

Ren kissed her forehead. "I think I probably deserve it tonight."

"Oh, come on. It can't be that bad. Besides, Lindsay is the sweetest. Just take her a bag of chocolate covered cinnamon bears. They're her favorite."

"I'll keep that in mind. Tell me about Brooke's dad. What is he like?"

"He's been a total jerk to Lindsay since the divorce. So has Brooke, but I think she's being a jerk to both of them. I hate when she does it in front of me, though. I love Lindsay. She's the coolest mom ever. Next to my mom, of course." Corey raised her head. "Also, she's really pretty. You guys make a super cute couple."

Ren smiled. "She is pretty. So pretty I might lose all of my brains."

Corey gave her a serious look. "Just don't take off your 'I'm going to Paris' crown. Not everybody gets a chance like that."

"No. My 'I'm going to Paris' crown is firmly attached to my head. It's just that I didn't expect to fall for someone in Salt Creek. That was definitely not in the plans."

"Ha. Like you had a choice." She wrapped her arms around Ren. "I'm so happy for you. We should have a party or something."

Ren held on to Corey's shoulders and looked her in the eye. "What do you mean I had no choice?"

"You know, because of the Roo is Ren, and Ren is Roo thing."

So literally everyone on earth knew about this *except* Ren. "Corey, does your mom know about this?"

Corey shook her head. "Brooke swore me to secrecy."

That was a relief. Ren wasn't sure how she'd feel if Deb had kept this information from her too.

"Okay," Corey said. "Now don't forget. Lindsay likes chocolate covered cinnamon bears. I know, it's weird, but we all have our little idiosyncrasies, right?"

"Right." Except Lindsay's idiosyncrasy had nothing to do with her taste in sweets and everything to do with the gigantic elephant in the room. Ren stood and put out her hand. "Let's go inside and warm up."

Chapter Twelve

Patty opened a cardboard box. She pulled out some dust masks and earplugs and handed them out. "Put these in your ears."

Mrs. Stokely leaned in and said, "I tried to convince her not to do this. Sometimes, things should be left as they are." She looked at Lindsay's shoes. "Good thing you're wearing closed toe shoes. There could be a rodent stampede when that wall comes down." She put the mask over her mouth and mumbled something unintelligible.

Lindsay cringed. A rodent stampede? Maybe Mrs. Stokely was just testing her mettle. Seeing if she'd bolt out of there before a single nail was pried loose. Well, that wasn't happening. Unless there really were rodents. In that case, she'd definitely bolt, and heaven help anyone who got in her way. She put her earplugs in and watched Patty and Mrs. Stokely do the same. She waited for Patty to reach in the box again, but she didn't. "Don't you have any safety glasses? My eyes get irritated easily," she yelled.

Patty shook her head and yelled back, "Did you just ask if we're having martinis?"

Lindsay threw her hands in the air, then grabbed her sunglasses out of her purse. She'd hoped for a hands-on experience. Breaking down a fake wall with a sledgehammer sounded like a good prescription for all of the hurt that had welled up inside her. She was angry at Ren for being so dismissive. Ben for tattling like a teenager. And Brooke for actually being a teenage tattler. She pulled her mask down and shouted, "Do you happen to have a sledgehammer in your box?" Patty's look of surprise let Lindsay know she was forming some sort of dirty interpretation of the question, so she waved her hand. "Never mind."

The three of them stood side by side and watched the handyman remove the screws in the plywood. Lindsay still had no idea how she knew what was behind that fake wall, but she'd be shocked if she turned out to be wrong.

The first piece of plywood came down, and dust flew everywhere. Patty and Mrs. Stokely turned away, but Lindsay stood firm in her dark sunglasses and dust mask. "Told you," she said. Of course, no one heard her.

She didn't wait for the next piece to fall. Once the dust settled a bit, she got closer. It was still pitch-black back there, but she took a step in anyway. She lifted her sunglasses and realized it wasn't so dark after all. *Duh.* And there were the words painted in distinct black writing with an arrow pointing to the right. *Ladies Dressing Room.*

Lindsay's chest tightened. Her pulse quickened. The room started spinning, and she couldn't seem to pull any air into her lungs. She ripped off the mask and backed out of the opening. Patty was saying something, but she couldn't hear anything. No air to breathe. No sound. Just dust and panic.

Lindsay stumbled out of the gallery in a desperate search for air. She bent over and took a few shallow breaths. Finally, some air. She was able to cough up some dust and spit it out.

Patty bent down next to her and handed her a bottle of water. "Are you okay, hon?"

Lindsay straightened up and took a sip. "I'm fine."

Mrs. Stokely handed her a tissue. "You were right, dear. Nothing but dressing rooms back there."

"I still don't understand how you could've known that," Patty said.

The images were so clear in Lindsay's mind. She could see Roo giggling as she led Katie into the dressing rooms. Pointing up at the sign and winking. Skirts being pushed up. Roo against the wall, panting for air. And then screams as Roo was ripped away.

It was more detail than she'd ever had before. It felt as if a few dots had been connected. Roo and Katie had lived in Salt Creek. What a relief it was to have something solid to cling to. But sharing the details of Roo with others hadn't exactly served her particularly well so far. And maybe now that she knew the truth, it was enough.

Maybe now, she could let Roo go once and for all.

❖

"This house is fabulous." Patty looked around in awe. "I can't believe Mrs. Stokely had such good taste back in the day."

Mrs. Stokely came out of the kitchen with a tray of coffee and cookies. "It was Millie's taste. She was the hippie, and I was the good girl who minded her mother and prayed for forgiveness every night." She stood there with the tray. "How many times do we have to do this before you realize that this tray is heavy, and I'm an old woman?"

"Oh, right." Lindsay grabbed the tray and set it on the coffee table. "Sorry, Mrs. Stokely."

"Call me Joyce." Mrs. Stokely sat and wiped her brow with a handkerchief. "Not you, Patty. I'm still Mrs. Stokely to you." She winked and then laughed. "I'd lost my sense of humor years ago, but I recently found some of it hiding under the bed." She laughed again and turned to a framed photo of Millie that Lindsay was pretty sure hadn't been on the fireplace mantel before. "I expected Ren too. Where is she?"

"Patty came with me today. She's been dying to see your beautiful home."

Lindsay hadn't wanted to make the visit at all. She missed Ren, and she wasn't in the mood to socialize in a place that held so many memories of their short time together. But Patty had insisted Lindsay go with her.

Patty scanned the room. "It's so retro. You even have embroidered owls."

"I stitched those back when my hands worked," Mrs. Stokely said.

Lindsay poured the coffee. "They still work. You're still painting, right?"

Mrs. Stokely spread her fingers. "Yes, but it pains me to do so." She grunted as she tried to straighten them completely. "How is the renovation coming along, dear?"

"It's going well, but I don't really understand who would've wasted so much space," Patty said. "I mean, why not do what I'm doing now and tear the dressing rooms out if they weren't needed anymore?"

"The store didn't change. They just closed off the dressing rooms to make a point."

Lindsay set her cup down. Mrs. Stokely *knew* what had happened? "What are you saying, exactly?"

"You have to understand the world at that time," Mrs. Stokely said. "It all seems very romantic now, and some of it was. The kids would dance until their feet hurt on Saturday night and then dress up in their finest for Sunday services. But there was also a lot of hate." Mrs. Stokely paused and seemed to wait for the memories to return. "I was maybe ten or eleven when it happened. Too young to really understand it at the time, but I knew whatever those girls had done in that dressing room was bad."

Patty bounced with excitement. "I knew there was a story behind that wall. Tell us, Mrs. Stokely."

"I can only tell you what I heard while standing next to my mama. She thought that by covering my ears, I couldn't hear the conversation she had with Mrs. Brown. And then the next day with Mrs. Eccles. And then…" She waved her hand. "Well, let's just say I'd heard several different versions of the salacious events."

"Salacious?" Patty rubbed her hands together in anticipation. "Now you're speaking my language."

"Well, in a sense, yes. I am speaking your language. And mine, if I'm truthful. Although, as it relates to the events in the dressing room, I didn't discover my own truth until much later." Her expression sobered. "Those poor girls were torn apart and humiliated in front of the entire town. It was a travesty all around."

Patty shook her head in confusion. "The girls were gay?"

"So it seems. And they were also naïve. Oblivious and blind. No one would ever accuse me of that, and no one would ever tear Millie from my arms. I made sure of that. We were always on guard. Always aware of who might be watching us. But those girls decided to go into a public dressing room and get intimate."

Patty looked at Lindsay, then at Mrs. Stokely again. "Did my grandfather do something to them?"

"Well, this is where the story gets a bit sketchy. I heard several versions, but the one I believe to be true is the worst one. I remember the look on Mrs. Brown's face as she recalled it. She looked stricken. Probably with guilt, since she claimed she was there at the time and did nothing about it." Mrs. Stokely looked them both in the eye and said, "He pushed his way into their dressing room, grabbed them both, and dragged them out, not stopping to let them get whatever clothes they'd taken off. The entire store watched as he tossed them out onto the street, yelling the entire time about what an abomination they were. In a town that small, it wasn't long before everyone knew their story."

Lindsay felt surprisingly calm. She didn't feel an urge to run from the details. She'd felt remnants of the pain of what had happened for most of her life. She knew the dread and shame. The loss. Lindsay had spent her adult life under the shadow of those feelings. Finally having some details was actually a relief. From the look on Patty's face, she felt something different.

"How dare he?" Patty said.

"Your grandfather? I'd imagine if it were a boy and a girl messing around in his dressing room, he'd have quietly put a stop to it. Maybe given the boy a pat on the back," Mrs. Stokely said.

"You mean he wouldn't have dragged them outside half-dressed with the guy's erection in full view? How surprising." Patty put her face in her hands.

"Patricia!"

"Sorry, Mrs. Stokely. I just can't believe my grandfather did this."

"I know this wasn't the news you were hoping for, dear."

"It's just so disappointing, you know? I barely knew my

grandfather, but I spent my life being told what a wonderful, kind man he was. He obviously wasn't the man I thought he was."

❖

Lindsay stood by the car and dug through her purse until she found a tissue. "I hate it when you cry, Cakes. Always have."

Patty took the tissue. "Were you even in the room with Mrs. Stokely? Of course I'm going to cry."

Lindsay got behind the wheel. "I only meant that it's hard because you get such a sad look on your face, but it's not like I can put you on my lap and kiss your boo-boo away like I have with Brooke."

Patty put her seat belt on. "Why not? Maybe my boo-boo would respond quite favorably to that."

Lindsay rolled her eyes. She'd walked right into that one.

"And I would like to reiterate that my boo-boo is not, in fact, a bushy boo-boo," Patty said. "I still haven't forgiven you for putting that image in Brooke's head." She put up a finger. "For the record, I do trim the hedge."

Lindsay gave her a side-eye. "Thank God."

They drove in silence until Lindsay parked in front of the gallery. Patty turned to her and said, "I'm going to find out who those girls were, and I'm going to make amends."

"Cakes, you realize this was like, seventy years ago, right? There's almost no chance they're still alive." Of course, Lindsay knew they weren't.

"I have a lot to think about." Patty opened the car door, then turned back. "Where's Ren? Mrs. Stokely asked, but you didn't answer."

"She's…I don't know. Ben told her about Roo. She asked me about it. It didn't go well."

"Well, shit. Are you going to talk to him about it?"

Lindsay shook her head. "No. I don't want to spend another minute on him. Brooke graduates next year. My time will be my own again. And Ben doesn't get a say in what I do with the rest of my life."

Patty smiled. "Good for you. But what about Ren?"

Lindsay took a deep breath. "How much longer can I let Roo control my life?"

Patty's eyes widened. "First Ben. Now Roo. Am I next?"

Lindsay nudged Patty's shoulder. "No, silly. You'll always be stuck with me. But Roo? I'm going to paint her once more, and that's it. You'll have it to sell soon, and I expect you to get top dollar for it. No lowball offers." Lindsay leaned over and kissed her cheek. "See you soon, Tater Tot."

Patty got out of the car and shut the door. "I miss your casserole," she shouted.

Lindsay flipped her the bird. "No, you don't!" She laughed as she drove away. Saying it out loud seemed to have lightened the load she'd carried with her for so long. Roo would finally rest in peace.

If only it were that easy. Just will it to be so, and poof, Roo would be a distant memory. Lindsay knew it didn't work that way, or at least, it hadn't in the past. But she had a newfound sense of hope that the memories, both bad and good, would fade so Lindsay could focus on her future. Enough of living in the past. She wanted a full life in the here and now. *Live before you die, Lindsay. Live before you die.*

CHAPTER THIRTEEN

L indsay locked up her studio and turned to leave. She stopped when she saw Ren standing a few feet away.

"The sign on your front door said to come back here if you didn't answer."

Lindsay stepped off the small porch. "Hi." Her tone was flat, but she'd been caught off guard by Ren's sudden presence. And why Ren was holding a carved pumpkin was baffling.

"Can we talk for a minute?"

"Maybe we should talk about the huge pumpkin in the room first."

"Oh. Right. This is for you. We carved pumpkins last night at Deb's house."

Lindsay tilted her head. "Is that Yoda?"

"A fan you are, hmm? Your doormat I saw."

Well, wasn't this the cutest thing Lindsay had ever seen? Ren, dressed in cropped jeans, black Chucks, and a gray hoodie, holding a Yoda pumpkin and using Yoda-speak. "Observant you are." Lindsay headed for the back door. "Brooke will love it." She opened the door and let Ren go in first. "You can put it on the counter."

Ren pulled out a stool and sat at the island. "I don't like the way we left things."

Lindsay opened the fridge. "Am I going to need alcohol for this conversation?"

"Linds, just listen to me for a minute. We both should've been more honest. I should've told you about the conversation with Ben, and you should've told me about Roo before we ever…" Ren stopped and took a breath. "I'm going to Paris. It would've been nice to know that you thought we had this big connection."

Lindsay turned around. "I'm not trying to keep you here."

"So you just wanted to have sex with your long-lost love from another life? I find that hard to believe."

"I didn't have any motives. It was just sex."

"Nice try, but it wasn't even *just sex* for me."

Lindsay lowered her gaze. She couldn't hear the word *sex* over and over while looking at Ren and not feel something she didn't want to feel again. She needed to stay strong in her convictions. She'd made the decision to let go of Roo, and that meant letting go of Ren too.

"What do you want, Lindsay? From me? What do you want?"

"I got what I wanted. I had a fling with a beautiful woman. I can check that off the bucket list now." Lies, lies, and more lies. A bucket list? Lindsay didn't have a bucket list, but hey, it sounded good.

Ren stood. "Is this fling over? Because the way your face is heating up right now tells me that maybe it isn't." She took a few steps and stopped. "What happens if I come over there, Linds? Because if that's all this is…just a fling…I don't leave for another five days."

❖

Ren usually liked to be in charge. Directing the show. That wasn't at all what was happening, and she was fine with it. She watched her shoe fly across Lindsay's bedroom and land somewhere behind her. Then the other. That one hit a potted plant and knocked it over. She was going to point it out, but the look on Lindsay's face told her she didn't give a fuck about some plant.

Ren's jeans came off next. Lindsay threw those behind her as well. She was still fully clothed, which was never how it went down with Ren. But Lindsay was special. And apparently, very horny.

Lindsay slowed her pace when she hooked her fingers into the sides of Ren's panties and pulled them down to her knees. She left them there while she ran her finger over Ren's pussy. "God, you're beautiful," she whispered.

Ren wanted to open her legs wider so Lindsay had better access, but the panties were snug around her knees. "Will you take off your shirt? And who are the Everetts, anyway?"

"A family I don't know. But I feel like they'd throw a good reunion. You know, the kind where they never run out of Flamin' Hot Cheetos." Lindsay pulled the T-shirt over her head and threw it behind her. Then her bra. She got up on her knees and put her hands on Ren's legs. "Better?"

"So much better."

Lindsay slid Ren's panties the rest of the way down. Ren didn't open her legs. She wanted Lindsay to do it. She wanted Lindsay to lie on her and grind into her. She wanted to wrap her legs around Lindsay's hips while their tongues collided. She wanted Lindsay inside her.

But none of that was happening fast enough, so Ren grabbed Lindsay's hands and pulled her down. "I'm all for slow, but only if you keep your tongue in my mouth."

Lindsay granted the request and kissed her deeply. She reached for the claw that held Lindsay's hair up and let it fall around their faces. She tossed the clip to the side and grabbed Lindsay's ass with both hands. Big denim pockets prevented her from getting a good grip. She pushed the overalls down with her hands and then her feet.

Lindsay leaned up on her hands while she pushed her hips into Ren. With the overalls gone, it was clear she could feel the friction against her clit too. She moaned and said, "Take my panties off."

Ren pushed them down and grabbed Lindsay's bare ass. She spread her legs farther and wrapped them around Lindsay. They rocked against each other while holding a stare. Ren pulled her down for another kiss. She took Lindsay's bottom lip between her teeth and bit it, then worked her way down her neck, all the while keeping a firm grip on her ass. Lindsay moaned and whispered, "You get me so turned on."

Ren grabbed her face and looked her in the eye. "Ditto." She tried to turn them over, but Lindsay held them where they were.

"No. I need you in my mouth." Lindsay pulled Ren's bra down and circled her nipple with her tongue.

Ren whimpered. "Okay. I'll just be up here, feeling things. Oh God." She put her hand on the back of Lindsay's head. She needed more pressure, and Lindsay responded by pulling Ren's nipple into her mouth and lightly biting. She did the same with the other one and then worked her way lower.

With the first flick of Lindsay's tongue against her clit, she knew she'd come like a house on fire. Lindsay's bravery was such a turn-on. She'd never been with a woman before Ren, but she showed no hesitation. She was all in, and she was rockin' it.

It didn't take long for the orgasm to build inside her. She ran her fingers into Lindsay's hair and closed her eyes. She thought back to the first time she saw Lindsay naked. How beautiful she was. How fucking sexy she looked on her hands and knees. Ren's body stilled, then she came with a fury, gripping Lindsay's hair, her hips bucking, her mind lost in memories.

Lindsay worked her way back up Ren's body and lay on top of her. They held each other's gaze while Ren caught her breath. It seemed like both of them were hesitant to say anything. Words would complicate things. Besides, Ren had other means of communication.

She rolled them over so she was on top and straddled Lindsay's body. She removed her bra and tossed it on the floor. "When does Brooke get home?"

"Not for a few hours."

"Perfect."

"A fling?" Deb leaned across the counter and knocked on Ren's head with her knuckles. "What's wrong with you? I thought you'd fallen hard for her. Not to mention the fact that I've made plans. *Big* plans for when you move here."

"I'm moving to Paris. That hasn't changed."

"I thought maybe you'd change your mind because of the past life thing."

"You know about that?"

"Corey couldn't keep it in anymore. She was bursting with excitement because she wants to throw you two a big party."

"What? No. That's not going to happen. And why are you acting like this past life thing is nothing? It's a big deal, and Lindsay kept it from me. I had to find out from her ex-husband that she thought I was this Roo person, and everyone else already knew. Talk about feeling like an idiot."

"And yet, you went to her house and got jiggy."

"Like I said, we talked it over and came to a mutual understanding. What we have is physical. That's it."

"And you don't see yourself ever having an emotional connection to her?"

"And have this Roo person always hanging over my head? I mean, how will I feel when she mixes up our names?" Ren shook her head. "No. It's easier this way."

"Then why do you look so sad right now?"

Patty walked into the coffee shop. "Oh, hey, girls. Deb, I'll have my regular."

"A small skinny mocha, no whip?"

Patty made a face. "What? Ew. I only ordered that so Mrs. Stokely wouldn't comment on my weight. It's a hobby of hers, trying to guess if I'm up ten pounds or down five. She usually guesses up."

Deb got up and went behind the counter. "One large iced coffee and a cherry bomb muffin with vanilla frosting, coming right up."

Patty sat where Deb had been. "You'll never guess what we found behind the plywood. Old dressing rooms from the 1950s. It was disgusting getting it all cleaned up. So much dust it had basically turned into a thick layer of dirt."

"Dressing rooms," Ren said. "That's odd." She glanced at Deb, then lowered her voice. "Patty, tell me about Roo."

"Oh. Quick subject change. Okay. Okay. It's not really my

place…" She paused and looked around, then leaned in. "Okay, so a long time ago in a faraway land, or close land, no one really knows—"

"I know that part. I just need to know how big a role this person—past person—plays in Lindsay's life."

"I'm not in her head, so I can't really say."

"You're her best friend," Ren said.

"She has dreams. About a past life with Roo. And dreams about the boy too. That's really all I can say. BFF code and all that. I mean, I can't have her telling all of my secrets. I've known her since elementary school. Can you imagine the things she knows?" She made a motion like she was zipping her lip. "Loose lips sink ships and all that."

Ren blinked. She had no idea what Patty was talking about, but she was getting used to Patty and her stream-of-consciousness conversations, so she was able to zero in on the pertinent information. "The boy. The boy in the painting I bought?"

"Don't expect to make any sense of this," Patty said. "I've been trying for years, and I finally decided that this is just Lindsay's thing. It's what she believes, and it doesn't have to make sense to anyone else. But you'll never find a better person, a better mom, or a better best friend."

"So you're aware that she thinks I'm the reborn version of Roo, right?"

"Of course."

Of course. Ren didn't even need to ask. She was the only one in Lindsay's life who'd been left in the dark. Deb set the to-go coffee and muffin on the table, then looked at her watch. "Patty, you have six minutes to get to the gallery and open it on time."

Patty scoffed. "Oh, please. I never open on time. See you girls later."

❖

Lindsay woke up from a short nap and sat up. The uncomfortable cot had given her a kink in her back. As she tried to massage it out, she took a good look at what she'd accomplished so far. Roo was coming to life again on the canvas. A much bigger canvas this time around.

Lindsay had positioned Roo with her back to the viewer, looking over her shoulder with a mischievous grin on her face. She was larger than life. Untamable. A thorn in the side of anyone who tried to control her. Those were the feelings the painting evoked in Lindsay. Roo was a force to be reckoned with. And she had loved a girl named Katie.

Lindsay got up and went back to work.

❖

"Okay, smile." Ren took a few shots of Mrs. Stokely from different angles. She'd just had her hair done when she stopped in for a coffee. "You look beautiful. Doesn't she look beautiful, Deb?"

"I thought I'd try something different," Mrs. Stokely said. "I told Michelle to go hog wild. Do whatever she wants to this old head of hair. There's nowhere to go but up."

Michelle had completely changed Mrs. Stokely's look by ditching the helmet hair and giving her a choppy, close cut. Ren also noticed that the therapeutic shoes had been replaced with a pair of red loafers that matched Mrs. Stokely's wool coat. Had she gone digging through her old clothes? It looked like she had indeed.

Deb set a small cup and saucer in front of Mrs. Stokely, similar to the ones she had in her own home. "This is your cup from now on, Mrs. Stokely. I think it suits you better than the larger cups."

"Why, thank you, dear. And call me Joyce."

Deb smiled. "Okay, Joyce. Enjoy."

Ren noticed Mrs. Stokely's fingernails had recently been painted too. "Do you have a hot date this weekend?" she asked in a teasing tone.

"Oh, don't be silly. The only date I have is with my new jumbo-sized crochet hook." Her eyes widened. "Oh my. That sounded bad." She slapped Ren's hand, and they both laughed.

Ren leaned in and lowered her voice. "Would you ever want to date again?"

Mrs. Stokely didn't say no, but she didn't say yes. After pondering the question for a moment, she said, "Who would want to date someone my age?"

"Another lesbian around your age." Ren brought up the photos she'd just taken on her phone. "We could post one of these shots on Ryder. It's a lesbian dating app for women of all ages. You might find someone to share the rest of your life with, or you might just find some friends. Either way, it seems like it might be worth a shot."

"I have to admit that I've had so much fun with you girls, I think I would enjoy knowing some like-minded women."

"Oh, this is going to be fun. Deb, get over here. We need to work up a profile for Mrs. Stokely."

Lindsay opened her front door, and Ren said, "I have news, but I wanted to tell you in person."

"Come in. I was just taking a pie out of the oven."

Ren followed Lindsay into the kitchen. "It smells delicious in here."

"I try to bake a few pies every winter. Brooke loves them."

"My God, that's such a turn-on. They only thing I ever bake is those premade tubes of cookie dough." Ren stood close to her. "Cute apron." She leaned in for a kiss.

"Brooke's home," Lindsay whispered.

Ren took a step back. "Right. Okay, well, I came by to tell you that Mrs. Stokely has her first date tomorrow."

Lindsay took off her oven mitts and tossed them on the counter. "What?"

"She came into You Mocha Me Crazy, and we got talking, and she said she'd like to meet some like-minded women, so I decided to make a profile for her and post it online."

"What?" Lindsay blinked a few times. "I'm in shock."

Brooke slid into the kitchen just like her mother made a habit of doing. "About what? Oh, hey, Ren."

"Mrs. Stokely," Lindsay said. "She's going on a date. I hope she'll be okay after all this time."

"Oh, don't worry about Mrs. Stokely. Worry about her poor date," Brooke said.

"Be nice, Brooke. Mrs. Stokely was in the closet her entire life. I'd be grumpy too." Lindsay looked at Ren. "We have to dress her. Do her hair. All of it."

Ren grinned. "She's kind of already taken care of that. Check it out." She handed her phone over.

"That's Mrs. Stokely?" Brooke exclaimed, her mouth gaping open. "She looks great."

Lindsay handed the phone back. "We have to see it happen."

Ren grinned. "I'll get the details. We'll hide in her bushes if we have to."

Lindsay put her hand out. "I'm in."

Brooke put her hand on top of Lindsay's. "I'm in too."

❖

Lindsay covered her mouth to keep from screaming. She knew Brooke didn't mean to slam a heel down on her big toe, but that didn't make it hurt any less. Mrs. Stokely's juniper trees had obviously been planted with three or four hapless souls in mind, not six.

"I feel so covert," Corey whispered. She'd painted black stripes under her eyes like the football players did. Brooke went all-in with her black knit facemask. Brookey the bank robber. Lindsay prayed the police didn't decide now was a good time for a neighborhood patrol.

Patty had on bright orange hunting gear. No one knew why, but they'd stuck her behind the largest tree so she didn't give them away.

Deb chose to wear normal clothes with mismatched rubber

boots and a black beanie pulled low. Again, no one knew why. Or at least Lindsay didn't.

And then there was Ren, who was standing the farthest away from her. Tight jeans, a black turtleneck, those old boots she was so attached to, and a red and black lumberjack's coat she was certain was another item stolen from Deb. God, she looked adorable. Lindsay wanted to take it all off and breathe Ren in for six hours straight, but things felt slightly tense between them. Friendly, but tense.

Lindsay wondered if maybe it was because she'd rebuffed a kiss from Ren the day before. It wasn't that she didn't want the kiss. She just didn't want Brooke to get attached to the idea of them dating in a serious way. Still, they could've stolen a quick kiss, and Lindsay found herself feeling regretful that she hadn't let it happen.

She wanted to be closer to Ren, so she worked her way through the small crowd. "Excuse me. Sorry. Can I get past? Hi."

"Hi," Ren whispered. "You really know how to make an entrance."

Brooke put her finger over her lips and shushed everyone. "I see car lights."

Lindsay got behind Ren and wrapped her arms around her. She'd get all kinds of good whiffs of her scent in this position. She smiled when Ren took their hands and tucked them into her pockets.

A car pulled into the driveway. Deb clasped her hands together and whispered, "Here we go, girls."

The car wasn't nearly as old as the Mistmobile. And the woman who got out of what looked like a Prius wasn't nearly as old as Mrs. Stokely, either. Or maybe she just dyed her hair. Lindsay felt a sense of panic rise up in her chest. What if this woman was too young for her? Would her heart be broken? And then the woman in the pretty blue pantsuit took her cane from the passenger seat and leaned heavily on it. Lindsay breathed a sigh of relief and whispered in Ren's ear, "What do we think so far?"

Ren put two thumbs up. Brooke and Corey were whispering to each other, and Patty was trying to make a pair of binoculars work.

Lindsay kissed Ren's ear. "You're amazing, you know that, right?"

Before Ren could answer, Patty whispered, "She's inside. Follow me, troops."

They all crouched down single file and made their way to a small side window where, if they had the living room mapped out right, neither Mrs. Stokely or her date would discover them. But that was only if Mrs. Stokely sat in her regular spot.

Patty, in her hunting gear and orange trapper's hat, decided she would have the first look. "I got this," she whispered. Then she made all these gestures with her hands like she was running a SWAT team operation. No one knew what any of it meant. Go left? Go right? Slice our necks open with our nonexistent knives?

Lindsay didn't think fast enough. If she had, she would've known to pull Patty and her loud hat away from the window before she peered in it and screamed at the top of her lungs, echoing Mrs. Stokely's scream.

Lindsay ran for the front door and knocked. "Mrs. Stokely? Mrs. Stokely, it's Lindsay."

Mrs. Stokely opened the door, holding her hand over her chest. "What in damnation? I thought a deer hunter had mistaken me for a five-pointer, and I'd breathed my last breath."

The other five gathered around. Patty had magically removed all of her hunting gear. "We chased him away," she said. "The hunter. Gone for good. No need to worry. How's your date going?"

Lindsay rolled her eyes. "We'll let you get back to it."

"Oh, no." Mrs. Stokely waved them in. "I'd love for Verna to meet my friends."

"We're not really dressed for it," Lindsay said. "Deb's boots don't match."

"Uh, your daughter looks like she just robbed a bank," Deb said.

Brooke pulled the mask off her face. "And Corey decided to join the football team. Tight end." Brooke slapped Corey's butt.

Mrs. Stokely stared at them with a blank look on her face, then whispered, "Does my hair look okay?"

She hadn't done too bad trying to recreate what her stylist had done. And the matching navy pants and sweater were very age-appropriate. Everyone gave her a big nod and a thumbs-up.

"Good. Now, get outta here. You'll get a full report tomorrow."

The door slammed shut. They all shrugged, then ran to Deb's minivan parked down the street.

Patty threw all of her gear in but kept the binoculars, which most likely did not have night vision, around her neck. She put her hand out, palm facedown. "Bring it in, cohorts. This mission was a success."

Lindsay put her limp hand in. She couldn't wait to hear what came out of Patty's mouth next. Would it be a big oorah like the Marines did? Would they get tattoos to commemorate their first team mission? And what would that tattoo look like? A rainbow flag with a trapper's hat hanging from it?

"Brooke," Patty said. "Stealth. Very stealth. Deb, excellent job creating confusion with the boots. Corey, the Dallas Cowboy Cheerleaders might be in your future. Ren, try harder next time. The lumberjack look didn't fool anyone. And Lindsay..." Patty motioned with her head toward Lindsay's coat pocket. "Yellow dishwashing gloves?"

Lindsay stuffed the gloves hanging out of her pocket in farther. "Whatever. If it turned out that we'd had to belly crawl through Mrs. Stokely's garden, I'd be the only one with clean hands right now."

Patty shrugged. "I guess that makes sense. Bring it back, boys. On three. Oh, wait. Here comes a car. Just act casual." Patty put one hand in her hair and another on her hip. "Nothing to see here."

Brooke and Corey started up a fake conversation with silent laughter. Lindsay turned to Ren and said, "You look so hot in that lumberjack coat, I just want to..." She stopped when she realized everyone was looking right at them and most likely heard what she'd said. "Borrow it. I want to borrow it."

Giggles ensued as everyone climbed into the van. "Sure, Mom," Brooke said.

Ren motioned with her hand. "Maybe you can finish that sentence another time."

"Maybe I'll do more than that."

❖

Ren wondered if Corey's last-minute slumber party had nothing to do with studying for an exam and everything to do with getting Brooke out of the house so they'd have some time alone. She'd have to thank Deb later.

As she followed Lindsay home, her thoughts turned to Paris. It was such a great job opportunity that she couldn't give up. At the same time, she loved Salt Creek. She loved the laid-back attitude, the slower pace, the people. One person, specifically.

She and Lindsay needed more time. They needed to get to know each other better. Ren needed to get a better understanding of all of this past life stuff so she wouldn't fear it so much. That would take time she didn't have.

Once inside Lindsay's home, Ren took off the now infamous jacket she'd borrowed from Deb's coat closet. She looked up and realized Lindsay was leaning against the wall, watching her. "I thought you were going to let me do that," Lindsay said.

"I just saved you the trouble."

"Undressing you would be a pleasure, not a hardship."

Ren stepped a little closer. She slid her hands into her back pockets and said, "What if I said I wanted to spend the night? Sleep naked with you. Wake up next to you. Trace the lines of your body with my finger until you stir. Bring you coffee in bed."

Lindsay folded her arms. "Sounds like heaven. But then what?"

"Then we both have a beautiful memory of our last time together." Ren couldn't read Lindsay's expression. Did she want this as much as Ren did? Would it feel too confusing? "Let's not waste what little time we have left together, Linds. Let's part on a good note, with good memories of each other."

Lindsay pushed off the wall. "I left a fan on in my studio. I'll meet you upstairs in a minute."

"I'll go with you. I love seeing your work."

Lindsay stiffened.

"What's wrong?"

"It's Roo I've been painting."

"Oh. Okay. Do you not want me to see it?"

"Do you want to?"

Ren wasn't sure what she wanted. Time with Lindsay. That's what it boiled down to. If that meant seeing this Roo person again, so be it. She forced a smile and said, "Let's go."

They walked hand in hand to the studio, but the minute Ren saw the huge painting through the window, she dropped Lindsay's hand. She wasn't working on the painting she'd already seen. This was a new one, and it was enormous. Twice, maybe three times the size of the first painting of Roo. And the look on Roo's face was as *come hither* as it got. Follow me to my boudoir and let me do naughty things to you, was the vibe Ren got.

They walked in, and Ren stood in a protective stance with her arms folded. Lindsay turned off the fan and sat on a stool. She gazed at the painting and said, "She's been such a huge part of me for so long. It's strange to look at her from a distance."

The work was extraordinary. Ren couldn't deny that. But it gave her such a feeling of inadequacy, she couldn't fully comprehend why. She felt vulnerable and small in the presence of this larger-than-life version of Roo. In fact, larger-than-life was the perfect description for her. A supposed dead woman had taken over Lindsay's life, and in Ren's estimation, there really wasn't room for anyone else.

"Is she going to hang in your living room?"

Lindsay turned to Ren. "What?"

"Your living room, Linds. Or maybe over your bed? Or better yet, on the ceiling above your bed so you don't have to crank your neck to look at her?"

"Wow. Where is this coming from?"

Ren shook her head. "I'm sorry, it's just too much. Even if I wanted to try to have more than a fling with you, would you ever really be mine?"

Lindsay stood. "I'm going to sell her. One day, I'll sell her."

Ren didn't believe it for a second. Lindsay would never sell that painting. Or any painting of Roo. If she struggled to sell paintings of a boy she didn't know, how would she ever bring herself to let go of Roo? "You won't. You won't ever sell her, Linds. And I can't compete with her. I won't even try."

Ren walked out of the studio and got in her car. She wanted to scream. She wanted to take that painting and throw it in the trash. She wanted to shout at Lindsay, wake up! Stop living in someone else's past. And stop pretending you could love anyone else but Roo.

CHAPTER FOURTEEN

It was for the best. Wasn't it? Ren could focus on her job in Paris. Her heart wouldn't be in two places at once. She could explore France without wishing her girlfriend was there with her. She could date French women, which she'd been looking forward to doing. The pros of ending it with Lindsay outweighed the cons. It never should've started in the first place. Deb was right. Ren was old enough to know better.

She hated the idea of having to say good-bye to Lindsay before she left the next day. She'd said some pretty rude things about the painting of Roo before she left in a bitter huff. She'd have to start with an apology. And then have an awkward hug while saying awkward things like, it was nice getting to know you. And having sex with you. And almost falling madly in love with you. Almost? Who was she kidding?

One good thing had come of it. Together, they'd managed to make Mrs. Stokely's life a little better. Ren felt a sense of pride about that. And when she turned the corner onto Main Street and saw the Mistmobile parked in front of the art gallery, she found herself hoping Mrs. Stokely would be visiting Patty so they'd have a few minutes to talk about how her date went.

Patty didn't look happy when Ren walked in. In fact, she scowled so hard, Ren was tempted to leave. "Oh, no," Patty said. "Oh, no, no, no. That sale was final."

A sense of relief washed over Ren. She wasn't scowling at her.

She was scowling at the paintings in her hands. "Wait. I'm not here to return them. I'd just like you to pack them up and ship them to me."

"Oh." Patty swiped a hand over her brow. "That could've been so awkward. I mean, I would've had to throw you out on your ass, which I kind of want to do anyway."

"Right. Okay." Ren noticed there was a new art installation against the back wall. In fact, it looked as if it was part of the building. She set the paintings down so she could get a closer look.

It wasn't graffiti on the walls. Just words painted haphazardly, sort of like what you'd find at a crime scene where the criminal felt the need to express a thought before he fled. The word "Ladies" with an arrow pointing to an opening had been crossed out and replaced with the words "Defiant Queens." On the other side, the word "Men" had been expanded to "Menstruate."

There were messages everywhere. Some large, some so small, Ren couldn't read them. The ones she could read were all messages of empowerment. The message right in the middle seemed like an important one since it had a black frame around it. She read it to herself.

Bad things happened here. Hearts were broken. Souls crushed. Young lives changed forever. This will stand as a monument to those who have suffered at the hand of bigotry and hate. It will stand for those who have lived in fear for far too long. For those who can't touch the one they love in public. For those whose rights are still ignored. This monument is your safe space.

"Too dramatic? Over the top? Angry?" Patty stood next to Ren and folded her arms. "Well, I never claimed to be a real artist, but I had something to say, and this is going to stay here until I…hey, wait, you don't want to go back there. It's just some old dressing rooms."

Ren was so moved by the work, she had to see more. She pushed on the first door. It swung open with a loud squeak. Her heart felt as if it would pound out of her chest, but she had to know what this was about. It was an urge she couldn't control, kind of like in the movies when the person was drawn to the strange noise coming from behind a closed door. The audience was yelling, "Don't open the door!" but the character did it anyway. Ren had to know what was behind those closed doors. The next dressing room door opened with an even louder squeak. The bench was dusty. It didn't matter. Ren sat on it anyway. The mirror was so dirty she could only see a blurred version of herself with what little light there was.

Her breath was shallow. If felt as if there wasn't enough oxygen in the air, but she couldn't leave. She put one hand on the mirror and the other on the opposite wall. She needed to dig her heels in. Or better yet, slam them up against the door. She pushed against a force that wasn't there.

A fluorescent light turned on above her head. "Ren? Are you okay back there?"

She could see more detail now. The broken lock on the door. The splintered wood around the lock. Patty pushed on the door, but Ren had her feet firmly planted against it. "I'm fine, Patty."

But Ren wasn't fine. She was on the verge of tears. She dropped her feet to the floor and flung the door open. She raced out of the gallery and only stopped when she was on the other side of the street. She bent over and inhaled the fresh air. At least she tried to.

She felt unsteady as she stumbled to her car. Like the Earth had tilted on its axis. She leaned against the trunk and tried to take deep breaths while frantically wiping soot on her jeans that had gotten on her hands. Patty put a hand on Ren's shoulder. She jerked around and said, "Sorry. I don't know what the fuck just happened, but I had to get out there."

"Lindsay reacted the same way, but she blamed it on the dust."

"It's not the fucking dust." Ren wiped her face with the back of her hands. "I'll email a forwarding address. And for God's sake, get a priest in there to perform an exorcism."

❖

Lindsay opened her front door. Patty pushed past her, turned, and put her hands on her hips. "What are you not telling me?"

Lindsay shook her head. "I'm not sure—"

"Ren came into the gallery today, and after a big scene where she's hyperventilating in the middle of the street, she basically ordered me to call the Ghostbusters, and you know what it reminded me of?"

Lindsay closed the door. "I thought you were going to board it back up."

"So you do know what I'm talking about. Damnit, Lindsay!"

Lindsay went into the kitchen and sat on a barstool. Patty followed, but the anger in her eyes remained. "Calm down, Cakes."

"I'll calm down when you tell me the truth."

"Okay," Lindsay said. "It was Roo and Katie. That's who your grandfather caught. Or at least, I think it was."

Patty didn't move for a moment. Then she threw her hands in the air. "What am I going to do with you, Linds? How could you have kept that from me?"

"Your words from before ran through my head when it happened. It all seemed a little bit too convenient."

"So you didn't tell me because you thought I wouldn't believe you?"

"Would you have?"

Patty started to say something but stopped. Tears filled her eyes. "I'd like to make a request to be in the safe zone right now, but the first time I did that, it bit me in the ass so hard."

"Let me say it for you. You would've thought I was making up everything about me and Roo again. Everything has to circle back to Roo for me, right?"

Patty nodded.

"I'm not angry, Cakes. I get it. I do. But you've stood by me for so long. Please don't ever stop being my best friend."

Patty went in for a hug. "Never. I'm here. Always."

❖

Patty poured two glasses of wine and put her feet up on the coffee table. She drank from one while still holding the other.

Lindsay stared her down until Patty said, "Oh, right," and handed her the second glass.

"It's like I'm invisible sometimes." Lindsay took a sip and rested her head on the back of the sofa.

"Not invisible. I was just thinking," Patty said. "What are you going to do about Ren?"

"I think Ren is done with me and my past life."

Patty shook her head. "Don't assume that."

"What good would it do to tell her the story? She wouldn't believe it. Why put myself through that? I'd rather she think it was paranormal activity."

"Two reasons. Number one, I know you have feelings for her. *Ren*, not just Roo. And number two, whatever she experienced in that dressing room has to mean something because I'm telling you, she was freaked out. And number three—"

"You said two things."

"And number three, I can't have rumors going around that my gallery has a poltergeist. Imagine what that would do to my business."

"Increase it tenfold?" Lindsay shrugged. "You probably wouldn't sell anything, but you'd get a lot of foot traffic. People love having the shit scared out of them. Hey, it's almost Halloween. You could turn it into a haunted house."

"Talk to Ren, or I walk."

Lindsay gasped. "Not even five minutes ago, you promised that we'd be BFFs forever."

Patty stood. "I just meant I'd walk out the door right now. See? This is me, backing my way to the front door. I'm almost there. Won't be long now."

Lindsay giggled. "That's what she said."

Patty opened the door. "I'm out." She slammed it shut.

"Okay, fine. I'll talk to her!"

Patty opened the door and blew Lindsay a kiss. "Sometime in this century, please."

❖

Ren hadn't moved for several minutes. It was cold enough that she'd kept her car running outside of You Mocha Me Crazy for the heat. She'd been driving for hours while going over and over the incident in Patty's gallery.

She'd been drawn to those dressing rooms, but once she was in there, the panic and the rage were so strong, she could feel the adrenaline coursing through her veins, and she had to get out.

She remembered Patty's proclamation to the world that something bad had happened there. What was she going to do, sell tickets? It infuriated her so much her fists clenched. Perfect for slugging the person who decided to bang on the driver's side window. Except it was Lindsay. Sweet, beautiful Lindsay. Ren unclenched her fists and rolled the window down. "Hey."

"Were you going to skip town without saying good-bye?"

"No. Of course not." Ren lowered her gaze. "I thought it might be awkward, so I was maybe, possibly, stalling."

"You know what isn't awkward? The way you kiss," Lindsay said. "You're like the queen of kissing. You make me want to live in the town of Lipsville, which is in the county of Kissington."

Ren blushed. How was it that Lindsay could make her drop her defenses with just a few words? "Is that anywhere near the Wet Tongue Cliffs?"

"Oh, you have to be careful if you go there. It gets slippery, and you could easily fall off one of those cliffs."

Ren motioned with her head. "Get in."

Lindsay hurried to the other side of the car and jumped in. "Hi."

Ren opened her arms. She pulled Lindsay in and nuzzled her neck. She inhaled her sweet scent and ran her lips over her soft skin. The frazzled, nervous feeling drifted away, and a sense of calm and safety washed over her. She took in a deep, cleansing breath. And then another.

Ren took in everything. She noticed the tight grip Lindsay had on her shoulder. How her hair smelled like strawberries, and her nose was cold from being outside. The way she seemed to melt into

Ren as if the only place she really fit in this world was in her arms. "I'm sorry," Ren whispered. "I've wasted so much time that we could've spent together." She held Lindsay's face so they were eye to eye. "I leave tomorrow."

"Then why are we still in this car?"

❖

They drove to the same hotel in Lake City. Lindsay stepped into the elevator first, key card in hand. Ren pushed the button for the third floor, then leaned against the wall. Before they got off the elevator, Lindsay knew what she wanted, and it wasn't to talk about Roo and those damned dressing rooms like she'd promised Patty she'd do.

She took Ren's hand as they walked down the hallway. So much would be left unsaid between them, but they'd have this, and maybe it was enough for both of them. It would have to be. Maybe it would be a perfect ending to their story. They wouldn't have to suffer through heartache and loss the way Katie and Roo had.

No, this was a gift, and Lindsay was determined to look at the next few hours that way. A parting gift. Like Ren had said, a good memory that would bring a smile to their faces when they thought of each other.

Lindsay put the key card in the door and opened it. Ren walked in, looked around and said, "I'd like to take a quick shower. I had to deal with some dust earlier."

"It's fine," Lindsay said. "Take your time."

She watched Ren take off her boots.

"Do you still want me to hang on to them for you?"

Ren paused. "Naw. I think I'll give them back to Deb. Can't have her running around town in mismatched boots. People would talk even more than they do now."

Lindsay sat on the bed and crossed her legs. Was it that, or was Ren avoiding anything that would keep a connection between them? She couldn't be sure either way. It was another reason to let their time in that hotel together be whatever it was meant to be. "You're so beautiful, Ren. Would you undress for me?" She leaned back on her hands and waited for a response. Yes, they were bold words, but she was so ready to get this party started.

Ren slowly unzipped her jeans. Lindsay leaned forward again because her request was actually going to be met, and she didn't want to miss a single detail.

"Join me," Ren said.

"In the shower?"

"That too, but I meant right now. Undress with me. Let me watch you too."

Talk about getting out of one's daily rut and enjoying life. Lindsay didn't see that coming when she'd made the request, but she stood and slipped her boots and socks off. She unzipped her jeans and waited for Ren to push hers off her hips.

Ren let her jeans fall to the floor, and Lindsay did the same. The look in Ren's eye told her she liked what she saw and wanted more. Lindsay made the first move this time. She pulled her sweater over her head and let it slide off her arms.

Ren only had her shirt to remove, which she did with speed and ease. Lindsay was about to remove her bra when Ren said, "No. Let me."

Her tender touch caused goose bumps to pop out all over Lindsay's body. Ren took off her own bra too and stepped into an embrace. She wrapped her arms around Lindsay's waist and pressed their breasts together, then their foreheads. They stood that way for what felt like a long time, breathing each other in. Warming each other up. Saying good-bye.

Lindsay took Ren's hands and intertwined their fingers. She wanted to hang on as tightly as she could for what little time they had left. She wanted Ren to believe the only thing that mattered was this moment. Not the past, not Roo, just Lindsay and Ren.

Words wouldn't work. Words had failed. Lindsay could never put into words how important her time with Ren had been. Knowing her had changed Lindsay's life forever. She no longer had to wonder why Roo had been such a big part of her life. She didn't have to pine for a woman she'd never known. She didn't have to wonder what it would feel like to be loved by a woman. She could rest now. Her heart could rest. Roo could rest.

Ren led Lindsay to the shower. She turned on the water, then slid Lindsay's panties down her legs. She did the same with her own and offered her hand. Lindsay stepped into the shower with her, and just like they'd done a few minutes ago, they clung to each other while the water washed over them.

❖

Ren felt Lindsay tighten around her fingers. She slowed her pace and gently circled her clit with her tongue. Lindsay's nipples were taut. Her chest heaved. Her stomach flexed with each buck of her hips. Ren took a mental snapshot.

When it felt like Lindsay was almost ready to climax, Ren pushed in as far as she could with her fingers and let her tongue flatten against Lindsay's clit. She watched her grip the sheets with both hands and press her shoulders into the mattress. Her breasts bounced, and again, Ren took a mental snapshot.

Ren knelt over her while she recovered. Their eyes locked, but no words were spoken. They didn't seem to need them this time. They'd let their bodies do the talking. Their hands. Their lips.

It surprised her when Lindsay rolled them over. She opened her legs, and when their bodies touched, Lindsay let out a little moan. They kissed deeply, letting their tongues explore while Ren ran her hands all over Lindsay's backside. She squeezed her ass and pushed her own hips up to create more contact.

Lindsay pushed up onto her hands and ground against Ren's clit. Again, Ren took a mental snapshot.

Lindsay slid down and took Ren's breast into her mouth. Ren ran her fingers into Lindsay's hair and held her there for a moment. It felt so good to have Lindsay on top of her, loving her this way. *Making* love to her. Because that's what it felt like.

Lindsay moved to the other breast. Ren held Lindsay's head and closed her eyes. She couldn't take a mental snapshot of this, but she would never forget this feeling of pure joy. Pure connection. She'd never forget Lindsay.

❖

"You didn't tell her?" Patty tossed her phone on Lindsay's kitchen counter.

"I got sidetracked."

"You realize that Ren thinks my gallery's address is 112 Ocean Avenue now, right?"

"What?"

"Oh, come on. How can you not remember the movie that kept you from sleeping for most of the eighth grade? The house in Amityville, Linds."

Lindsay threw her hands over her eyes. "Don't say that word in my house."

"Fine." Patty folded her arms and shook her head. "But I won't leave it like this. I'm telling her the truth."

Lindsay uncovered her eyes. "What truth is that, Cakes? The story you probably would have had trouble believing if I'd told you?"

Patty held up three fingers. "I have three corroborating facts. Yours, Mrs. Stokely's, and now, Ren's. And for the record, Linds, I've always believed you. Sometimes it just took me a minute to absorb it all, you know?"

Lindsay wrapped her arms around herself. There was absolutely no way she was going to march over to Deb's house and ruin the way she'd left things with Ren. They couldn't *be* together, and they both knew it. Ren had a fantastic job opportunity in Paris, and Lindsay had her life in Salt Creek. It was what it was, even if it hurt like hell to say good-bye.

"I do know. I'm letting go of all of this, Cakes. Everything. I'm putting Roo to bed once and for all. And you're going to support me in that like a best friend would."

"If you've had so much control over this, why didn't you let go of it a long time ago?"

"I don't know that I do have control, but I'm going to try." Lindsay's emotions got the best of her, and she started to cry. "Please, Cakes. Just leave it alone."

Patty sighed, then wrapped her arms around Lindsay. "I've got you, girl. I've got you."

❖

Ren closed the trunk of her car. She'd said her good-byes to Deb's family already. Now, only Deb was left, and it wouldn't be easy. Her friendship meant so much to Ren. Besides her parents, it was the longest lasting relationship she'd had in her life.

Deb came out carrying those damned boots. She held them up and said, "You forgot something, and don't say you're not taking them. I need you to take them. I need to know a part of me is always with you."

Damnit. There was no holding back the tears now. "You're always with me. Always." Ren barely got the words out before the tears showed up. "Oh God. Here we go with the waterworks." Ren knew she shouldn't have bothered putting on any makeup. Leaving Salt Creek had never been easy for her. Deb's family had become her family.

"Really, Soda Pop? We've been over this so many times. I'm married."

"But you mocha me so horny."

They laughed through their tears and held each other close. Deb tried to say something, but her emotions prevented the words from coming out. Ren decided to help her. "I know you're going to miss me like crazy because I'm the best friend you've ever had, and no one will ever replace me."

Deb nodded and kissed her cheek. "Come back for Christmas. It won't be the same without you."

Ren didn't think she could make it happen, but she didn't want to tell Deb that. She returned the kiss and said, "I'll try."

Ren's eyes filled with tears while she waited for the last stoplight to turn green. Part of her wanted it to stay red forever. In less than a mile, she'd be out of Salt Creek with no plans to return. Her fingers tightened around the steering wheel. Should she turn around? Speed past the coffee shop and Patty's gallery and the high school? Rush up Lindsay's sidewalk and shout her name into the cold air?

But this wasn't a romantic comedy. This was real life where doorbells were used and certain things couldn't be overcome, no matter how loud you shouted. Things like past lives and a woman named Roo.

The honk of a horn behind her shook Ren from her thoughts. She wiped the tears from her eyes and pressed hard on the gas pedal, putting Salt Creek behind her.

EPILOGUE

Ren stepped out of her favorite bakery with a croissant in one hand and a coffee in the other. Her apartment building was only two doors down, so she'd become a regular at the café. Gilbert, which she found out way too late was pronounced with a soft G and silent T—kind of like Jill-bear, only fancier—flirted with her every time she went in. He was a sweet enough guy, and the coffee was great. The croissants, however, were to die for.

She held up the croissant and said, "Hello, my love. I dreamt about you last night. It was...exciting and buttery and—" Her speech was interrupted when someone moved into her space. She nearly dropped everything. "Patty?"

"You talk to your food now? Seduce it before you devour it? How very French of you. God, I wish I could stay in this city for months on end and just soak it all in."

Patty. Salt Creek Patty was standing right in front of Ren's building wearing a raspberry beret, of all things. Because of course she was. "What are you doing here?"

"Chaperone. I know, right? Who would ask me to chaperone a bunch of teenagers?" Patty cleared her throat. "They didn't ask. I volunteered. It was the only way Brooke could go. I think Ben's watched *Taken* one too many times." Patty tilted her beret to the side a little more. "I've had this forever. No one in Salt Creek appreciates its significance except Lindsay, but boy, have I gotten some great looks here. Even a few double takes. What do you think?"

"It's fabulous. And now I'll have the song in my head for days. So where's Brooke?"

"She's with the rest of the choir group. I took the train from Lyon to see you."

Ren laughed lightly. "You're not much of a chaperone, are you?"

"Oh God, no. I'm the worst!"

Ren couldn't believe she was standing in Paris, looking at Patty. They'd emailed a few times. Patty wanted to make sure the paintings had arrived safely, which they had. "It's good to see you," Ren said. "I'd give you a hug, but my hands are kind of full."

Patty leaned in. "We can air kiss." She made a loud kissing noise. "See? All good."

Patty was such a quirky thing but so cute. Ren felt excited that they'd get to catch up. "Do me a favor. Reach into my front pocket and pull out my key."

"Wow. You really are in love with that croissant," Patty said. "You won't even risk dropping it."

"Wait until you have a bite. Then you'll understand. You wouldn't want to break up with this croissant either. Marriage material. That's what this croissant is."

"Actually, I need to get back to the group in Lyon. I just wanted to drop this envelope off. Lindsay hasn't seen it yet. We thought maybe you could tell her. Brooke came up with the idea. She sends her love and wishes she could've come with, but Ben would have my head on a platter if we deviated from the itinerary at all."

"How's Brooke?"

"Brooke is seventeen. It really depends on the minute you ask that question," Patty said. "But overall, she's good. Ready to graduate and go off to college."

"Patty, you have to come up for a few minutes at least. Please. I need to hear more about everyone in Salt Creek. I miss it so much. I have croissants. Buttery, delicious croissants."

"Ha. I knew you were a little bit crazy, but that's why you fit right in, I guess."

"What does that mean?"

"It means you're in Paris, eating delicious croissants and looking fabulous, I might add. But you're missing Salt Creek. Is the scarf Hermès?" Patty took the croissant. "Open up." She stuffed it into Ren's mouth and said, "Hang on to that." She put Ren's key in her hand and tucked a large envelope under her arm. "Take care, Ren. Hope we see you soon."

Ren shouted, "Wait! Patty!" But it came out unintelligible due to the croissant hanging from her mouth.

❖

Patty said she had a surprise for Lindsay at the gallery. Lindsay hated surprises just as much as she hated taking down the Christmas decorations. It wasn't putting it all up that bothered her. She loved Christmas. It was taking it all back down in January. The house felt cold and empty without all of the lights, greenery, and shiny ornaments. A Christmas hangover was what it always felt like to her.

Even with the house lit up and the tree decorated, December had felt cold for lots of reasons. Lindsay had packed up all the paintings of the boy and put them in storage along with the paintings of Roo. Then Brooke went to Europe for ten days. Lindsay had found it difficult to get in the Christmas spirit with so much missing from her life.

She thought of Ren every day. Longed for her touch and to hear her voice again. Nothing was keeping her from making contact. Of course, nothing was keeping Ren from making contact either. And yet, neither of them did. They'd left it where it was, a beautiful memory.

That night, the school choir was putting on a Christmas performance for the town as a thank you for supporting their efforts to make the trip to Europe. She chose to wear a blue and gray scarf instead of the more festive red or green like everyone else was sure to do. "No reason," she said out loud to no one. She wrapped the scarf around her neck a couple of times and tucked a matching knit hat in her coat pocket.

❖

You Mocha Me Crazy was You Mocha Me Busy. Lindsay circled the block again, looking for an open parking spot. She wasn't walking into the coldest place in town without a tall Americano, extra hot, in her hand. Patty blamed the lack of heat in her gallery on the renovations. Lindsay blamed it on Patty's early menopause. There were other symptoms. Paranoia. Nervousness. Indecisiveness. Moodiness. All the nesses, Patty had them lately.

And the headaches. Patty couldn't get lunch because she had a headache. She couldn't come over for dinner because she had a headache. Lindsay was starting to feel like a sexually deprived husband. If Patty had found a new best friend or something, she should just be honest about it. The headache excuse was getting old.

"Yes!" Lindsay slammed on the brakes and waited for a car to reverse out of the parking space.

Deb knew how to heat a building. Or maybe it was all of the warm bodies filling up the tables. Lindsay gave her a wave from the back of the line. She acknowledged a few people she knew and waited because cold gallery plus no hot coffee would make for a cranky Lindsay.

Deb came from behind the counter. "Hey, Linds. What are you doing here?"

Lindsay furrowed her brow. "Um…coffee?"

"Right. Right. Um, so how are you? I love that jacket. What is that, teal?"

Lindsay looked at her Patagonia jacket. "I know, not exactly Christmasy, but I just couldn't bring myself to wear the ugly sweater this year."

"The one with the injured squirrel climbing up your arm and the holly that's really poison ivy?"

Lindsay put up her finger. "Wait. Are you telling me that my ugly sweater is infamous?"

"Some of us wait all year to see it again," Deb said.

"Well, crap. I should go home and change. I didn't think anyone would even notice. Don't want to disappoint my sweater fans." One of the high school kids Deb had hired came around the counter with a to-go cup and handed it to her. "Oh. I could've waited in line like everyone else, but thank you."

"Please. Perks of knowing the owner." Deb took her arm and led her to the front door. "I think you have someplace to be, don't you?"

Lindsay looked at her watch. "Yeah, gotta run. Patty's waiting for me." She opened the door and turned back around. "How did you know?"

Deb smiled and gave Lindsay a small push out the door. "Enjoy your surprise."

❖

The gallery felt warm. "Cakes? It's actually a reasonable temperature in here. Have the hot flashes subsided? What about the secrecy and paranoia? And don't tell me you're not here because you have a headache." The door was unlocked. Of course Patty was there. "Cakes?"

"I'm back here!"

Her reply came from behind a large sheet of plastic that covered the dressing room area. "I don't want to go back there. Come out."

Patty came through an opening in the sheet. "It's not dusty anymore. Wanna see?"

"Can I stand right here and see?"

Patty gave the sheet a good tug, and it fell to the ground. Behind it was a wide-open space with bright white walls. New lighting lit up the space. "It looks fantastic, Cakes. But what about the memorial you painted? You know, with all the words."

"Two things," Patty said. "Number one, my best friend wouldn't come into my gallery anymore because she hated the memorial so much, and number two, it's still a memorial."

"How so?"

Patty went to the far wall where a sheet covered something on the wall. "Are you ready?"

"So it's not menopause? I'm so relieved. You're way too young."

"Focus, Linds."

Lindsay cleared her throat. "Right. I'm ready. Always dangerous words where you're concerned, but yep, ready. Hit me."

Patty pulled the sheet away, and Lindsay gasped. "Cakes!"

Patty stood behind Lindsay and put her hands on her shoulders. "She's too beautiful to keep locked away. The world should see her and know who she was."

Lindsay stood there, stunned. It was the painting of Roo. The one where she was looking over her shoulder, lit up and on display for the whole world to see. Roo, who had suffered in that very spot, was there again, looking larger than life and full of joy. Patty was right. It was the perfect memorial. Lindsay wiped a tear from her cheek and turned. "This is amazing, Cakes. Just amazing."

"That's not all," Patty said. "Go in the first dressing room."

Lindsay opened the door and found a book sitting on the bench. She sat and opened it. Her mouth dropped open when she saw a photo of Roo. Below it was her name, *Eleanor Roosevelt Allred*. Lindsay had painted her image almost perfectly. "Roo," she whispered through her tears.

Lindsay took the book and rushed out of the dressing room. "Cakes! I can't believe—" She stopped short when she saw Ren.

"If you keep reading," Ren said. "You'll see that Roo and Katie's story didn't end in this place."

"No?" Lindsay said.

Ren took a step closer. "Roo's family was wealthy, so after the incident, she was shipped off to Europe to finishing school. Katie's family didn't have much, but she had the talent and big dreams to become a famous artist." Ren pointed. "Just like you."

Lindsay shook her head in disbelief. "You know who Katie was?"

"Kathryn Beck. But she didn't paint under that name. She ran off to Europe to find Roo and changed her identity. They raised a child together, Linds. A *boy*."

Lindsay covered her mouth with her hands. The boy she'd

painted over and over but never knew who he was had an identity now. It was almost too much to take.

"You don't have to feel sad anymore," Ren said. "They found each other again and shared a happy life for twenty great years."

Lindsay went still. "Twenty years? What happened after that?"

"There was a terrible car accident," Ren said. "Neither of them survived. But before that tragic day, they built a life together. A good life. And if my research is correct, Katie painted under the name K.C. Allred. She took Roo's name, Linds. They were as good as married. Just like Millie and Mrs. Stokely."

Lindsay's hand shook as she reached for Ren. "And the boy?"

Ren stepped closer. "I thought maybe we could find that part out together. He lives in a nursing home in Switzerland. His name is Matthew Allred."

Lindsay let out a little laugh through her tears. "I'll have to get used to the new name. I love your new hairstyle." Ren had a shorter, blunt cut. She looked amazing. Lindsay took out her phone. She held it up and took a photo.

"What are you doing?"

"Capturing this moment. You at this moment. So I can paint you later." Lindsay looked at the photo. Her voice full of wonder, she said, "I don't think we know anything about the universe. Nothing at all."

Ren took Lindsay's hand. "Paint us going to Switzerland to visit Matthew. Then paint us living in Paris together while you attend that art school you had to put off for Brooke." She took Lindsay's other hand. "Paint us happy and in love because I'm already in love with you. We just need the happily ever after part."

"I'm in love with you too," Lindsay said. "I always have been."

When their lips met, Patty cheered from outside. She rushed back in with Brooke in tow, grinning from ear to ear. Lindsay and Ren pulled them into a group hug. Lindsay glanced at the painting of Roo. She wasn't meant to let her go. And the woman in her arms—Ren—she was meant to love forever. "Now," Ren said. "About this ugly sweater I keeping hearing about…"

About the Author

Elle Spencer (http://ellespencerbooks.com) is the author of several best-selling lesbian romances, including *Casting Lacey*, a Goldie finalist. She is a hopeless romantic and firm believer in true love, although she knows the path to happily ever after is rarely an easy one—not for Elle and not for her characters.

When she's not writing, Elle loves working on home improvement projects, hiking up tall mountains (not really, but it sounds cool), floating in the pool with a good book, and spending quality time with her pillow in a never-ending quest to prove that napping is the new working.

Elle grew up in Denver, and she and her wife now live in Southern California.

Books Available From Bold Strokes Books

Forging a Desire Line by Mary P. Burns. When Charley's ex-wife, Tricia, is diagnosed with inoperable cancer, the private duty nurse Tricia hires turns out to be the handsome and aloof Joanna, who ignites something inside Charley she isn't ready to face. (978-1-63555-665-0)

Journey to Cash by Ashley Bartlett. Cash Braddock thought everything was great, but it looks like her history is about to become her right now. Which is a real bummer. (978-1-63555-464-9)

Love on the Night Shift by Radclyffe. Between ruling the night shift in the ER at the Rivers and raising her teenage daughter, Blaise Richilieu has all the drama she needs in her life, until a dashing young attending appears on the scene and relentlessly pursues her. (978-1-63555-668-1)

Olivia's Awakening by Ronica Black. When the daring and dangerously gorgeous Eve Monroe is hired to get Olivia Savage into shape, a fierce passion ignites, causing both to question everything they've ever known about love. (978-1-63555-613-1)

The Duchess and the Dreamer by Jenny Frame. Clementine Fitzroy has lost her faith and love of life. Can dreamer Evan Fox make her believe in life and dream again? (978-1-63555-601-8)

The Road Home by Erin Zak. Hollywood actress Gwendolyn Carter is about to discover that losing someone you love sometimes means gaining someone to fall for. (978-1-63555-633-9)

Waiting for You by Elle Spencer. When passionate past-life lovers meet again in the present day, one remembers it vividly and the other isn't so sure. (978-1-63555-635-3)

While My Heart Beats by Erin McKenzie. Can a love born amidst the horrors of the Great War survive? (978-1-63555-589-9)

Face the Music by Ali Vali. Sweet music is the last thing that happens when Nashville music producer Mason Liner and daughter of country royalty Victoria Roddy are thrown together in an effort to save country star Sophie Roddy's career. (978-1-63555-532-5)

Flavor of the Month by Georgia Beers. What happens when baker Charlie and chef Emma realize their differing paths have led them right back to each other? (978-1-63555-616-2)

Mending Fences by Angie Williams. Rancher Bobbie Del Rey and veterinarian Grace Hammond are about to discover if heartbreaks of the past can ever truly be mended. (978-1-63555-708-4)

Silk and Leather: Lesbian Erotica with an Edge, edited by Victoria Villaseñor. This collection of stories by award-winning authors offers fantasies as soft as silk and tough as leather. The only question is: How far will you go to make your deepest desires come true? (978-1-63555-587-5)

The Last Place You Look by Aurora Rey. Dumped by her wife and looking for anything but love, Julia Pierce retreats to her hometown only to rediscover high school friend Taylor Winslow, who's secretly crushed on her for years. (978-1-63555-574-5)

The Mortician's Daughter by Nan Higgins. A singer on the verge of stardom discovers she must give up her dreams to live a life in service to ghosts. (978-1-63555-594-3)

The Real Thing by Laney Webber. When passion flares between actress Virginia Green and masseuse Allison McDonald, can they be sure it's the real thing? (978-1-63555-478-6)

What the Heart Remembers Most by M. Ullrich. For college sweethearts Jax Levine and Gretchen Mills, could an accident be the second chance neither knew they wanted? (978-1-63555-401-4)

White Horse Point by Andrews & Austin. Mystery writer Taylor James finds herself falling for the mysterious woman on White Horse Point who lives alone, protecting a secret she can't share about a murderer who walks among them. (978-1-63555-695-7)

Femme Tales by Anne Shade. Six women find themselves in their own real-life fairy tales when true love finds them in the most unexpected ways. (978-1-63555-657-5)

Jellicle Girl by Stevie Mikayne. One dark summer night, Beth and Jackie go out to the canoe dock. Two years later, Beth is still carrying the weight of what happened to Jackie. (978-1-63555-691-9)

My Date with a Wendigo by Genevieve McCluer. Elizabeth Rosseau finds her long-lost love and the secret community of fiends she's now a part of. (978-1-63555-679-7)

On the Run by Charlotte Greene. Even when they're cute blondes, it's stupid to pick up hitchhikers, especially when they've just broken out of prison, but doing so is about to change Gwen's life forever. (978-1-63555-682-7)

Perfect Timing by Dena Blake. The choice between love and family has never been so difficult, and Lynn's and Maggie's different visions of the future may end their romance before it's begun. (978-1-63555-466-3)

The Mail Order Bride by R. Kent. When a mail order bride is thrust on Austin, he must choose between the bride he never wanted or the dream he lives for. (978-1-63555-678-0)

Through Love's Eyes by C.A. Popovich. When fate reunites Brittany Yardin and Amy Jansons, can they move beyond the pain of their past to find love? (978-1-63555-629-2)

To the Moon and Back by Melissa Brayden. Film actress Carly Daniel thinks that stage work is boring and unexciting, but when she accepts a lead role in a new play, stage manager Lauren Prescott tests both her heart and her ability to share the limelight. (978-1-63555-618-6)

Tokyo Love by Diana Jean. When Kathleen Schmitt is given the opportunity to be on the cutting edge of AI technology, she never thought a failed robotic love companion would bring her closer to her neighbor, Yuriko Velucci, and finding love in unexpected places. (978-1-63555-681-0)